CYNDA

MILTON J. DAVIS

MVmedia, LLC
Fayetteville Georgia

MVmedia, LLC
PO Box 143052
Fayetteville, GA 30215
info@mvmediaatl.com
www.mvmediaatl.com

Publisher's Note: This is a work of fiction. Names, characters, places, and incidents are a product of the author's imagination. Locales and public names are sometimes used for atmospheric purposes. Any resemblance to actual people, living or dead, or to businesses, companies, events, institutions, or locales is completely coincidental.

Ordering Information:
Quantity sales. Special discounts are available on quantity purchases by corporations, associations, and others. For details, contact the "Special Sales Department" at the address above.

Cynda/ Milton J. Davis. -- 1st ed.
ISBN 979-8-9905121-4-6

Contents

To Vickie. I love you always and forever.

1

The Eiffel Tower lights blinked in perfect synchronicity against the spring night sky, a pulse that matched the rhythm of Cynda's racing heart. She sighed as the beautiful brown man standing before her touched her waist before he slid his arm around her then leaned close to whisper in her ear.

"So, did I do good?" he asked.

She gazed at the five-carat diamond on her ring finger. "Yeah, baby. You did really good."

They faced each other, the bright streetlight obscuring his features. Cynda didn't need to see them; she knew every inch of him by heart. Their lips met and his tongue teased hers. This was it. This was love.

He pulled away from her suddenly.

"Look baby, there's something I need to..."

A loud beep interrupted him. The tower brightened, hurting Cynda's eyes.

"What is it?"

"I just wanted to say..."

The beeping intruded again. This time it didn't stop but thumped in time with the lights. The lights grew brighter and brighter until all she could see was flashing red and all she could hear was the constant beeping. Dread filled her head and her heart.

"No," she cried. "No, no, no..."

Cynda opened her eyes to the sight of her ceiling fan spinning lazily above her. Her alarm clock chirped incessantly, the red numbers flashing at 5:00 a.m.

"A dream," she sighed. "It was a stupid dream."

Cynda Ella Jones threw her arms open and sighed. Monday morning crushed her like a boulder. It was the worst day of the week, the one day that everything had to be done at once. But she was tired despite a full night's sleep. She wasn't going to get out of bed until she had to.

"Auntie Cynda!" the twins cried in unison.

Cynda slammed her hand on the alarm clock then fumbled about until she found the shut off switch. She threw her bare legs over the edge of the bed and dug into her hair with her fingers.

"I need a perm," she moaned.

"Auntie!"

"I'm coming babies," she answered as cheerfully as she could manage. Malon and Sha'kwon were up and active before her as always, two twin balls of crazy energy. She stopped for a moment, the same question popping into her head every time she thought of their names. *Why in the hell did Tiffany name those boys that?*

Cynda slipped on her worn out house shoes then grabbed her housecoat from the foot of her queen size bed, the same bed she'd slept in since high school. She shuffled into her bathroom, looked in the mirror, and moaned again. She was about to brush her teeth when a crash made her jump.

"Oh Jesus!"

She ran out of the room then down the hallway to the kitchen. Malon looked at her with tears in his eyes, expecting the spanking he was about to get. Sha'kwon stared at her triumphantly, holding the box of Honey Nut Cheerios in his hand as he stood on a kitchen stool, totally ignoring the broken dish on the floor.

"We're making breakfast!" he announced. "We're big boys!"

Cynda stormed over to Sha'kwon, snatched the cereal box from his hands then slammed it on the counter. She scooped him from the chair under one arm, tucked Malon under the other arm, marched to their rooms then dropped them in their beds.

"Do not move out of this room until I come get you, you here?"

They nodded in unison.

No sooner had she closed the door did Mama call out, her voice tight with concern.

"Baby, is everything alright?"

Cynda took a deep breath before walking down the hall to Mama's room. She eased the door open then forced a smile. Mama was sitting on the edge of the bed adjusting her night cap.

"What you doing up so early?" Cynda said.

"The babies woke me," Mama replied. "You want me to fix them some breakfast?"

"No Mama, I got it. I'm just a little tired this morning."

"Cynda, I'm sick but I ain't helpless."

"I know Mama. I'll let you do it tomorrow."

"Okay, baby. I'm going to lay back down."

"Okay Mama."

Cynda waited until Mama was back under the covers before she backed out of the room. Seeing Mama calmed her somewhat. No matter what she was going through it was nothing compared to Mama. Her thoughts were interrupted by knocking. She stopped in front of Terrence's room.

"Breakfast ready yet?" he called through the door.

"Not for your lazy ass," she hissed back.

"Come on, Cynda! You know what's up."

"All I know is that you need to get a job!" she shot back.

And just like that she was back in a bad mood.

She went back into the kitchen, cleaned up the broken bowl, and prepared breakfast for the twins. She'd planned to make a big breakfast like she usually did on Mondays but she slept late. She always did when she had that dream, that beautiful, wonderful, impossible dream. She filled the bowls with cereal and milk, poured orange juice in the juice glasses then set them beside the bowls. She'd be lucky to get a weekend in Chattanooga, let alone two weeks in Paris. She rushed to the twins' room then opened the door. They stood in perfect attention, their eyes wide and expectant. Cynda couldn't help but laugh.

"Alright, cereal is on the table."

They rushed by her.

"Hold it down now. Grandma is still asleep."

Cynda went back to her room and dressed while the twins ate. She was doing what she had to do, not what she wanted to do. In the end it was about what needed to be done. That's what Daddy told her. Her family needed her. She was the strong one, Daddy said. The oldest child usually is. She left Fort Valley University when daddy died to help Mama sort things out. She'd planned to enroll at Georgia State but while Daddy was a sweet and loving man, he wasn't very good with money. Cynda took a job to help pay off the bills he left behind. She'd been working ever since.

She glanced at the clock. It was six thirty. "Damn! Got to get a move on."

She grabbed her make up bag then stuffed it in her large purse. She could put on her make up at work. She hurried into the kitchen; the twins were finishing their cereal.

"Y'all go and get dressed," she said. "I laid out your clothes last night."

The twins jumped from the table then raced to their room. Cynda didn't have time to clean the table. She made a bowl of cereal then scarfed it down while the twins dressed.

Giggles and laughter caught her attention. The twins stood before her dressed in each other's clothing.

"So y'all being funny this morning," she said. "I'm taking you to daycare just like that."

"No!" they shouted then ran back to the room. In moments they returned properly dressed.

"Now that's more like it," she said. She glanced at her watch.

"Let's go, men!" she announced.

They headed to the garage door.

"Terrence, make Mama some cereal then wash the dishes!" she shouted.

"Okay!" he shouted back.

"I mean it!" she shouted as she walked through the door.

"I mean it, too!" he shouted back.

Cynda took a minute to look at changing colors of the trees in their front yard. The tall maple oak was in full fall glory, its bright yellow leaves resembling muted sunlight. It was one of the reasons fall was her favorite time of year.

Cynda strapped the twins in her SUV and they were off to Bright Lites Daycare on Sullivan Street. Talisa Cameron, an old friend from high school, was the owner and gave her a good rate for the twins. She couldn't afford other daycares, and Talisa ran a good operation. She was waiting at the door when Cynda pulled into the roundabout driveway, greeting the parents as she did every day. Cynda was always the last to arrive.

"Hey girl!" she squealed. She always greeted Cynda as if she was seeing her for the first time in years.

"Hey, girl!" Cynda replied. They hugged tight.

"So when you going to come party with me?" Talisa asked.

"When these boys grow up," Cynda replied.

"We'll be too old to get in trouble then." Talisa winked at her.

"Girl, take these babies and leave me alone," Cynda said.

Talisa laughed as Cynda walked back to the SUV.

"See you this evening!" she shouted.

Cynda waved without looking back. She hopped into the car and then sped down Highway 85 to Jonesboro Road. When she arrived at work the early birds waited at the door, their arms folded across their chests. Cynda rolled her eyes.

"Like they in a hurry," she whispered.

She took a moment to gather herself before stepping from the car.

"Good morning!" she sang.

"Morning," they replied in ragged unison. Cynda took the keys from her purse then unlocked the door. The others followed her in, trudging to their offices. Benson Realty was officially in operation.

Her phone rang as soon as she sat in her chair.

"Hi Miss Laura," she said.

"Right on time, Cynda. Right on time. I'll be in about 10:30. I have a breakfast meeting then a few homes to show in McDonough. Is everyone in?"

"Everyone but Ray."

"I know you're glad for that," Laura said.

Cynda scowled. "You should fire that man."

"I would if he wasn't so good," Laura replied. "Don't mind him. He's harmless."

"He's not trying to date you, with his old ass," Cynda said.

Laura's boisterous laugh made her smile. Benson Realty was one of the largest independent realty companies in Metro Atlanta. Laura Benson built the business by herself, and Cynda worked for her for the last five years. The middle-aged Atlanta native was tall, beautiful, and fierce, with the energy of someone half her age. She was Cynda's role model, but she was also disorganized as all get out.

"If you were selling houses instead of warming this desk, you wouldn't have to deal with him," Laura said.

"You'd go out of business if I wasn't here to keep you straight," Cynda replied.

"Lord knows that's true. Hey, are we having lunch today?"

"Yes, ma'am."

"You know the place. I got to run Cynda. See you later!"

No sooner had she hung up did Ray enter the building. The middle-aged man flashed his perfect smile, licking his lips like he always did when he looked at Cynda. She lowered her head so he wouldn't see her roll her eyes.

"Hey Ray, "she said.

"Hey beautiful," Ray said in his rough baritone voice. Twenty years ago, he must have been something else, and for women his age he was still quite the catch. Ray was Miss Laura's top agent, garnering Realtor of the Year five times since becoming an agent fifteen years ago. The ex-Atlanta Falcon's magnetic personality drew women and men of all ages into his orbit, but Cynda wasn't interested. At all.

"I can't think of a better way to start the day than to see your lovely face," Ray said.

"Thank you," Cynda managed to reply. "You have a 9:30 in Alpharetta."

"Yes, I do," Ray said. "That's a done deal. All they need to do is sign the papers and that's a hundred houses sold this year. We should celebrate."

"No, we shouldn't," Cynda said. "You know I don't date co-workers. Especially if they're old enough to be my grandfather. I've told you that about a million times."

Ray laughed. "Yes, you have. But I'm pleasantly persistent. You'll see the error of your ways one day."

"Goodbye Ray."

"See you later, Cynda."

The morning hours flew by. The pandemic was a bitter memory and people were in the market for homes again. Cynda distributed the new leads to the agents based on experience and proximity. She shut down the system at 11:30, locked up the office then jumped into her SUV. Twenty minutes later she exited off International Avenue, her destination, the CNN Center. She parked in the deck behind Phillips Arena then hurried across the street to McCormick's and Schmick's. Laura waited at her favorite table, sipping on her favorite bourbon. Cynda smiled at her boss and friend. Laura raised her glass and waved her over.

"Come on over here, girl," she said. "You know I hate drinking alone."

Cynda sat then took off her coat. A waiter appeared at once, a clean cut college-aged brother with an eager smile.

"Welcome to McCormick's and Schmick's," he said. "What would you like to drink?"

"Sweet tea and water with lemon," Cynda said.

"Is the lovely lady ready to order as well?" the waiter said.

Cynda grinned as she shook her head. "No, young man. I'm not. Keep working on that tip though."

The waiter chuckled. "I'll be right back with your drinks, Ms.?"

"Customer," Cynda finished.

The waiter nodded then eased away.

Laura shook her head.

"Why you shoot that young man down like that? He's cute."

"And I'm busy," Cynda said.

"I should fire you," Laura replied. "Maybe then you'd have time to get you some."

Cynda laughed. "Some what? Sleep? Because that's what I'd do. Sleep for three months at least."

The waiter arrived with her drinks.

"Is Ms. Customer ready to order now?" he asked.

"Let me have the Low Country Shrimp and Grits," Cynda said.

Laura shuddered. "Ooh child! I don't see how you can eat that mess."

Cynda laughed. "You say that every time."

"I mean it every time, too."

"And what would you like, ma'am?"

I'd like the blackened rainbow trout."

"Low Country Shrimp and Grits and Blackened Rainbow Trout," the waiter said as he wrote. "Your meals will be out right away."

Laura sipped on her bourbon. "This is the year, Cynda," she said. "It has to be."

"You found a new potential investor?" Cynda asked.

Laura's face sagged. "No, but I feel it. Whenever I want something this bad, I usually get it."

Cynda sipped on her water as she glanced out the window. Laura's dream rose fourteen stories a block away, the last abandoned building in the Centennial Park entertainment district. It stood out among the newly renovated structures surrounding it, a beautiful scar among modern perfection.

"I don't know Laura," Cynda said. "Every time a new development goes up your baby gets that much more expensive."

"You don't have to tell me," Laura replied. "I checked the property value today. I liked to had a heart attack."

"Maybe we should go after something more accessible," Cynda said.

"No!" Laura slammed her drink on the table, causing those sitting nearby to glance at them. Cynda cursed silently. Never intrude on Miss Laura's Dream. She braced for the speech.

"Let me tell you something, girl," Laura said as she wagged her finger. "I've been slinging houses in this damn city for over forty years! Nobody knows real estate like I do. That building is a diamond in the rough just waiting for somebody like me to give it the care it needs to come to life."

"I know, Miss Laura," Cynda said.

Laura finished her drink. "And stop calling me Miss Laura. Makes me feel old as hell."

Cynda laughed. "Okay, Laura."

The waiter returned with their meals. The rest of lunch was small talk, updates, and new assignments for the day. The worst news came as their waiter cleared the table.

"We need to let Josie go," Laura said.

"Josie, really?" Cynda replied. She liked Josie. She was the only agent close to her age and had a sweet disposition.

"I know you like her and she's a sweet child, but she couldn't close a deal to save her life. This is a business, and she has to learn how to sell a house, not just show it."

"Can't you work with her?" Cynda said.

Laura shook her head. "I don't have that kind of time anymore."

"Give her another month," Cynda said.

Laura shook her head again. "Another month of losing money."

"I'll be responsible for her," Cynda said.

"Girl, what do you know about selling houses?"

"More that Josie," Cynda replied.

Cynda

"Okay, one month," Laura said. "Cynda, you got to stop trying to be everyone's savior. Some folks don't deserve to be saved."

"I know," Cynda said. "But Josie does. Now if you told me you were firing Ray, I'd set off fireworks."

Laura laughed. "Get back to work girl. I'll see this evening."

Cynda hurried back to the office. There were fifteen messages waiting and a ton of mail, a typical Monday morning. It was five o'clock before she caught up, time for her to pick up the twins. She locked up then hurried to the daycare. Talisa stood at the door, the twins running to her then hugging her tired legs.

"This weekend?" Talisa called out.

"I'll try," Cynda said.

"You're lying," Talisa replied.

"I know," Cynda confessed.

She secured the twins in their car seats, jumped into the car then sped home to fix dinner. One day down, four to go, she said to herself. *And none of them are mine.*

MILTON J DAVIS

2

P. Nelson Carter woke to a gentle tug on his sleeve. He opened his eyes to the pleasant smile of Gertrude, the Lufthansa flight attendant, the Afro-German sister who flirted with him the entire flight. He stretched in his first-class seat then covered his mouth as he yawned.

"Rise and shine, lovely man," Gertrude said. "I need you to buckle in and raise your seat. We're preparing for landing."

Nelson did as he was told then smiled.

"That's a good boy," the attendant said. She winked then went about inspecting the other passengers.

Nelson yawned again. He was tired; no, he was exhausted. Three weeks ago, he climbed on a plane at O'Hara to begin a business trip that took him literally around the world. It was his first time visiting the international real estate investment empire his father had built and it made him respect the old man's hustle more than he had before, if that was possible. He scheduled a redeye from Frankfurt without notifying anyone, hoping to sneak into town and get some much-needed sleep. So far, so good.

His plane landed at six thirty a.m. By seven thirty he was in a rideshare on his way to his condo. The car pulled up to the 820 North High Rise; Nelson paid the driver with a hefty tip then gave a quick wave to the concierge as he hurried through the door to the elevator. He fumbled his keycard before opening the door then stepping inside. It was so good to be home again. He didn't know how his father did it for so many years. But he was a man at home wherever his feet touched ground. Nelson was more like his mother. He tolerated travel but was always more comfortable in familiar surroundings.

"Welcome home!"

Nelson jumped even though he recognized the sultry voice. Veronica emerged from his bedroom.

"Ronsie! What are you doing here?"

"I should be asking you the same question."

She sauntered over to him wearing his Chicago Bears jersey and tap pants. If he hadn't been so tired he might have been happy to see her. Instead, he was annoyed.

"You weren't supposed to be back until tomorrow," she said.

"I decided to come back early to rest."

Veronica pulled him close then kissed him hard while pressing against him.

"Well, it looks like you won't be getting that," she said. "I have something better in mind."

Nelson broke off the kiss then pushed her away.

"Baby, I'm really, really tired right now."

Veronica stepped away then placed her hands on her hips.

"You know it's not nice to turn a woman down."

"I'm not turning you down. I'm just asking for a rain check. What are you doing here anyway?"

"I missed you."

"I knew I shouldn't have given you a keycard."

Veronica shrugged. "Too late now. I'll give you a pass this time. Besides, I wasn't expecting you. I have to go to work."

She pranced back into the bedroom. Nelson collapsed onto the sofa, rubbing his tired eyes. Veronica was the last person he wanted to see. He had to tell her soon. The longer he waited, the worse it would be. But not today. He'd get some sleep, go into the office the tomorrow and get back up to speed.

He closed his eyes and dozed off; Veronica's kiss on his cheek woke him.

"You are tired," she said. She was dressed for work, a simple blue blouse and black slacks, her hair pulled back into a ponytail.

"Don't go into work," she said. "I want you well rested when I get back."

Nelson gave her a weak wave. "Have a good day, baby."

"You, too," she said.

Nelson pulled himself from the couch then trudged into the bedroom. He took off his clothes and left them on the floor as he went into the bathroom and turned on the shower. The hot water woke him somewhat, at least enough to get him through the morning meeting. After the shower he dressed casually, a pair of jeans with a polo shirt and sports coat. He hoped his dad didn't mind; if he did, he didn't care.

Nelson caught another quick nap during the ride to the office. The driver dropped him off at the curb and he trudged into the office foyer. Darrell, the office manager, shared a smile as he entered.

"Welcome back, stranger," he said.

"Hi Darrell. The old man in?"

"Yes, he is," Darrell replied. "He's not expecting you."

"Exactly."

Nelson eased into his father's office. Thomas Martin Carter sat at his desk, his chair facing the spectacular view of Lake Michigan, his face buried in the latest edition of the Chicago Tribune.

"Hey Pops!" Nelson exclaimed.

Thomas jerked his head about.

"What...boy, what are you doing here?"

His father dropped the paper and hurried around the desk then gave him a tight hug.

"I caught the red eye from Frankfurt," Nelson said. "I was anxious to get home."

Nelson sat in the guest chair before the desk.

"So did I miss anything?"

"No, but I heard good things about you," his father said.

"Already? I just got back."

His father laughed. "You know I was keeping tabs on you. All of my colleagues were impressed. A few of them suggested that you take over their accounts. That kind of hurt my feelings."

They laughed together.

"I can't replace you," Nelson said.

"But one day you'll have to," his father replied.

Nelson's smile faded. Taking over the business was something that had been on his father's mind a lot lately. Nelson understood how important it was but it wasn't a conversation he wanted to have at the moment. His father seemed to sense his mood. He reached into his desk then pulled out a portfolio.

"I want you to take a look at this," he said.

He slid the documents to Nelson. Nelson opened the folder. Inside was a photo of a multi-story building in desperate need of repair. The other documents were city grid maps and property specifications.

"A fixer-upper? You're usually not interested in property like this."

His father shrugged. "Usually not, but this is in a prime location in Atlanta. I figure a return on the renovation investment in two years depending on how much work needs to be done. A local real estate owner has been sending me letters for years hoping to form a partnership to buy it."

"So why haven't you?"

"She's into home real estate. I'm not confident in her evaluation. I'd like to get another pair of eyes on it."

Nelson closed the folder. "My eyes?"

"Why not? You proved yourself, son. It's time you had your own project."

Nelson grinned. "So this is mine."

"Yes. From beginning to end."

"Pops, I'm grateful but just got back," he said. "I'm a little tired."

"No rush. That folder's been on my desk for years. What's a few more weeks?"

"Thanks, Pops. I won't let you down."

"Of course you won't. You're a Carter. Now go back home and get some sleep. I'll see you tomorrow."

His father didn't have to say it twice. He headed back to his condo, shed his clothes, and fell immediately to sleep. A soft kiss on his cheek woke him. He opened his eyes to Veronica's sweet smile. She was under the covers pressed against him naked.

"You rested?" she asked.

"Yes, I am," he replied.

"Well let's give you a proper welcome home."

3

Saturdays were golden. When Cynda woke it was almost 9:00 a.m. She stretched then kicked off the sheets. She could hear the television, the twins watching some cartoon or another. She sat up, felt a tinge of sleepiness then lay back down. When she woke again it was to the insistent calls from the twins outside her locked door.

"Auntie Cynda! Auntie Cynda! Are we going to talk to mommy today?"

"Shit!" Cynda sat up then looked at her calendar. Yes, it was the fourth Saturday of the month.

"Yes, babies," she said. "We're going to talk to mommy today."

"Yay!"

Cynda dragged out of bed then into the bathroom. She'd forgotten about Tiffany's call, which wasn't like her. Tiffany was the looker of the family; tall, pretty and with intense green eyes that brought people to their knees. But just like a flower can't control which bees it attracts, Tiffany was constantly swarmed by unsuitable men. Unfortunately, she married one. Four years and two children later she was divorced and struggling. Mama and Daddy helped her as much as they could, but when Daddy died that help disappeared. With too many bills and too few options she joined the National Guard to help support herself and Mama. She never suspected she would be stationed overseas. Cynda took in the kids. And so it had been for the last year.

Cynda logged in on her laptop then signed on. She found Tiffany's account then called.

"Come on, babies!" she shouted. The twins came barreling into her room, jumping on the bed.

"Mommy! Mommy!" they shouted.

"Not yet," Tiffany's picture popped up as her account rang, the twins squealing at the image. Moments later Tiffany appeared, smiling only like a mother can when she sees her children.

"Hey babies!" she exclaimed.

"Hey mommy!" the twins shouted. They rushed to the computer and kissed the screen.

"Eww!" Cynda said. "I told y'all about that."

Cynda left the room as Tiffany talked to her babies. She peeked in on Mama, who sat on her bed watching the morning news.

"Hey Mama, Tiffany's on the computer. I'll bring it in when she's done talking to the twins.

Mama smiled. "Thank you, Cynda."

"You need anything?"

"No, I'm all right baby. You go on in there and talk to your sister."

The twins were still sharing all the details of their day with Tiffany, and she listened with parental patience. It was only when they began to repeat themselves that Tiffany gently brought the conversation to a close.

"Hey babies, let me speak to your auntie for a little while, okay?"

"Auntie Cynda!" the twins shouted.

"I'm right here," she said. The twins scampered back to their room.

"How you doing, sis?" she asked.

"I've been better," Tiffany said. "Cynda, I need to talk."

Cynda knew what that meant. Tiffany was about to tell her something she didn't want to hear.

"Talk to Mama first," she said. "I need to fix the twins their breakfast."

"Okay," Tiffany replied.

Mama was sitting up against the headboard when Cynda entered the room, a glowing smile on her face. Although she would never admit it, Tiffany was her favorite. They were practically twins twenty-five years apart; same eyes, same smile. Cynda took after daddy.

Cynda set the laptop on Mama's lap then tilted the screen so they could see each other.

"You call me when y'all are done," Cynda said.

Mama nodded as she stared at Tiffany.

"Hey baby!" she said.

"Hey Mama!" Tiffany replied.

Cynda grinned as she went to the kitchen to prepare breakfast. She loved Saturdays because she had the time to create a proper breakfast for everybody. She started the coffee then heated the pan for bacon and sausage. She also prepared the water for grits then took out the pancake mix. Mama always wanted pancakes for Saturday breakfast; she and the twins preferred grits. Terrence ate whatever was left. She made the twins' plates then grilled pancakes for Mama and Terrence.

"Cynda?"

Cynda shuffled to Mama's room then took the laptop from her lap.

"I'll bring your breakfast," she said.

"That's all right. I feel good today. I'll come into the kitchen."

Cynda set the laptop down on Mama's dresser to help her get out of bed. Mama waved her away.

"I got it, baby," she said.

Cynda watched Mama ease out of the bed, ready to help. Mama stood then tipped to the kitchen; Cynda looked at Tiffany and smiled.

"Give me one more minute," she said.

She hurried to Terrence 's room then banged on the door.

"What?" he shouted.

"I need you out here. Mama's in the kitchen eating breakfast."

She heard Terrence jump from the bed. The door cracked opened.

"Is that a good thing?" he said.

"I don't know, but I need you out here to keep an eye on her. I got Tiffany on the computer."

He closed his door then stepped out a few minutes later in mix-matched pajamas. Cynda crinkled her nose as he walked by.

"You need to take shower," she commented.

Terrence grunted as he headed for the kitchen. Cynda took the computer into her bedroom then closed the door.

"So what's up sis?"

"Serving my time in this man's army," Tiffany said.

"You okay?"

"As good as someone can be in the desert. Hey, I got some bad news."

Cynda stiffened. "What?"

"My tour has been extended. I'm going to need you to watch my babies for six more months."

"Done," Cynda said. "You know I got you. This is family."

"I know, but I hate asking you. I should be home raising my kids."

"You're doing what you have to do," Cynda said. "We all are."

"I know, but still . . ."

"Look girl, stop worrying about it. I'll let Mama and Terrence know. I'll tell the kids when they ask."

"Okay. I love you so much, Cynda."

"I love you too. Now tell me about those fine soldiers you're serving with."

Tiffany laughed. "Girl, you crazy."

Tiffany went on about her tour while Cynda half listened. She loved her sister and she loved the twins, but she was really looking forward to the end of Tiffany's tour. She needed a break so she could begin putting her life back together. That was going to take another six months.

Cynda and Tiffany talked until the twins finished their breakfast. Cynda signed off then marched the boys into the bathroom to wash up and get dressed. When they were done she sat them in front of the television as she helped Mama back to her room. She made her plate and ate then cleared the table, ignoring Terrence's moaning as he washed the dishes. There was no sympathy for him. Two years out of college and he still wasn't working a steady job, talking about how he was creating the next great electronic game. If it wasn't for Mama, she'd give him an ultimatum; get a job or get out.

Cynda let the twins play games while she washed up then changed clothes. As soon as she was done, she marched into the family room and turned off the television. "Let's go!" she said.

"Wait."

It was Terrence.

"What do you want?"

"You taking the kids to the park?"

Cynda frowned. "I do it every Saturday unless it's raining."

"I got some things I need to work on today."

Cynda shook her head. "Nope. You're watching Mama. I'm taking the kids to the park. Unless you want to take them."

Terrence stomped. "You enjoy doing this to me! You know what I'm doing!"

"No, I don't know what the hell you're doing!" Cynda shouted. "What I do know is that you don't pay rent, you barely help out, and every time I ask you to do something you start bitching about that game ain't nobody seen. Now I'm taking the kids to the god damn park, and you're going to watch Mama!"

Terrence stepped closer to her. "You don't care about what I do. You're like everybody else!"

"Look, boy," Cynda began. "If I didn't care about you, you wouldn't be in this house. Quit whining and do what I asked you to do."

"You two quit fussing!" Mama called out.

"See what you did?" Cynda said.

"Just go," Terrence replied.

"Like I wasn't," Cynda retorted.

Cynda felt someone tug on her pants leg. She looked down to see Sha'kwon staring at her.

"You gonna whup Uncle Terrence?"

"Not yet," Cynda answered. "Come on, babies. Let's go play."

Cynda and the twins loaded into her car and she drove to the local playground. It was early; they had the entire park to themselves, at least for the time being. She parked and let the little ones free. They ran to the equipment and began playing with unbridled enthusiasm. Cynda watched them and couldn't help but smile. She remembered when her life had been that simple. The weight of everything she had to do began to settle on her mind and she pushed it away. This was Saturday, and she was going to enjoy it. She left the bench and joined the twins, swinging, sliding, and climbing until she was exhausted. They left the park and found a nearby Krystals for lunch. After lunch they found another park to play, then after another exhausting round she took them for ice cream. By the time they reached home the twins were asleep.

"Okay warriors," she said. "Wake up! I can't carry both of you inside."

The twins tumbled out of the car. Cynda grabbed their arms and led them to the back door. When she opened it, Terrence was standing there waiting.

"You didn't say you'd be gone all day!"

Cynda brushed by him, leading the twins to their room.

"Y'all need to bath before dinner," she said. "Sha'kwon, you first.

Sha'kwon took his pajamas from the drawer then trudged into the bathroom. Malon collapsed on his bed. Cynda ignored Terrence 's glare as she went to the kitchen to prepare dinner.

"Baby is that you?" Mama called out.

"Yeah, Mama. It's me."

"Did you and the babies have a good time?"

"We did, Mama. I'm about to fix dinner."

"Okay, baby."

Cynda looked at the sink. The same dishes from breakfast were there.

"Terrence, what did you fix you and Mama for lunch?"

Terrence didn't answer. Cynda flushed with anger. She rushed up to Terrence, their noses almost touching.

"Goddammit, Terrence! There's leftover spaghetti in the fridge. All you had to do was warm it up!

Terrence backed away. "I didn't know!"

"You didn't know because you didn't look! I bet you went back to your room the minute I walked out the door."

"I checked in on Mama to see if she was okay."

"Checked in?" Cynda closed her eyes, her fingers rolling into fists. "Get out of my face, Terrence. I can't with you right now."

"I'm sorry, Cynda. I . . ."

"Just go. I got to fix dinner."

Terrence sulked to his room. Cynda went to the cabinet and took out the Saltine crackers. She placed them on a plate then poured a glass of water. Setting the crackers and the water on a tray, she carried the snack to Mama. Mama sat up in the bed and smiled as she entered the room.

"Here you go," Cynda said. "A little something while I cook dinner."

She set the tray on Mama's lap. Mama picked up a cracker and nibbled on it.

"Thank you, Cynda."

"I can't believe that boy didn't make y'all lunch."

Mama took a sip of her water.

"It's alright," she said. "I wasn't that hungry anyway."

"It's not just that," Cynda said. "What if something had happened?"

"It didn't," Mama said. "I'm sure he'll do better the next time."

"You said that the last time," Cynda said. "If he's not going to pay attention to anybody, the least he can do is get a job."

"Now you know he can't do that," Mama said. "He's working on his game."

Cynda opened her mouth but stop. She wasn't going to lose her joy because of Terrence.

"I'll have dinner ready in a minute."

"Take your time," Mama said. "I'm okay with these crackers and water."

Cynda fixed dinner, bratwurst for her, Mama and Terrence; hot dogs, and French fries for the twins. She ate dinner in the room with Mama while the twins watched a video in the family room. Terrence fixed his plate the returned to his room. After dinner she helped Mama pick out something for church the next day then prepare for bed. She took their plates to the kitchen and discovered the twins asleep on the floor, French fries scattered everywhere. She put them to bed then cleaned up the room. After washing the dishes, she took a quick shower, put on her pajamas, grabbed her laptop, and placed it on the kitchen table. She took a beer from the fridge then pulled up her French language program. She'd been taking lessons for two years and was getting proficient, at least according to the program. She was having a conversation with her tutor when Terrence came into the room and sat beside her.

"Terrence, not tonight," she said.

"I came to apologize."

Cynda rolled her eyes. "You're always apologizing. What I need you to do is be responsible. Just do what I ask you to do, that's all."

"Okay," Terrence said. "I promise."

"So, make it up to me," Cynda said.

Terrence fell back on the couch then grabbed a throw pillow and put it over his face.

"I know what you're going to ask."

"So?" Cynda took the pillow from his face.

"Okay," he said.

Cynda grinned then hit him on the head with the pillow.

"Iron your shirt tonight. I'll find you a tie."

Terrence took the pillow then hit Cynda on the head.

"Okay. Goodnight."

Cynda smiled. Mama would be happy that Terrence was joining them for church. She completed the lesson then decided to watch the science fiction movie, Redeemer. Balogun Ojetade was one her favorite writers, so she was anxious to see how they adapted the book. She sipped on her beer as she watched, the day finally catching up with her. She fell asleep on the couch.

4

Nelson arrived at the office early Monday morning. He let himself in and shut off the office alarm, surprised he beat his father to work. That was rare. For a moment he wondered if there was something wrong, but he shushed it away. His mother would have contacted him. He'd never seen his father ill, but he knew time was catching up with him. It was the reason he was being sent on more assignments and given more responsibility. Pops was getting old and was preparing him to receive the torch.

His desk was covered with paperwork. Pops could have shared the documents with him in the cloud, but some things never changed. Nelson sat down, loosened his tie, and went to work. Most of the papers were acquisitions already closed, but Pops passed them to Nelson as instruction. He smiled as he read them; his father had a style that stood out in every deal he made. A few were negotiations waiting on his feedback. Knowing Pops, he'd already made up his mind; he wanted to run it by Nelson for his opinion, not that it would change anything. After over thirty years building one of the largest REITs in the country and the largest Black-owned REIT in the world, his father had all the confidence in the world when it came to making decisions. This was his way of instilling the same certainty in Nelson.

It was almost noon when he reached the bottom of the pile. He picked up the Atlanta file and smiled.

"Finally," he said. He was about to open it when his phone buzzed. It was Veronica.

He answered the phone. "Hey Ronsie? What's up?"

"You have time for lunch with a beautiful woman?"

"Sure, what's her number?"

"I'd kick you in the balls if you were standing in front of me."

Nelson laughed. "I'm sure you would. I'll come to you. Be there at twelve."

"Okay, love you."

"Love you, too."

As he hung up a pall settled over Nelson. He was going to have to talk to Ronsie eventually. He'd been distracted during the entire European trip, and that same distraction threatened to interfere with this new acquisition. That wasn't acceptable. This was his test, the project that would prove to Pops he was ready. He wouldn't tell her at lunch, though. He would wait until Friday night.

The truth was that he loved Ronsie, but not the way she wanted him to. They grew up together; he didn't have one memory without her. Their parents were life-long friends and prominent people in Chicago society. It was during high school that their friendship became more; the official announcement of them as a couple was when he asked her to the senior prom. Everything was good until recently.

"So, what do you think?"

Nelson looked up to see his father standing in the door.

"I haven't really had a chance to study it," he said. "You dumped all this other work on me."

"No hurry," his father said. "What are you doing for lunch?"

"I'm hooking up with Ronsie."

"When are you going to marry that woman and make us some grandkids?"

Nelson rolled his eyes.

"Come on, Pops. It doesn't work like that."

"It works exactly like that," Pops replied. "Your Mama and I want grandkids while we're still young enough to spoil them."

Nelson held up the Atlanta folder and Pops raised his hands in surrender.

"Okay, okay. Never let it be said that I interfered with a man making money. But we're going to talk about this again. Soon."

"Okay, Pops."

Pops went to his office and Nelson sighed. He was going to have to tell Ronsie, and everyone else. The sooner, the better.

He studied the file. The property was in the midst of an area experiencing intense gentrification. The word gave him a bitter taste in his mouth. Although he understood the business logic, he hated what it was doing to traditional communities, especially Black communities. Still, the property value was rising every day, so they had a limited window of opportunity to buy it at a good price. He switched to his computer, taking a detailed look at the building. It would take a sizable investment to bring it up to speed, but with the rising property value they would make up the expense in that alone. The only drawback was Pops was not fond of repairing property unless it was a flip opportunity. He'd leave those details for later. The only way he could make a good assessment was to see it firsthand. It was what Pops would do.

He rummaged through the file for the letter then read it again. His first instinct was to send an e-mail, but he decided to call. He had to let Pops know first. He picked up his phone and texted him.

Hey Pops. I'm contacting the Atlanta folks. Going to schedule a visit.

His phone buzzed and he laughed.

"Hey Pops," he said.

"You know I don't text."

"You should. It would save us both some time."

Pops sighed. "Anyway, let me give them a call. Ms. Benson is expecting to hear from me. I suggest you fly down on Friday. Take the weekend to check things out."

"Yes sir."

Nelson hung up then searched his contact list for the forbidden number. He looked around before texting.

Hey, Red.

A few minutes passed before the response popped on his screen.

"Nelly? Is that you?"
"The one and only."
"Daddy must not be around."
"LOL! He's not. Hey, I'm coming to Atlanta this weekend. You free?"
"No, but I'm free for you."
"What's happening?"
"Got a show at a local gallery."
"Excellent! Perfect timing!'
"When is your flight arriving?"
"Don't know yet. Don't worry about meeting me. I'll hit you up once I get settled in my hotel."
"No hotel. You're staying with me."
"You sure? I don't want to intrude."
"You're my brother. You're staying with me."
"Okay. Looking forward to seeing you."
"Me too. Love you."
"Love you, too."

He switched to the office phone and called his assistant, Kadija. The intern worked from her home office, visiting only when necessary.

"Hi Nelson," she said. "What do you need?"

"Can you book me a flight to Atlanta on Friday, returning on Sunday?"

"Transportation?"

"No. I'll catch a rideshare."

"Good. Give me a minute."

Nelson busied himself with paperwork. His phone pinged seconds later, his itinerary complete.

He was reviewing property on the Westside of the city when his phone buzzed. It was Ronsie. Time had slipped by him; it was past noon. He picked up the phone and texted her back.

"On my way."

Nelson jumped from his desk and hurried out of the building. Luckily, the restaurant they chose was nearby. As he entered the maître d' greeted him.

"How many?" he asked.

Nelson looked over the man's shoulder and saw Ronsie at their favorite table.

"My lunch date is waiting for me," he said.

The man turned to see Ronsie.

"Go right ahead sir."

Ronsie smiled when she saw him.

"There he is," she said.

"Here I am," Nelson replied.

He went to her side, and they shared a kiss.

"Busy today?" she asked.

"Always," Nelson replied as he took his seat. "Going to Atlanta next week,"

"You just got back!" Ronsie said.

"Yea, I know, but there's a piece of property Pops wants me to check out. It might be my first solo project."

Ronsie eyebrows rose and she clapped her hands lightly.

"Congratulations! I know how Papa Carter can be."

The server interrupted them for their orders. Nelson ordered the prime rib sandwich, his usual, and Ronsie ordered the chicken salad.

"Still watching your weight," Nelson said.

"You weren't here to watch it for me," she replied.

Nelson rose up in his seat to gaze at her. "Looks good to me."

"Sit down, silly" Veronica gave him the once over. "Looks like you gained a few pounds."

"Guilty. It's hard to get in a good workout while traveling."

"Seriously though, do you have to leave so soon?" Veronica asked.

"You know Pops," Nelson said. "Don't put off tomorrow what you can do three days ago."

"You going to see Darla?"

"I'm staying with her. She insisted."

"Give her my love, will you?"

"Of course."

They ate in silence for a while. Nelson could tell something was amiss.

"What's up, Ronsie?" he asked.

"Nothing," Ronsie replied.

"Really, what's up?" Nelson said. "Something's bothering you. I can tell."

"This isn't the time," Ronsie said.

"It's always the time," Nelson said. "No secrets, remember?"

Ronsie put down her fork. "Nelson, how do you feel about me?"

Nelson froze. "What do you mean how do I feel about you? I love you."

"I love you, too," Ronsie said. "But what kind of love do you have for me?"

"Why are you asking me this?" Nelson replied. "What's going on?"

"We've been together all our lives," Ronsie said. "Everybody expected us to end up like this. But I need to know something. Is this what you want? Is this what we want?"

Nelson began to speak and Ronsie raised her hand.

"No lies, Nelson."

"To tell the truth, I don't know," Nelson said. "I've been asking myself that question ever since I got back from Europe."

"Me, too," Ronsie confessed. "I didn't miss you like I should have. Not like I wanted to."

"Could have fooled me," Nelson said with a mischievous grin.

Veronica smiled. "Well . . . you know."

"So, what do we do about it?" Nelson asked.

"Well, we can either go back to your place and sex our way through it, or we can break up."

Nelson hesitated before answering. This was the conversation he wanted to have and he was relieved he wasn't the only one with doubts. Still, he didn't want to be the bad guy.

"What do you want to do?" Nelson asked.

"I think we should take a break to sort things out," Ronsie said.

Nelson was about to agree when a thought popped in his head.

"Ronsie, have you met someone?"

Ronsie picked up her fork and began playing with the remains of her salad.

"Sort of," she replied.

Mixed emotions roiled through Nelson. A part of him wanted to be angry, but another part of him wasn't surprised.

"I wasn't trying to," Ronsie explained. "It began as small talk. Caught me by surprise. I never felt this way about anyone other than you."

"Really?" Nelson said.

"Please don't hate me," Ronsie said. "I couldn't stand it if you did. Despite everything you're my best friend."

"With benefits," Nelson added.

"How can you joke at a time like this?" Ronsie said. "We're breaking up!"

"I don't know what else to do," Nelson replied. "Truth be told, I've been wondering about how it would be to be with someone else."

"Wondering?" Ronsie said. "I figured you already knew, with all the traveling you do."

"Why would you think that?" Nelson said.

"You know how men are," Ronsie said.

"I know how women are, too," Nelson said. "I have an older sister and cousins that aren't saints."

"So, you're telling me I'm the only woman you've ever been with?"

Nelson shrugged. "What can I say? I'm a one-woman man."

"Now I really feel bad."

Nelson reached across the table and took her hand.

"Don't. It's been you and me for a long time. Maybe too long."

"So, what do we do?" Ronsie asked.

"We break up," Nelson said. There it was.

Ronsie looked stunned for a moment, then she sighed.

"Okay," she said.

The server showed up and took their plates. Nelson took the bill and paid for lunch.

"Walk you back to your office?" he asked.

"Walk me to my condo," she said.

Nelson took her hand.

"How can I refuse?"

They left the restaurant together, one last time.

5

Cynda took off her headset then tossed it onto the desk. It was a busy day so far. Good for the company, bad for her. The real estate market in the ATL was hot and they were reaping the benefits. But it was a bittersweet success. The homes they sold were the homes of people she knew, families and people forced to sell because of rising property values.

The phone rang, bringing Cynda back to reality.

"Benson Realty. How can I help you?"

"Hello, this is Kadija Dumare, calling on behalf of Thomas Carter of Carter Enterprises. Is Miss Benson available?"

Cynda's mouth opened but nothing came out.

"Hello?"

"What did you say?" Cynda finally said.

"I'm Kadija Dumare. I'm . . ."

"Calling from Carter Enterprises," Cynda said. "Sorry about that. We weren't expecting your call. Miss Benson isn't in the office right now, but I can transfer you to her cell. One minute please."

Cynda put Kadija on hold then jumped from her desk and danced as she called Laura.

"What is it, Cynda?"

"It's him!" Cynda yelled.

"That was loud. Him who?"

"Thomas Carter!"

"Where?"

"On hold. Thomas Carter is on hold!"

"Well damn, girl! Transfer him!"

Cynda sat down, transferred the call to Laura's phone then bounced as she waited. Five minutes later the transfer light on the office phone went off and her cell buzzed.

"Well?" she asked.

"He's coming to Atlanta!"

Cynda jumped out of her seat then pumped her fist.

"Yes!"

"Close the office and meet me at Communion Coffee," Laura said "We got a thousand and one things to do to get ready. This is our chance, Cynda. It's finally happening!"

"I'll be right down!"

Cynda hung up then texted all the realtors that the office was closed until tomorrow morning. She ran into Laura's office, rifling through the filing cabinet for the specs for the building. Laura had an amazing space but hated working on big projects there. Cynda found Laura's portfolio tucked between the file cabinet and the end table where she always put it and forgot it. She filled it with the plans then sprinted out of the office, through the building, out the door, then to her car.

"Where you going in such a hurry?"

Cynda rolled her eyes before turning her head to see Ray sauntering her way.

"Not today," she said.

"Where are you . . ."

Cynda spun around, her eyes narrowed.

"I said not today! Didn't you get the text? The office is closed. Bye!"

"Well, excuse me! I was just . . ."

Cynda jumped in the car and slammed the door, cutting off Ray's response. She sped out of the parking lot, her destination Communion Coffee House. It was Laura's favorite place to brainstorm, a quaint oasis in the middle of the Summerhill District. It took her all of twenty minutes to get there, dodging the crazy traffic on Highway 85 and the wannabe NASCAR drivers in their souped-up Dodge Daytonas. She exited onto Langford Parkway then drove through the neighborhood, noting the encroaching gentrification. Newly renovated homes selling for six figures sat beside untouched homes in various states of disrepair. Some of the older homes displayed 'Not For Sale' signs. The area was another battleground between the haves and the have nots.

Cynda pulled into the Communion parking lot. Laura was there still in her Jeep, talking on her cell. Cynda gathered her things, trotted to the vehicle then tapped on the window. Laura jumped then jerked her head toward the window, her eyes wide. They softened and she smiled as her window slid down.

"Girl, you scared the hell out of me!" she said.

Laura exited the car and they hurried to the entrance.

"You got everything?" Laura asked.

"Yep," Cynda replied.

An elderly man opened the door for them, a generous smile on his rugged face. Cynda smiled back then held the door for him as he shuffled out into the crisp fall air.

Cynda handed Laura the file then went to the counter to order their usual, two turkey club sandwiches, chips, and bottled water. Laura had the files spread out and the laptop booted up when she reached the table.

"I can't believe this is happening!" she said. "All these years."

"Good things come to those who wait," Cynda replied.

Laura twisted her mouth. "Whoever came up with that saying can kiss my Black ass."

Cynda almost knocked the files off the table trying to stifle a laugh. "You're crazy."

Laura smiled. "So here's what I need you to do, Cynda. I need you to confirm the value of our baby. It's been a minute, and I know she's probably sky high now."

"You think Mr. Carter will be interested if the property value is high?"

"Uh huh," Laura replied. "He knows the market here is hot. That's why he's finally interested. That man keeps his eye on real estate everywhere. He could quote you a yurt in Mongolia."

"Got it," Cynda said.

"In the meantime, I'm going to make arrangements," Laura said. "I'm calling in all my favors; the best hotels, the best restaurants, the best events. By the time I'm done this man is gonna think he's the second Black president!"

Cynda frowned. Laura's eyebrows rose and she folded her arms across her chest.

"What?" Laura asked.

"Nothing," Cynda replied.

Laura sucked her teeth. "Girl, what?"

Cynda shrugged. "I don't know. I know Mr. Carter is important, and I know you want to make a great impression, but all that seems a bit much."

Laura leaned back into her chair.

"Really? So, what do you think we should do, Miss-never-planned-an-event-for-a-major-client before?"

"This is our home," Cynda replied. "I think we should just show him the city and stick to the numbers. If he's everything you say he is, that should be enough."

Laura looked away as if contemplating Cynda's suggestion. When she looked back, she was not smiling.

"Just do what I told you to do," Laura finally said. "Let me handle the rest."

"I'm on it."

Cynda left the coffee shop as Laura tapped her cell keyboard, her feelings bruised. Laura rarely disagreed with her. It felt like a setback. She sat in her car then started it, leaning her head on the steering wheel as she took a deep breath. This deal was extremely important to Laura and the firm. The best she could do was follow orders, even if she didn't agree. That was probably best, because if it didn't work out, she wouldn't have to share the blame. On the other hand, she'd worked for Laura for so long, the deal was important to her, too. She sighed. "Not your company, Cynda," she said aloud. "Lord knows you have enough to worry about. Do your job."

She pulled out of the parking lot, her destination the old high rise. She drove through the neighborhood, noting the mix of dilapidated and new homes, each with a different owner but with the same property taxes. Gentrification was happening everywhere, in almost every city in the country, but this was home and it hurt her to see people losing their houses because of the latest land rush. By the time she reached the office she was in a sour mood. Luckily, none of the agents were waiting, so she hurried inside, finding and downloading the information Laura requested then emailing it to her. The flashing numbers in the corner of the screen told her it was time to pick up the twins so she closed up the office then headed to the school. Luckily, the traffic wasn't as heavy as normal. The twins jumped up and down when they saw the car, acting as if it was the first time they'd seen her in years. Their exuberance lifted her mood.

Cynda parked and the teacher on parking lot duty opened the door for the children. Cynda strapped them into their car seats and they were on their way.

"What do y'all want for dinner?" she asked.

"Pizza!" they said in unison.

"Pizza it is!"

She called Terrence.

"What?"

"Call Junie's and order two large pepperoni and Italian sausage pizzas."

"I'm busy."

"Boy, order the pizzas. I got the kids."

"You order them. I'm working on my game. You think I can just drop everything on your whim?"

"It's been a long day, Tee. Don't start."

"How you know if my day wasn't rough?"

"Well, first off you don't have a job," Cynda said. "Second, Mama sleeps most of the day, so you ain't taking care of her."

"I don't have time to order no damn pizza!"

"Which means you don't have time to eat. If I pick it up, I'm getting just enough for me, Mama, and the twins. You do you."

Terrence sighed. "What kind of pizza?"

Cynda grinned. "Pepperoni and Italian sausage."

"Can we get mushrooms and green peppers on one side."

"Yes, but you better eat it all. I'll pay when I pick it up."

"Okay."

Cynda hung up then shook her head. That boy needed a job. A good job. Two years out of college and still playing with that computer. If it was up to her, she'd give him an ultimatum; get a job or get out. No, she wouldn't. It wasn't her way. She couldn't put him out even if she wanted. It was Mama's house, and she was still in her right mind. But sometimes the weight of what she carried settled on her shoulders and she wondered how long she could handle it. At least until Tiffany ended her tour and took the twins. That would take off a big load.

She pulled into Junie's and was about get out the car when she saw her favorite server, Antonio, walking to the car with her order. She rolled down the window.

"Thank you so much, Antonio!"

Antonio smiled. "You're welcome. You're a busy woman."

"At least you noticed."

She gave him her card. Cynda was usually extra cautious about her card, but she'd known Antonio for years and knew he was cool. He returned moments later with the card and the receipt. Cynda gave him a generous tip.

"Until next time," he said.

"See you later," she replied.

The twins moaned about how hungry they were as the pizza smell wafted throughout the car. By the time they reached the house they wailed liked they hadn't eaten in weeks.

"Y'all calm down," Cynda said as she unhooked them from their seats. "I want y'all to go inside, put up your things, wash your hands then meet me at the table. Okay?"

They nodded their heads. As soon as she unbuckled them, they sprinted to the door. Cynda took her purse from the car then ambled to the door and opened it. The twins rushed inside to their rooms. Cynda set the pizza on the table and turned on the oven. When she turned around, Terrence was opening one of the boxes.

"Did you wash your hands? No," Cynda said. "You know what to do."

"I ain't been nowhere!" Terrence said as he went to the bathroom.

"No telling where your hands have been. Cooped up in that room all day," Cynda shot back.

"Baby? You home?"

Cynda washed her hands then went to Mama's room. Mama was sitting up watching TV, a smile on her face.

"Hey Mama," Cynda said. "How was your day?"

"The same," Mama replied. "You cooking dinner?"

"I stopped for pizza. Pepperoni and Italian sausage."

"Okay. You get Terrence his mushrooms?"

Cynda rolled her eyes. "I did."

"Good." Mama straightened up a bit. "Cynda, you are too hard on that boy."

"Mama, you ain't hard enough," Cynda replied. "He's two years out of college and two years in that room. He should have been found a job by now."

"Terrence is a dreamer," Mama said. "Always has been. Dreamers need time to grow."

"But it's my time, Mama!" Cynda said. "I'm out here trying to support everybody. Whose supporting me?"

"Baby, you know . . ."

Cynda didn't let Mama finish. She stormed back to the kitchen. Terrence was at the table with the twins eating pizza.

"Terrence, can you take Mama a slice?"

"You can't do it?"

"No. I'm going outside for a minute."

"Outside? What . . ."

"Terrence, take Mama a damn piece of pizza!" Cynda shouted before storming out of the house and into the backyard. She stopped under the canopy of the huge white oak, tears running from her eyes and down her cheeks. She looked up into the leaves, listening to the wind as it flowed through the branches like an invisible stream. Her thoughts went to Daddy.

"What's that you used to say, Daddy? Life is hard but it ain't harder than me! A Jones might bend, but they don't break."

She wiped her tears away before sitting on the old stone bench he put under the tree when they moved in fifteen years ago.

"I'm bending daddy. As a matter of fact, I'm bent all the way over."

She closed her eyes as she remembered days gone by, the days when she was a girl and everyone took care of her. She took so much for granted back then, but one thing she did learn was that you do for family. You sacrifice for family. Because in the end, family is going to be there for you when nobody else is.

"Cynda?"

She looked up to see Terrence.

"You okay?"

Cynda stood and brushed at her clothes. "I'm okay. I just needed a few minutes alone."

"I took Mama her pizza. She wanted two slices."

Cynda's eyes widened. "She must have been hungry."

"It's pizza," Terrence replied. "The twins finished and I washed their plates. I'll get the dishes once you're done."

Cynda began walking back to the house and Terrence fell in step with her.

"I'm sorry," he said. "I was working on a code that's been giving me hell for the last few hours and I was in a bad mood."

"It's okay," Cynda said.

"No, it's not okay," Terrence replied. "You're taking care of all of us. You don't need to deal with my mess. But I swear, when this game blows up, I'm gonna set you straight. You'll never have to work again."

Cynda smirked. "Thank you, brother."

The kitchen was empty, and the children were doing homework. Cynda sat alone at the table, taking her time as she ate her pizza. Terrence's apology made her feel a little better; she'd be ecstatic if he announced he had found a job. But she'd take her victories where she could get them. And today, it was eating pizza alone.

MILTON J DAVIS

6

Nelson checked his email and texts while waiting for the other passengers to disembark from the Airbus. He was two days early, so with this being his first visit to the A he was going to make the best of it. And Darla was the perfect person to make that happen.

His phone buzzed as he exited the plane. It was Darla.

"Hey Red! Big brother is here!"

"Nelly! I'm waiting inside at the top of the main terminal escalator. Can't wait to see you!"

Nelson hurried to the trains, following the overhead signs. He was at Concourse C, so it wouldn't take long to reach the terminal. He travelled light, only checking a bag because Mama had a ton of stuff she wanted to send Darla. He'd leave the bag with her when he returned to Chicago.

He exited the train at the terminal, surrounded by the joyful faces of those returning home after a long trip and those excited about their visit. Mixed in were the frowning and blank expressions of the road-weary, those to whom the ATL was just another stop. He knew the feeling too well.

The escalator to the main floor was steep and slow, a few passengers jogging up the left side. Nelson waited patiently, checking his phone along the way. He'd barely set foot on the ceramic floor when he heard his name shouted. He looked up to see Darla holding up a big sign of his head, jumping up and down with a mischievous smile on her honey-brown face. It always amazed him that such a petite woman could make so much noise.

"Look at you!" Nelson said.

Darla was stylishly dressed as always, wearing a cute top, jacket, and designer jeans that fit her perfectly. Her frosted tipped dreadlocks brushed her shoulders. The family resemblance was obvious. She dropped the sign then hugged him tight.

"Welcome to the A!" she said. "Let's go!"

Darla grabbed his hand then dragged him to baggage claim, holding the sign in her other hand.

"So how long are you here?" Darla asked.

"A couple of days," Nelson replied. "Going to meet with the realtors then view the property. I can do everything else from my desk."

"You have to stay an extra day so I can show you off. None of my friends here have met any of my family."

"Okay, I'll stay one more day. But you better show me a good time."

"I have a couple of friends who will love you. Speaking of which, how are you and Ronsie doing? Making wedding plans yet?"

Nelson's smile faded. "Me and Ronsie are taking a break."

Darla froze. "What!?!" Her voice echoed across the baggage claim area.

Nelson walked by her then checked to see which baggage carousel would be receiving his suitcase.

"We agreed to take some time to see what else might be out there," he said. "I told her my eyes have been wandering, and she said the same thing."

"Wow," Darla replied. "Y'all have a very mature relationship. If Simone told me that I would have straight cussed her out."

Nelson laughed. "We're friends before anything else and we want the best for each other. If it's meant to be, we'll get back together."

Nelson found the baggage terminal for his flight. A few minutes later the carousel began moving and the bags spilled out. His purple suitcase was one of the first to emerge; he grabbed it and they were off.

"This is for you," he said. "Mama said hi."

"Yay, Mommy!" Darla said. "You hungry?"

"Always," Nelson replied.

"Excellent! Simone's at the house cooking as we speak."

"Simone's at the house? Is everything all right?"

"Yes. She's been working from home since the pandemic. It's been great. The dogs got attached to us being home all the time so her being there kept them from having to readjust."

"Dogs?"

"Yep. Two goldendoodles, Sammy and Max. You'll love them!"

"No, I won't," Nelson said. "You know how I feel about pets, especially giant ones. Looks like I'll have to get a room after all."

"No! At least stay with us one night!"

Nelson looked into her sad eyes then laughed. "Okay. One night."

"Great! You're gonna love our house!"

He followed Darla to her Mercedes SUV.

"Nice," he commented. "The artist life has been good to you, I see."

Darla smirked. "You don't know the half of it."

Nelson and Darla caught up during the drive from the airport to her home in Grant Park. Atlanta traffic was as bad as he heard, so he was glad he wasn't driving. Darla's house was directly across the street from Grant Park, a stylish wooden frame abode with a modest yard. Nelson guessed it was worth somewhere between six hundred fifty thousand to eight hundred thousand in value. Not a bad investment if she bought it original and renovated it.

Darla parked the car on the street.

"Home sweet home!" Darla said.

Simone and the dogs waited on the front porch. Simone greeted them with a wide, warm smile; Sammy and Max bolted down the stairs and swarmed Darla before turning their attention to Nelson. After a brief smell inspection, they were all over him, rising on their hind legs for head rubs.

"Leave him alone!" Darla said.

Nelson squeezed by the dogs to the stairs. Simone gave him a hug. She wore a blue warm up and house shoes, her dark brown skin glowing. Her pixie haircut fit her dimpled oval face perfectly.

"Welcome to our home, irmão!"

"Hi Simone," he said.

The dogs double teamed him again. Nelson scowled.

"I see you're still not a fan of dogs," Simone said.

"Does it show?" he replied.

Simone let loose that cute laugh that made Darla fall in love with her.

"They're not going to stop until you love on them," she said.

"She's right," Darla agreed.

"Will they really stop if I do?" Nelson asked.

"Maybe," Darla said.

"Okay then."

Nelson set down his bag, knelt, and began a hug fest with both dogs. They responded enthusiastically, wagging tails and trying to lick his face. A minute of attention was just enough; the dogs turned their attention to Simone and Darla.

"Come on," Darla said. "We'll get you settled then visit the gallery. It's not far."

Nelson followed his sister through the house's main living space. It was open concept with wooden floors and a large island in the modern style kitchen. The main suite was to the right of the open space, the guest rooms to the left at the back of the house. The first room was Simone's office, the second the guest bedroom. It was of modest size, with an inviting looking queen rice bed. There was an attractive ensuite with a shower and quartz vanity.

"This is nice," Nelson said.

"Thank you," Simone replied. "I designed it myself."

"You did a great job."

"Sure you only want to stay only one night?" Darla asked. "You got a great room and home-cooked meals."

"I'm tempted," Nelson said.

"I'm making Bacalhaus-a-bras," Simone said.

"What's that?" Nelson asked.

"Something you're going to love. Trust me," Darla said.

The dogs came into the room, brushing against Nelson's legs.

"I guess I can stay two days," he said.

"Yes!" Darla replied. "Let's get your things stashed."

Nelson and Darla unpacked his bag, Darla chatting the entire time. He realized he missed her energy and her ability to fill every moment with conversation. After they were done, Darla left the room to change. Simone appeared moments later.

"I'm glad you decided to stay," she said. "Darla was excited when you told her you were coming. She loves you very much."

"Me and Red were close coming up," he said. "I've missed her a lot, too. Pops keeps me busy with the business these days. As a matter of fact, me being here is a test."

"Really?" Simone said.

Nelson nodded. "This is the first deal he's given me free reign on. I went to Germany to close a deal for him and his partners were impressed. So I guess it's time for me to show what I got for real."

"If everything Darla says about you is true, you've got this," Simone said.

"Thanks. And thank you for making my sister happy," Nelson said. "It took her a long time to get where she needed to be."

"And thank you for supporting her along the way," Simone replied.

"That's what big brothers are for," Nelson said.

"Simone!" Darla called out. "Come get ready!"

"Okay!" Simone called back. She smiled and left the room.

Nelson sat on the bed then patted the mattress. This was a good firm bed, and the prospect of home cooked meals was hard to pass on. He decided he could put up with the dogs for a couple of days. Staying with family was always better than hotels, and to be honest, he was a bit weary of them. Pops must be a real road warrior to have done it for so long. He fell back on the bed and closed his eyes.

"Thank you for your sacrifice," he whispered.

"Oh no you don't!"

Darla stood at the door; arms folded across her chest as she patted her foot. Simone was behind her, hiding a grin. Simone had changed into an outfit that complimented Darla's.

Nelson sat up and stretched. "Just resting a bit."

"You'll have time to do that tonight."

"Can't stay out too long," Nelson replied. "I have a meeting in the morning."

"We won't. We're coming back here for dinner, remember?"

"Well, let's go! You know I love your art."

"You and millions of others," Simone said. "Your little sister is the current darling of the artworld."

They climbed into the car, Nelson sitting up front with Darla, Simone in the back with the dogs. After they were on their way, Nelson glanced in the back.

"The gallery allows dogs?" he asked.

Darla nodded. "We don't go anywhere that doesn't, even if we don't have the dogs with us."

"Besides, our babies are well behaved," Simone added.

The gallery was a few blocks away. It occupied a space surrounded by new restaurants and other businesses close to Atlanta's Beltline. It was revitalized neighborhoods like these that made Ms. Benson's hotel interesting to his father.

The inside of the gallery was a model of fashionable minimalism with very little to take attention away from the art. A few people strolled through, stopping at each image. Darla hurried over to a middle-aged couple studying one of her abstract pieces.

"I call this one Tempest," Darla said. "I painted it when I was in a stormy mood."

The couple turned to look at Darla and their eyes went wide. A lively conversation ensued, with Darla leading them to each painting. By the third painting, everyone in the gallery was captured by her celebrity and energy.

"She loves doing that," Simone said.

"Darla's always been the outgoing one," Nelson replied. "So tell me, how did you two meet?"

"In a gallery in Portugal, just like this," Simone said. "But while everyone else was staring at the paintings, I was staring at her. I didn't think she noticed until her tour was over and I was leaving. She grasped my arm and it felt electric. I knew it was her before I turned around. And we've been together since."

"Vintage Darla," Nelson said. "Honest and straightforward. So you moved to Atlanta?"

"Yes, after she promised me that when she became famous, we would return to Lisbon and buy a house. We would spend six months in America, and six months in Portugal. We bought the house in Lisbon two months ago."

"Congratulations!" Nelson said.

"Now she's learning Portuguese," Simone said.

They followed Darla and her entourage to the next painting.

"Has it been tough establishing your interior design business in the States?"

"Not at all," Simone replied. "Darla knows so many people, and many of them gave me a chance just on her recommendation. I owe it to her."

"You better treat my baby sister right," Nelson said. "Or you'll have to answer to me."

"You don't have to worry about that," Simone said. "She's my forever love."

"I know," Nelson replied. "I see it when I look at you two. It's just part of my duty as big brother."

"She told me you were very protective of her," Simone said. "She said your support got her through some difficult times."

"Family is everything," Nelson replied. "That's what our parents instilled in us."

"What are you two doing?"

Nelson looked at Darla's frowning face. They'd made the rounds of the gallery and the visitors had dispersed.

"Just catching up," he said.

"You were supposed to be on the tour," she replied.

"I wasn't going to listen to you talk about your art with a bunch of strangers. I'm your brother. Membership has its privileges."

Darla grinned. "I'll let you off the hook this time. Now come on. Let me tell you about my finger paintings."

"Lead the way," Nelson said.

Simone leaned close to him then whispered. "You got out of that one."

Cynda

Nelson winked before following Darla to the first painting.

MILTON J DAVIS

7

Cynda pulled into the parking lot of Cherry Hill Baptist Church with a frown on her face. It wasn't because she didn't want to be there; it had been too long since she attended church. Her frown was for who she would see there. But Mama insisted on going, so she obliged. It wasn't often she felt good enough to want to go outside, and she wasn't going to be the person to deprive her of her simple pleasures.

The twins had been a mess getting dressed, but once it was done, they settled down. She'd expected more resistance from Terrence, but he agreed without an argument. She wished he hadn't. He had nothing decent to wear, so she had to salvage something from what remained in Daddy's wardrobe. Seeing him in one of Daddy's favorite suits almost made her cry. She didn't realize how much Terrence resembled him until the moment he stepped out of his room. 'My, my, my,' Mama said when she saw him. Cynda felt the same way.

The church members greeted them with hoots and shouts of blessing. It had been almost a year since they attended and Mama's old friends were happy to see her. Miss Myra was the first to greet them, looking elegant in her black dress and ivory church hat so wide that anyone sitting next to her would have to lean away.

"Bless the Lord!" she said. "If this ain't a sight for sore eyes!"

She bent over and gave Mama a hug while she was still in her wheelchair.

"Hey Myra," Mama said. "It has been a long time. I feel bad not coming sooner."

Miss Myra waved her hand as if shooing away a fly.

"Ain't nobody worrying about that, Justine," she said. "We just glad you here."

Miss Myra's eyes fell on Cynda and she smiled and beamed again.

"And just look at you, Cynda Ella Jones! Just as beautiful as ever. No wonder Reverend Smith asks about you so much!"

"Hey Miss Myra," Cynda said. She hugged Mama's best friend while keeping a lookout for the reverend. It was her plan to spend as little as time as possible with him.

"And the babies!"

Miss Myra released her to hug the twins. They were polite, their little faces cute and confused.

"So the babies are still with y'all?" she asked.

"Yes, ma'am," Cynda replied. "Until Tiffany comes back."

"You are an angel," Miss Myra said. "Taking care of your family like this. Your daddy would be proud of you."

A spark of sadness flared in Cynda's chest as Miss Myra turned her attention to Terrence.

"Terrence Jones, Jr.! Don't you look like the spitting image of your daddy!"

74

Terrence gave Miss Myra a half smile and an anemic hug.

"I have so much to tell you Justine, but service is about to start. Let's go inside!"

Cynda and the family followed Miss Myra into the sanctuary. Cynda was about to sit in the rear pew when Mama touched her arm.

"I want to sit up front with Myra," she said.

"Okay, Mama. I'll take you up front then come back."

"I want y'all to sit with me," Mama said.

Cynda didn't answer because she didn't want to curse in church. She pushed Mama to the front aisle then helped her out of her chair and onto the pew. The twins jumped to sit beside her and Miss Myra sat opposite them. Terrence refused to come up front. He sat on the last pew, an 'I dare you' look on his face.

"Cynda."

Cynda did her best not to cringe when she heard Reverend Bowden's rumbling voice. She turned to see him, forcing a smile to her face.

"Hi Reverend," she said with false joy.

"Curtis," he said. "I told you to call me Curtis. We're friends, right?"

He pulled her into a hug before she could answer, an embrace that lasted too long.

"It's good to see you and the family here today. It's been too long. I was thinking that y'all had joined another church."

"Mama wouldn't have it," Cynda said. It wasn't that Curtis was a bad looking man. He was handsome, and the beard he'd grown worked in his favor. He was in relatively good shape, and he was always charming and polite. But there was something about him that didn't sit well with her. His attitude didn't come off as sincere. And there was also the fact that Curtis Bowden was looking for a wife. Many of the older church members had a problem with an unmarried pastor. It's not a proper church without a first lady, they would say. That's what Mama used to say. And while Reverend Bowden's fiery sermons and community activity increased church membership and tithes significantly, the deacons and the trustees wouldn't be satisfied until Cherry Hill Baptist Church had a Mrs. Bowden. And Cynda was determined not to be that person.

"Are y'all staying for church brunch?" he asked.

"I doubt it, Reverend," she replied.

"Curtis," he corrected.

"I doubt if we'll stay . . . Curtis," she said. "Every day is busy for me, and Sundays are my only day of rest."

"I understand," Curtis said. "It's admirable what you're doing. Taking care of your mother, watching your sister's children, and supporting your brother. Not to mention the great work you do for Laura. You know she gave a generous donation to our youth soccer league last month."

"Did she?"

"Yes. I was under the impression that you had something to do with that."

Cynda shook her head. "I didn't know. I'm not involved in that part of the business. But I'm sure Laura felt it was worth it."

"We have started a few programs that are having a positive impact on the community. A number of local businesses have noticed and given support, financially and otherwise. We've been blessed."

"All due to you, no doubt," Cynda said. She admonished herself silently. She'd given him a compliment. That was not good.

Curtis smiled. "I give it all to God."

"Reverend?"

Cynda looked over Curtis's shoulder to see Brittany Lanier frowning at him . . . or her. Brittany was a statuesque, brilliant woman who had moved to Jonesboro from New Orleans to expand her thriving tech business. Church gossip was she was working hard to become Mrs. Bowden, but so far, the reverend wasn't interested. Curtis's smile faded as he turned. Brittany's expression became joyful.

"It's almost time for service to start," she sang.

"Thank you, Miss Lanier." The reverend turned his attention back to Cynda.

"Maybe I can call on you sometime in the near future. I still haven't had time to see the city, and since you're a rare native Atlantan, I'm sure you can show me around."

"I wish I had time, Curtis."

"Make some time for yourself Cynda," he replied. "You'll look up one day and you'll wonder where it all went."

His words hit her between the eyes. She thought about that often. When would she have time for herself? When would she finally have time to do the things she always wanted without worrying about the welfare of everyone else?

"I will," she replied.

Service began promptly at ten. By eleven tithes had been collected and the parishioners moved to the church kitchen and dining space for brunch or strolled to the parking lot to their cars.

"I think I want to eat brunch here," Mama said.

"Really Mama?" Cynda replied.

"We don't know the next time we'll be here," Mama said. "I want to spend some time with my friends in the Lord's house."

Cynda's shoulders slumped.

"Okay, Mama."

They made their way into the church events room, sharing a table with Miss Myra. Curtis came over, sitting beside her with a big grin on his face. Things weren't as bad as she imagined. The twins enjoyed eating and playing with the other children, and it had been some time since she'd seen Mama so happy. Miss Myra and her friends lightened her mood. Curtis's attention was made bearable by interruptions from old friends and Brittany dragging him off to take care of 'urgent matters.' Terrence sat alone in a corner, his attention transfixed by his phone. By twelve they were on their way back to the house. Everyone changed into more comfortable clothes. Terrence retreated into his room but came out to watch the twins while Cynda helped Mama change. She left the room so Mama could take a nap.

Cynda finally had a few hours to herself. She retreated into her room, turned on some good jazz then did her latest French lesson. Afterwards, she picked up the romance novel from her nightstand she'd been trying to finish for the past month. She was just settling in when the familiar fire alarm ring from her cellphone blared.

"On a Sunday?" she said. She picked up the phone.

"Hi Laura. What's up?"

"Girl, I hate to bother you on a Sunday, but this is urgent."

"You sound terrible!" Cynda replied.

"All this time, and I pick now to get Covid. Good thing I took the vaccine."

"All you can do is rest. Can I bring you anything?"

"No. I'm good. But I'm going to need you to meet with Mr. Carter in the morning."

Cynda sat up straight. "Me?"

"Yes, you," Laura replied. "You know this project almost better than I do. You can brief him on the details, take him to the site, and answer any preliminary questions he might have."

"But this is the big one," Cynda said. "I'm not ready for this."

"You have to be, Cynda. I can't do it. It's on you."

Cynda's relaxing day had just crashed and burned.

"Okay. I'll go to the office and get the file."

"Thank you so much!" Laura said. "Call me if you have any questions. You can do this."

"Thank you. Now get off this phone and get some rest. The sooner you're well, the better."

Cynda fell back on her bed and sighed.

"One day," she said. "One day."

8

Nelson's rideshare pulled into the parking lot of Benson Realty a few minutes ahead of schedule. The renovated home didn't look like the headquarters of a real estate mogul, but Mrs. Benson had her roots in home realty, and using a former home as an office seemed right. There were a few cars in the lot, which meant the agents were out making their rounds. Another sign of a successful business. Nelson had done his research, so he wasn't surprised. Still, it was good to see a visual confirmation.

Nelson entered the home office. The foyer had been renovated into a reception seating area, with a few comfortable chairs and a counter set to the side. No one sat at the desk, so Nelson had no way of letting anyone know he had arrived. He was about to dial Mrs. Benson's number when a young woman with a mahogany complexion and curly hair walked from the back, wearing a sharp business dress. She shared a warm smile that immediately brought forth one from him. She extended her well-manicured hand and they shook.

"Mr. Carter, welcome to Atlanta," she said. "I'm Cynda Jones, Miss Benson's assistant. I have to apologize for her absence. She got sick last night."

"I'm sorry to hear that," Nelson replied. "We can postpone for another time."

"No need to," Cynda said. "I'm up to speed with the project, and who knows when we'll get this opportunity again."

Nelson smiled. "I understand. This proposal has been on my father's desk for a long time."

Cynda smiled. "Please follow me to the conference room."

They ambled down a long hallway. The old bedrooms on either side had been transformed into comfortable offices. Most were empty. Nelson kept looking to either side to keep from watching Cynda's hips. Be professional, he thought to himself. Yes, she's appealing, but this is business.

The conference room was a converted dining space. The original chandelier hung over a large rectangular antique table, giving the room an air of class. A coffee station occupied one of the corners, supporting a standard coffee maker and an expensive expresso machine.

"Coffee?" Cynda asked.

"I would like a cup of expresso," Nelson replied.

"You just went over my head," Cynda said. "That's Ms. Benson's baby. She's the only one in the office that knows how to use it."

"I'll give it a shot," Nelson replied. "I have a similar one at home. Would you like a cup?"

"If you're making it, of course," Cynda said.

Nelson put down his satchel and went to the machine. After familiarizing himself with the model, he went to work.

"So tell me about the building," he said.

"It's the Peabody Hotel," Cynda said. "The nickname was Freedom Inn."

"Why was that?"

"Before the Civil Rights Movement, it was one of the few hotels where Black people could stay. During the movement, many of the leaders and protesters visiting the city would rent rooms there. Of course it was the victim of vandalism until the Nation of Islam began protecting it."

"That's fascinating!" Nelson replied.

He finished a cup of expresso and took it to Cynda, placing it in front of her.

"Thank you," she said. "I feel kinda bad about this. You're the guest. I should be making coffee for you."

"Good thing the bosses aren't here," Nelson said. He smiled at Cynda and she smiled back before sipping the expresso.

"Wow. This is good," she said. "Better than what Laura . . . I mean Ms. Benson makes."

"I know how to handle precious things," Nelson said, then quickly regretted it. He was flirting.

"I'm sure you do," Cynda replied. She was flirting back, and that made him smile. He waited until he calmed down before turning around with his cup and taking a seat opposite Cynda.

"So what makes this project so important to Ms. Benson, and why should we invest?"

"It has sentimental and historical value to the community," Cynda began, "but of course that's not enough when it comes to investment. What makes it truly valuable is the increase in property value and community investment over the past ten years. Ms. Benson predicted it would happen, she just didn't predict how."

Cynda moved to his side of the table with her charts and sat beside him.

"I hope you don't mind shuffling through papers," she said. "I hate presentation software."

Cynda opened the folder then spread out the charts. "The property value took a jump when the interstate was built years ago, but it really got hot with gentrification."

"Is that the word we want to use?" Nelson asked.

"No need to sugar coat it," Cynda replied. "It is what it is."

"Do I hear a little emotion in your tone?"

Cynda closed her eyes and took a breath. "I'm sorry. It's just that I grew up in a neighborhood that's going through this. It's hard for me to be objective when I see people I know losing their homes."

"Is the Peabody in your neighborhood?"

"No," Cynda said. "My parents moved to the suburbs around the time I was high school age. Wanted me to go to a 'better' school."

"I see. Was it?"

"Yes and no."

Cynda looked at him and he got that feeling again.

"So what's the valuation now?" he asked, turning his attention back to business.

Cynda shared another chart. "Even without renovation the value has increased fourfold. Add the future mixed-use development planned for the area over the next ten years, this property could be a gold mine."

"I know you're aware that our company isn't in the business of long term investments," Nelson said. "We're interested in properties that will give us the desired return on our investment in five years."

"Peabody Hotel will do that and then some," Cynda replied.

Nelson leaned back in his chair.

"Well, you've convinced me on paper. Let's see this hotel of yours."

"Excellent!" Cynda said. "We'll take my car."

Nelson followed Cynda outside to a black SUV. She unlocked the doors and Nelson entered on the passenger side. He noticed two child seats in the back.

"Sorry about the mess," Cynda said. "I didn't have time to clean out the car. It's hard to do everything with two kids."

"What's their names?"

Cynda hesitated. "Malon and Sha'kwon. Don't ask me why my sister gave them those names."

"So you babysit them sometimes?" he asked.

"A year so far," Cynda replied. "Tiffany got stationed in Germany. She's in the National Guard. I'm watching the kids until she comes home."

"And when will that be?"

"In a few months." Cynda looked at Nelson. "Wait a minute. Why are you in my business? And why am I telling you?"

They both laughed.

"I apologize," Nelson replied. "It's a habit. I like to get to know the people I'm working with. Gives me insight into their motivations."

"I can save you the trouble," Cynda replied. "We want to make money. Lots of it. And your company does, too."

They drove to the site, Cynda sticking to the surface streets like a true native Atlantan. He found himself staring at her profile, then turned away.

"Where are you staying?" Cynda asked.

"At my sister's," Nelson replied. "I booked a hotel, but she insisted I stay with her. It's been a while since we've seen each other."

"That's great. Always good to stay with family. Where does she live?"

"Her and her partner have a house across the street from Grant Park."

Cynda whistled. "Sister is making some money!"

"She's doing okay," Nelson replied. "Her artist career is taking off. It's her partner that brings it home. She's an interior designer."

"That area is a perfect example of the changes in the city. When I was little, the park and the zoo were surrounded by low rent houses and duplexes. Now you can't buy a house there below six hundred thousand."

"Changing times, changing places," Nelson commented.

They drove a few more minutes before a ten-story hotel rose above the horizon.

"There she is," Cynda said.

Cynda parked the car in a lot across the street because chains blocked the hotel parking lot. The building was in worse shape than Nelson imagined. It had apparently been abandoned for quite some time. Most of the windows were broken, and graffiti decorated the lower walls.

"I know," Cynda said. "She needs a lot of work. At least two million dollars worth. But we're sure we'll get that back and some."

They walked around the base of the building, avoiding piles of trash.

"When was the last time someone's been inside?" Nelson asked.

"Officially? Two years ago. It was still structurally sound," Cynda replied.

Nelson took photos then they returned to Cynda's car.

"I don't know," he said. "We usually purchase in use properties. This will take some work, which makes it riskier. We'll have to renovate and then convince a REIT that it's worth the investment."

"I agree," Cynda said. "But we know it's worth it."

They were basically done, but Nelson wasn't ready to part company with Cynda.

"It would probably help if I knew more about the city," he said. "A tour would be nice."

Cynda smiled. "You got the right person. No one knows these streets better than me."

They walked back to the car.

"I know a good place we can stop for lunch too," Cynda said. "It looks like a dump, but the food is fire. Hope you're not on a diet." Cynda eyed him up and down. "You look like you work out."

Nelson face flushed. "I do a little something now and then."

"I bet you do. Let's go. I'm getting hungry thinking about it."

"Lead the way."

They set out again. Nelson had a decent sense of direction, so he knew they were heading west. Cynda pointed to their left.

"That exit will take you to the West End. It's also the exit for the AU Center."

"Ah," Nelson said. "Did you attend school there?"

"Yes," Cynda replied. "Clark-Atlanta. Didn't finish though. My daddy got sick and I had to leave and help out. I've been working ever since."

"Any plans to return?"

"Someday. Can't think about it right now. I have to be present for family."

"I understand that. Family first."

"You know it. How about you? What prestigious college did your family send you to?"

"Howard," Nelson replied. "It's become sort of a family tradition. Mama and Daddy both graduated there, my sister, too."

"Here's our exit," Cynda said. She steered off to the right, then took a left down a two-lane road. The homes and businesses in this part of the city were old and worn, a stark contrast to the area they just left.

"For a long time, a lot of the neighborhoods in South Atlanta suffered from lack of investment," Cynda said. "People say that the residents didn't care, but that's a lie. They did; they just couldn't get the loans and grants to make a difference."

Cynda pulled into the parking lot of a small strip mall. There was a convenience store, a barbershop, and a restaurant. The sign over the restaurant read 'Mama Bee's.'

"This is it!" Cynda said. "We're early, but if we waited another thirty minutes it would take us an hour to get in."

"This looks . . . quaint," Nelson said.

Cynda laughed. "That's a nice way to put it. Believe me, once you eat, you'll want to pay me for bringing you here."

"You know I'm from Chicago, right?" Nelson said.

"I heard y'all got some good food there, but that's that second generation Southern cooking," Cynda replied. "I'm not going to say anything else. I'll let the food do the talking."

A bell rang as they entered.

"Welcome, welcome!" the staff said in unison. A stout middle-aged woman came from the back, wearing clothes resembling a school cafeteria worker, covered by a blue apron. Her smile was like a slice of sunshine.

"Hey, Cynda!" she said.

"Hey, Miss Clara!"

They hugged and Miss Clara looked over Cynda's shoulder at Nelson.

"Who you done brought with you this time?"

"Nelson Carter," Cynda said. "He's here on business from Chicago."

Nelson extended his hand. Miss Clara pushed it aside and pulled him into a hug. She smelled like cocoa butter and fried chicken.

"Y'all sit where y'all want," she said. "I'll bring y'all menus."

"Just bring one," Cynda said. "You know what I want."

Nelson and Cynda sat at a worn table near the kitchen entrance, and a few minutes later Miss Clara returned with a laminated menu. The list had the usual meals served at most soul food restaurants, staples that had sustained the Black community for generations. It had been a long time since he ate like this. He wondered if his stomach could handle it.

"What do you recommend?" he asked.

"You can't go wrong with the fried chicken," Cynda replied. "But if you don't eat fried food, the baked chicken is great, too. The mac and cheese is amazing, and this is one of the few restaurants I've been to that does collard greens right. Actually, there's not a bad item on the menu."

"The fried catfish is great today," Miss Clara said. "It's fresh. Joney caught it this morning."

"I'll try that," Nelson said. "I'll get the rice, collards and mac and cheese, too."

"What do you like to drink?" Miss Clara asked.

"You got bottled water?" Nelson asked.

"Sure do. I'll be back with your meals in a few minutes."

Miss Clara took his menu then strolled away. Other customers had entered the restaurant, and Miss Clara greeted them on her way back to the kitchen.

"This is not the place Ms. Benson would recommend for lunch," Cynda said. "She prefers fancier eating establishments."

"I have a thing for them myself," Nelson admitted. "But I trust your judgement."

Cynda's eyes widened. "Do you? Why? You just met me."

"You did good work on the proposal," Nelson replied. "And before you say it was a team effort, don't. I know better. I can tell by how you read those numbers. This project means a lot to you. Just like this city."

"It does," Cynda admitted.

Miss Clara returned with their plates. Nelson's mouth watered when he saw his food. He hoped it tasted as good as it looked. He looked at Cynda's plate and his eyes widened.

"Is that oxtails?"

Cynda nodded. She stabbed one with her fork and put it on his plate.

"Try it. They're great."

"I'm not much of an oxtail fan," Nelson replied.

Cynda smiled. "That's because you haven't had Miss Clara's."

"I think I should eat my food before I eat yours," Nelson said.

Cynda laughed, a joyful sound that made him laughed as well.

"You better hurry up then," she said. "There might not be any left by the time you're done. That's why I put one on your plate. I might take it back."

Nelson tasted his food. It was excellent, especially the fried catfish.

"So?" Cynda said.

"You didn't lie," Nelson replied. "This is good. Good thing I don't live in Atlanta. I'd be as big as a house. I don't see how you stay so . . ."

Cynda put down her fork and stared at Nelson. "So . . . what?"

Nelson grinned, embarrassed. "So fit."

"Fit. That's a good way to say it," Cynda replied.

Miss Clara arrived, saving Nelson from further embarrassment.

"How is everything, Chicago?" she asked.

"Very good," Nelson replied.

"Better than Chicago?"

"There may be a place in Chi-Town that's better, but I haven't found it."

"And you won't," Miss Clara said. "I'm gonna let y'all finish y'alls meal."

Miss Clara began walking away but turned around.

"I know this is all business, but y'all look good together."

Nelson eyes met Cynda's and they both looked down at their food. They ate quietly until their plates were empty. When they dared to look up, Miss Clara was at their table again holding a pitcher of sweet tea.

"Now that's the best compliment a cook can receive. A clean plate."

"This was amazing," Nelson said. "I'll have to tell all my friends to make Mama Bee's a definite stop when they visit."

Nelson reached into his pocket for his wallet.

"No," Cynda said. "You're the client, remember?"

Cynda was about to open her purse when Miss Clara shook her head.

"No. This is on the house. You brought me a new customer. And as much as you're here, I'll get my money back and some. Y'all go on and have a good day."

Nelson and Cynda hugged Miss Clara then returned to Cynda's car.

"That was great," Nelson said. "Thank you."

"You're welcome. Anything else you'd like to see?"

"No, I think I've seen enough for now. I'd like to sit down and go over the numbers again."

"Of course," Cynda replied. "We'll go back to the office and do just that."

They returned to the realty office. A few agents were at the building, winding up the day. Nelson and Cynda went over the numbers on the project, Cynda answering questions that Nelson knew his father would ask. He glanced at his phone; it was almost five o'clock.

"Wow. The time flew by," he said.

"It did," Cynda replied.

"I guess I should be getting back. I need to call a rideshare."

"I'll drop you off," Cynda replied.

"You sure? I don't want you going out of your way."

Cynda waved. "It's fine. My brother Terrence picked up the kids from school today because I knew our meeting would run late. Won't hurt for him to baby sit a little longer."

"Great," Nelson said. "Can I repay you by taking you to dinner?"

"I'd love to, but I need to get home," Cynda replied. "Terrence can be trusted only so long. I don't want to come home and find the twins running in the streets."

Nelson laughed. "You're funny. Smart, funny . . . and beautiful."

Nelson did it again. Cynda's face went through a range of expressions.

"I'm sorry," Nelson said. "I didn't mean to make you uncomfortable."

"No. It's okay," Cynda replied. "It's just that it's been a while since I've been complimented. Thank you."

She grabbed her purse and keys from the table then headed for the conference room entrance. She stopped then gestured.

"After you," she said.

Nelson led the way to the parking lot, joining the procession of agents. Cynda locked the building after everyone left. Once they were inside the car, Cynda asked for his sister's address. She put it into her navigation system and they set out for his sister's house.

"So, you run it all," Nelson said.

"Yes. Been doing it for five years," Cynda replied.

"Only five? You've got it down. I can see how people would mistake you for Ms. Benson."

"You'll change that thought when you finally meet her," Cynda said. "She's a powerhouse. You either love her or hate her. There's no in between."

"But you don't have a problem working with her."

Cynda shook her head. "That's my superpower. I get along with most people. We butt heads from time to time but we respect each other. My Mama used to say, 'if Cynda can't get along with you, ain't no hope for you.'"

They finally arrived at his sister's home. Cynda extended her hand, Nelson took it. Instead of shaking, he held it still. She didn't pull it way.

"It was nice meeting you, Nelson," Cynda said. "I hope you feel this is a sound investment."

"It was nice to meet you too," Nelson said. "I'm encouraged by what I've seen."

"What time does your flight leave tomorrow?" Cynda asked.

"I'm not going back tomorrow," Nelson replied. "Gonna spend a few days hanging with my sister. I'll work remote until then." Nelson's eyes widened. "Hey, since I'll be here, how about doing that payback dinner tomorrow?"

"Ah . . . um, okay," Cynda replied. "I guess Terrence can handle the kids another evening. And I can answer any additional questions you might have about the project."

"Great!" Nelson said. "So it's a . . . go."

Cynda grinned. "Yes, A go it is."

Nelson let go of her hand then exited the car. He stood in the driveway, watching as she drove away.

"That doesn't look like a rideshare to me."

He turned around to see Darla standing on the porch.

"It wasn't," he replied. "Cynda gave me a ride from the realty office.

"Cynda?"

"Yes. Ms. Benson took ill and her assistant Cynda made the presentation."

The dogs wandered onto the porch and Nelson petted them.

"How did it go?"

"It went very well," Nelson replied. "It's a promising project. Not sure how Pops will feel about it. We'll have to invest more money than we normally do."

"If it's your project, that should be your decision," Darla said.

"You know how Pops is," Nelson said. "Nothing is your decision."

Darla laughed. "Yes indeed."

She opened the door. "Your timing is perfect. Simone just finished dinner. You're gonna love it!"

"If it's anything like yesterday, I know I will."

They entered the house and Nelson headed for his room.

"That Cynda is cute," Darla said.

"I didn't notice," Nelson replied.

"Yeah, right."

He took off his jacket then tossed it on the bed.

"Y'all look good together," Darla said.

Nelson dropped his head and grinned.

"That's the second time I've heard that today." He hugged Darla.

"Look, I'm here for business. On Friday I'm on my way back home. Once Ms. Benson feels better, I'll be dealing with her. Now let's get to that dinner."

"Follow me!"

They sauntered to the kitchen, the dogs loping behind.

MILTON J DAVIS

9

Cynda backed out of the driveway and began the drive home. The meeting went well, much better than she expected. The late-night cramming paid off; Nelson said she knew her stuff. The truth was that she was very familiar with the project. It was all Laura talked about since she bought the building five years ago. No matter what happened, she gave it her best shot. All they could do now was wait.

And then there was Nelson. He was a surprise, a pleasant surprise. Attractive, interesting, and attentive. Smart, too. That was the only thing that should have mattered, but she had to admit there was more to it. She couldn't remember the last time she spent time with a man that was more interested in getting to know her than bragging on himself, even if it was about business. But was it? There were a couple of times that he was clearly flirting. He even admitted it. Well not really admit, but he did apologize, which he didn't need to.

"Damn girl has it been that long?" she said aloud. She was getting dating signals from a business meeting. That was not good.

Cynda broke her musing and called Laura. The phone barely rang before Laura answered.

"So, how did it go?"

"I'm fine, how are you?"

"Girl, I don't have time for your smart ass attitude. Don't leave a sick woman hanging. How did it go?"

"It went very well," Cynda replied. "First off it wasn't Mr. Carter. It was his son, Nelson."

"What? He sent his son? That's terrible!" Cynda's stomach twitched. "Why?"

"By sending his son, he's telling us our project isn't a priority."

"Why wouldn't he just tell us that over the phone?"

"I don't know," Laura replied. "Maybe he's telling us he's more interested than most but not quite there."

"I don't know," Cynda said. "Nelson was very interested. I told him about the history of the building and the growth occurring in the city near the area. I even took him to lunch at Mama Bee's."

"You took him to Mama Bee's!?! Please tell me he didn't get food poisoning."

Cynda laughed. "He's just fine. He actually enjoyed it."

"That was a risky choice," Laura said. "But it worked out."

"It did."

"So what's the verdict?"

"It would have been the first thing I told you if I knew," Cynda replied. "He didn't say we had a deal, but he was very positive. I think we have a good chance. I'll find out more tomorrow at dinner."

"Wait, what?" Laura said. "You're going to dinner tomorrow? I figured he'd be on his way back to Chicago."

"He's staying a few extra days. His sister lives here, near Grant Park."

"And you're going to dinner because?"

"I gave him a ride back to his sister's house."

Laura was quiet for too long.

"What?" Cynda said.

"How old is this Nelson?"

"I don't know," Cynda replied. "Late twenties probably. About my age I think."

"Uh huh."

"It's not like that," Cynda said. "You know me. Strictly business."

"Is he attractive?"

"He's handsome. Fit, too. But again, you know me."

"But I don't know him."

"Laura, stop!"

Laura laughed then coughed. "I'm sorry. I have to get my laughs when I can. This covid is kicking my butt. Sounds like you did a good job. But please don't take him to another one of your hole in the wall restaurants. Wine and dine the man. Use your company card."

"Isn't that just for supplies?"

"You can use it anywhere. Dinner is on the company."

"In that case, I have a few places in mind. What's my budget?"

"Whatever you think is necessary," Laura replied. "I trust you."

"I got it, boss."

"Eww. I hate it when you call me that. Let me get back in this bed. Call me after the dinner, okay?"

"Okay. Get better."

"I'm trying."

Cynda hung up then called Terrence.

"What?" her brother answered.

"How did everything go?"

"Terrible."

Cynda's radar flared. "What happened?"

"I had to watch those damn twins all day AND wait on Mama. I had no time to get anything done!"

"Sounds like my life every day," Cynda said. "Welcome to the party. Hey, thank you for doing it. I'm picking up Chinese on the way home. You get to have whatever you want."

"Anything?"

Cynda laughed. "Yes, anything."

"Get me the Peking Duck with four chicken egg rolls and hot and sour soup."

"See, this is why I don't do this. You trying to spend all a sister's little money."

"You offered."

"It's all good. I got you. I don't need retirement money. As long as my brother is full that's all that matters."

"You're not going to make me feel guilty, Cee Cee," Terrence said, using her nickname.

"I didn't think so. See y'all in a little while."

"See you."

Cynda

Cynda called ahead for the order. With the exception of Terrence 's order, she knew what everyone else wanted. Everything was ready when she reached the restaurant.

It was almost dark when she made it home. The twins stood in the small foyer, their hands reaching out with mischievous smiles on their faces.

"Give us food. Give us food!"

"No!" Cynda replied. She ran by them and they chased her into the kitchen.

"Y'all go wash your hands while I make your plates," she said.

Terrence sauntered into the kitchen.

"Which box is mine?"

Cynda took out his meal and sat in the counter. He picked it up then went back to his room.

"Cynda?"

Cynda began putting Mama's meal together.

"Hey Mama!" she shouted. "I'm making your plate right now. I stopped by Royal House and got you some shrimp fried rice."

"That's wonderful, baby."

She made the children's plates and let them sit in the family room in front of the big screen. She'd have rice to clean up later, but she didn't mind. She was in a good mood because of today's meeting and Laura's compliments. She made Mama's tray then carried it into the room. Mama was sitting up, looking bright and warm. She sat the food on her bed tray then went to get hers. She didn't make a plate for herself; she was eating out of the boxes.

"You want to watch the news?" Cynda asked.
Mama shook her head. "Too depressing."
Mama ate a forkful of fried rice and smiled.
"Royal House has the best shrimp fried rice."
"They do," Cynda replied.
"What did you get?" Mama asked.
"Mongolian Beef," Cynda replied.
"Never understood why they serve Mongolian Beef at a Chinese restaurant. Don't make no sense."
"It might not make sense, but it tastes good," Cynda said. "You want to watch the romance channel?"
Mama shook her head. "Dr. Curtis called today. She wanted to make sure I made my appointment next week."
"Next week?"
Cynda set down her food and picked up her phone. She pulled up her calendar. "Yep. Next week. Time for your check up."
"We don't need to go if you don't want to," Mama said. "She's just going to tell us the same thing."
"We're going," Cynda replied. "Need to see how fast you're getting better."
Mama laughed. "Baby, I'm old. Old people don't get better. We just don't get worse as fast if we go to the doctor."
"Don't talk like that," Cynda said. "We'll let the doctor tell us what's going on."
Cynda picked up the remote. "Let's watch some home improvement. You can show me

what you want to do to the house when I get rich."

Mama laughed. "You're so silly. Okay, let's watch."

Cynda and Mama watched television while they finished dinner. Cynda took Mama's dishes to the kitchen; when she returned, Mama was asleep. She turned off the TV and went to check on the kids. They were mesmerized by the cartoon they watched, with Terrence sitting beside them just as enthralled.

"Terrence, bring me y'alls plates," Cynda said.

Terrence gathered the plates from the twins then walked backwards into the kitchen, never taking his eyes of the screen. Cynda rolled her eyes as she took the plates from him.

"Gonna break your damn neck," she said under her breath.

She rinsed the dishes before putting them into the dishwasher. Her thoughts drifted back to the day's meeting. She should have been thinking about the deal, but she kept seeing Nelson. She wanted to be sure that what she saw in him was strictly professional, but something inside said it was more than that.

"Girl stop," she whispered to herself. "It's just business."

Cynda glanced at the clock. It was past the twins' bedtime. She marched into the family room.

"Okay, bath time after this one," she announced.

"One more!" Malon pleaded.

"One more!" Terrence echoed, a big grin on his face.

"You're no help," Cynda said. "This is the last one."

The twins sighed and turned their attention back to the cartoon.

"I'll help," Terrence said.

Cynda was shocked. "Why are you so helpful all of a sudden?"

Terrence grinned. "I got my reasons."

"No, I can't loan you any money," Cynda said.

"Not even close," Terrence replied. "All will be revealed in time."

Cynda didn't have the time or energy for Terrence's cryptic statements.

"I hope it's a job offer," Cynda said. Terrence didn't reply.

The show ended and Cynda marched the little ones to the bathroom for their baths. Terrence helped as promised, which turned out to be a bad idea. The twins wanted to play and he obliged.

"Get out, Tee," Cynda said. Terrence raised his hands in confusion.

"But I'm helping!"

"No you're not."

Terrence shrugged his shoulders then left the bathroom. Cynda finally got the twins to calm down and finish their baths. She led them to their rooms then read them a story before tucking them in.

Terrence had retreated to his lair. Mama was fast asleep. Cynda took a shower then donned her night clothes. Normally she went directly to bed, but she decided to have a glass of wine. She didn't drink during the week, but tonight she needed it. As she sipped the merlot, she found herself thinking about Nelson again. She considered calling Telisa to talk about it but decided against it. What she needed was a night out hanging with friends and getting some attention from an interested man or two. She didn't think she was a beauty, but she knew she could turn a head or two with the right wardrobe. Then maybe she wouldn't be obsessing over a client. That was the plan. This weekend she would get a house sitter to watch Mama and the kids and she would go out, even if she had to go alone. She refilled her glass then took a long sip.

"Work is work," she said aloud. "Everything has its place."

Despite it all, she was still looking forward to dinner the next day.

MILTON J DAVIS

10

The day dragged on like an old school miniseries. Cynda should have felt overwhelmed having to handle Laura's work as well as her own, but she didn't. The agents picked up the slack as they usually did when Laura was out. Cynda kept checking the time, anticipating tonight's dinner. She stopped fighting her feelings, deciding to let things run their course. Once the business talk began, she'd come back down to reality and handle things like the professional she was.

Five o'clock came and Cynda began shutting down the office. Her phone buzzed; it was Laura.

"How did everything go today?" she asked.

"Fine," Cynda replied. "The reps closed a few deals today. I found a few new properties on the market and passed them on."

"Stay on top of that," Laura said. "These corporate sharks are snatching up everything before we can get close."

"Oh yeah, I cancelled your speech at the Chamber of Commerce lunch," Cynda said.

"Oh my goodness! I'd forgotten all about that! Thank you!"

"You're welcome."

"So are you ready for dinner tonight?"

Cynda cleared her throat. "As ready as I can be."

"See if you can find out what he's going to tell his father."

"I'll try."

"What are you wearing?" Laura asked.

"Slacks, a nice blouse," Cynda replied.

"Let me see."

Cynda held the phone back and stared at it.

"What?"

"I said let me see."

"It's fine," Cynda said.

"Cynda, let me see what you're wearing."

Cynda switched the phone to video then did a sweep.

"Happy now?"

"No, I'm not," Lauren said. "You look good for work, but that won't do for a dinner meeting."

"It's dinner with a client," Cynda said. "It's not a date."

"It isn't, but it is," Laura replied. "You have to be your best on all levels. Despite all the numbers, deals come down to whether or not the person across the table likes you."

"I think he does," Cynda replied.

"It doesn't hurt to make sure. It's like an interview. So ask yourself; would you wear what you have on now to an interview?"

Cynda inspected herself then frowned.

"No, I wouldn't."

Laura smiled. "What time is dinner?"

"Seven."

"You have time. Head over to Justine's right now."

"Wait a minute! I'm not buying new clothes just to impress a client."

"Of course you're not. I am. This is the big one, Cynda. We can't mess this up. I'm calling ahead so they'll be waiting when you arrive. I'm texting the address. Now go!"

Cynda closed the office then drove to Justine's. She'd been to the exclusive clothing store a few times to pick up items for Laura, but she never paid much attention to their selection. She had a habit of not noticing things she couldn't afford. The shop was in Buckhead on a side road off Peachtree Street, tucked among a row of exclusive clothing and furniture shops. She found a parking space in front of the store and hurried inside. A tall woman with an enormous afro and glittering smile met her as she entered.

"Cynda!" the woman said, greeting her as if she was a long-lost friend. "I'm Justine. Laura didn't exaggerate. You are lovely!"

"Hey, Justine." Cynda extended her hand and Justine pushed it aside, drawing her into a warm hug.

"Any friend of Laura's is a friend of mine," she said. She stepped away from Cynda then studied her.

"We don't have much time," Justine said. "I wish Laura had called me earlier. We could have made something custom. Come, come!"

Cynda followed Justine into the shop. A man entered from the back of the store, dressed in a black shirt and pants, a mane of dreads covering his head. His dimpled smile felt genuine.

"Stephan, this is Cynda, Laura's assistant. We're going to dress her for dinner." Justine said.

"Outstanding," Stephan replied. "I know just the thing. I have something that would be perfect for her!"

Stephan disappeared to the back then returned a moment later with a stunning dress. It was just the right blend of business and fun, perfect wear for the meeting.

"Come on," he said. "Let's get you measured."

"Measured?" Cynda said. "I thought this was my size."

Stephan laughed. "You are SO funny! The dress is your size, and it's going to look great on you, but we want it to fit perfectly. So come over here and get this dress then take it to a dressing room."

Cynda did as she was told. She checked the time before entering the dressing room and changed into the dress. She looked at herself in the mirror and smiled. It did look good on her. She stepped out and did a twirl.

"Now that's the attitude I'm looking for!" Stephan said. "Come over here and let me fit you."

Cynda stood still while Stephan pinched the dress and added pins where it needed alterations.

"Okay, take it off," he said. "I'll be done in seconds."

Cynda went back into the dressing room. As she was changing, a Justine's robe appeared on the door.

"Put this on," Justine said.

Cynda put on the robe. When she emerged from the dressing room, she was met by Justine, Stephan, and a woman sporting a short afro and wearing a tight t-shirt and ripped jeans. Stephan took the dress and hurried away.

"I'll be done in a few!" he called out.

"Cynda, this is Cinnamon," Justine said. "She's going to touch up your makeup and hair while we wait on Stephan."

"My makeup and hair are fine," Cynda said.

Justine and Cinnamon looked at each other then laughed.

"It wasn't that funny," Cynda said.

"We're sorry love," Justine said. "Come sit over here. Cinnamon's not doing anything drastic, just a few highlights."

"I'm just freshening your look," Cinnamon said in a husky voice. "You have been at work all day. Wouldn't you touch up if you were going on a date afterwards?"

Cynda followed Justine to a makeup chair then sat.

"I would, but this is not a date," Cynda said.

"It's not," Justine replied. "According to Laura, it's much more important."

Cynda closed her eyes and let Cinnamon have her way. A few minutes later the makeup artist stepped away.

"There," she said as she handed Cynda a hand mirror. Cynda's eyes went wide.

"Wow," she said. "That's really good."

"I'm a professional, honey," Cinnamon said. "Give me an hour and you'd look like a goddess."

"Finished!"

Stephan fast walked from the back, dress in hand. He hesitated when he saw Cynda.

"Excuse me, ma'am, have you seen Cynda?" he said.

Cynda smirked as she snatched the dress from Stephan then walked to the dressing room.

"Ha. Ha."

When she appeared, the others applauded. Cynda looked into the mirror and her hand flew to her mouth.

"Oh my," she said.

"You're welcome," Justine replied. "Now go close this deal, you savage!"

Cynda hurried to her car and continued to Urban Hits. If the traffic didn't get too bad, she'd make it just in time. But of course, Atlanta's traffic never fails. Cynda arrived ten minutes late. The valet parked her car and she hurried inside.

"Cynda?"

She looked to her left. Nelson was standing before the bar at the entrance, dressed in black slacks, a polo shirt and blazer. She didn't think the man could look any better than he did earlier, but she was wrong. He strolled up to her, clasping her hand with both of his.

"Wow," he said. "You look wonderful."

"You don't look too bad yourself," she replied. *This is not a date.*

"So did you have any trouble getting here?" she asked.

"Not at all," Nelson replied. "Good thing I wasn't driving."

Nelson's phone buzzed.

"Good timing," he said. "Our table is ready."

They walked together to the maître d's stand. She shared a generous smile.

"Mr. and Mrs. Carter, your table is ready," she said.

"It's just Mr. Carter," Cynda corrected her.

"Oh, I'm sorry," the woman replied. "You look so good together."

Nelson laughed while Cynda shook her head. They followed the woman upstairs to a table that gave them an unobstructed view of the Atlanta skyline. Nelson pulled out her chair and she sat.

"Your server will be with you momentarily," the woman said. "I hope you enjoy your meal."

Nelson folded his hands and rested his chin on them.

"So, Mrs. Carter, how did you find this restaurant?"

Cynda rolled her eyes. "A friend of mine told me about it. I drove by it at least five times before I decided to stop and try it. It's really cool, the food is great, and it's next to the Beltline."

"Was that friend a male friend?" Nelson asked.

Cynda ignored Nelson's question and picked up her menu.

"Like I said, the food is great. I'm partial to the duck, but their beef meals are excellent, too."

Nelson picked up his menu. "Interesting choices."

The server, a tall man with a bald head and a glittering septum ring, stopped at their table. "Welcome to Urban Hits," he said. "I'm Khalid, and I'll be your server. Is this your first visit?"

"I've been a few times," Cynda said.

"It's my first time," Nelson replied. "I'm visiting from Chicago."

"Ah!" Khalid said. "I love Chicago! Great foodie town. Let me assure you that you won't be disappointed. Would you like to start with something to drink and an appetizer?"

"You should ask my wife first," Nelson said.

"You're not gonna let that go, are you?" Cynda said.

Nelson laughed. Since Laura gave her free reign, she decided to go all out.

"May I?" she asked Nelson.

"Go ahead," he replied. "I'm not a picky eater."

"We'd like the calamari and pork belly appetizers," Cynda said. "And bring us a bottle of your best white wine."

Khalid nodded. "Excellent choices."

Nelson tilted his head as he looked at her.

"You sure you've only been here a few times? You order like a pro."

"I make every visit count," Cynda replied. "But enough about me, let's talk about you. Who am I sitting across the table from?"

Nelson leaned back in his chair. "Not much to tell. Born and raised in Chicago. Grew up with a silver spoon in my mouth. Private school my entire life then off to college to major in business. I hope to become a partner in the business and one day run it."

"Looks like you're on track," Cynda said.

"I hope so," Nelson replied.

"Your parents had a plan, and you're following it."

"It's a good plan," Nelson replied.

"Is it what you want?" Cynda asked.

Nelson looked puzzled. "What do you mean?"

Khalid returned with the wine and two glasses. He poured a part into Cynda's glass and she tasted it.

"Excellent," she said.

Khalid filled her glass and then Nelson's. He sipped his wine and nodded. They sipped as they talked.

"This is good," he said. "Now what do you mean is this what I want?"

"Sometimes people have a plan for us, but don't ask us if we want it," Cynda said.

"Why wouldn't I?" Nelson replied. "My parents are highly successful. They're well respected and influential in Chicago and beyond."

Cynda shrugged. "When I was about to go to college, my Mama and Daddy sat me down and asked me what made me happy. I told them, and they said that's what I should go for. They said don't worry about making money, because if I loved what I do, I'd do well because I'd be good at it."

"Are you?" Nelson asked.

"I never got to find out," Cynda replied. "Daddy got sick and I had to drop out of school to help out. He passed away a year later."

"I'm sorry," Nelson said.

Cynda shrugged. "Thank you. But that's life. I'm doing okay. Working with Miss Laura has been rewarding, but I still hope to go back to school, even if it's just to finish what I started."

Nelson raised his glass. "Here's to that."

They toasted and their eyes met. Cynda felt a flush of warmth on her cheeks. She looked away.

Khalid arrived just in time. "Are you ready to order?"

"Yes," Cynda replied. "I'll have the Crispy Skin Duck breast."

"And I'll have the Braised Wagyu Beef Cheeks," Nelson said.

Khalid repeated their orders before taking their menus and walking away.

"Back to you," she said. "Are you doing what you want to do?"

"Yes," Nelson said. "I can't imagine anything else."

"Have you tried?" she asked.

"No," Nelson replied.

"Then how do you know?"

Nelson looked thoughtful. "That's a good question."

Cynda

Khalid arrived with their appetizers. Cynda watched Nelson tasted both and grinned when he closed his eyes.

"This is good," he said. "Real good."

"Better than Chicago?" she asked.

"I'm not going that far," Nelson replied. "I have my pride."

"Fair enough," she said.

They finished the appetizers just before the main meals arrived. Again, she watched him sample everything on his plate as he nodded.

"You made good choices," Nelson said. "How did you know I would like these?"

"I didn't," Cynda said. "I knew I did. If you didn't, I'd have some delicious leftovers to take home."

Nelson laughed "That won't happen tonight."

They ate and enjoyed the wine. Khalid came and took the plates. When he returned, he was about to give the check to Nelson. Cynda stopped him.

"I'm taking care of this," she said.

"I'm sorry," Khalid said. "Pay whenever you're ready."

The server left the bill then walked away. Cynda looked at it and couldn't help but whistle.

"I can get that," Nelson said.

"No, you can't," Cynda replied. "You're the guest, remember?"

Khalid returned and Cynda paid the bill.

"Well, I guess we need to make this an official business meeting," Nelson said. "So what is this beltline you speak of?"

"It's a project that began in 2005," Cynda replied. "The goal was to have a series of walkways that connect certain areas of the city. The result was an explosion of building and property values. The project should be completed by 2030. Some of the gentrification of the city is a direct result of the plan. Let me show you."

Cynda took his hand. There was that rush again, but this time she held back a smile. Nelson didn't. He stood, gripping her hand tighter.

"Lead the way."

They walked to the wall window at the opposite side of the restaurant. Below them was the Beltline, a paved walkway bustling with pedestrians, bikers, and people in other forms of off-road transportation.

"This is interesting," Nelson said.

"It is," Cynda replied. "But just like every good idea, there's a bad side as things grow."

"Meaning?"

"Crime, congestion, gentrification," Cynda replied.

Nelson turned to look at her. "You keep bringing up gentrification."

"Do I?" Cynda asked.

"Yes," Nelson answered. "You do know that one of the reasons we're interested in your property is because of the increased property values in the area, which are a direct result of the gentrification in Atlanta."

Cynda felt the warmth drain from her. She turned to Nelson as she let go of his hand.

"I'm aware of it," she replied. "But . . ."

"But, what?" Nelson asked.

Cynda walked back to their table, Nelson close behind. His serious look didn't waver.

"Look Cynda, I think this is a good deal," he said. "And after I meet with my father, he will too. But I need to know that whoever I work with is behind the projects they present one hundred percent. If they're not, then the deal won't live up to everything we want it to be."

Cynda cringed inside. She'd gotten too personal and shared with Nelson how she really felt about the project. That had nothing to do with this deal.

"I can assure you that we're fully invested. Converting the hotel into valuable and useful property has been Laura's dream for a long time. She's never been this close."

"What about you?" Nelson asked. "Is this your dream?"

"It's not my company," Cynda replied. "You'll understand once you meet Laura and I'll work to make sure everything goes as it should like I always have."

Nelson leaned back into his seat. "I'm sure you will. I'm looking forward to meeting Laura, but I must admit I'm going to be disappointed not working directly with you."

"I'm sure we'll interact, when necessary," Cynda replied. "And I truly hope my personal opinion doesn't sway your opinion of her."

"It doesn't," Nelson replied.

Cynda looked at her phone. "It's getting late. I think it's time to call it a night."

"Really?" Nelson replied. "I'm curious about the Beltline, and since we're so close it would be ashamed not to take a look."

"Neither one of us is dressed for it," Cynda replied.

"We're not, which means we won't be long," Nelson said.

He keeps trying to make this a date, Cynda thought. Or was she reading the signals wrong?

"I guess a short stroll wouldn't hurt," she said. "But if my feet ache tomorrow, it's your fault."

They exited the restaurant from the Beltline entrance.

"Which way?" Nelson asked.

"This way," Cynda said.

They walked in silence, enjoying the spectacle of people. Despite her personal opinion Cynda had to admit the walkway was nice. City lights glittered in the distance, the temperature just warm enough for a leisurely walk. Nelson seemed content as well. This was her first business dinner, and it wasn't what she expected. She suspected she was seeing Nelson's business persona but whatever it was, it was nice. Very nice.

They walked a few more yards before Cynda's high heels disagreed with her feet.

"Let's go back," she said. "My feet are talking to me."

Nelson laughed. "Okay. If it gets any worse, I'll carry you."

"I don't think that's appropriate for a business meeting," Cynda said.

"I won't tell if you won't," Nelson replied.

They returned to the restaurant. Cynda gave her ticket to the valet while Nelson called a rideshare.

"This was nice," Nelson said. "Thank you for dinner."

"You're welcome," Cynda replied. "I hope you see how important this project is. I think this would be a great partnership."

"I do, too."

The valet returned with her car, handing her the key pod and opening the door.

"It was nice meeting you, Nelson," she said. "I hope I'll see you again soon."

They shook hands, then continued to hold on, their eyes meeting as Nelson smiled.

"I hope so, too."

Cynda finally let go of his hand, climbed into her car, and drove away.

MILTON J DAVIS

11

Nelson looked at Atlanta from the window of his rideshare. He'd heard a few negative comments about the city from his colleagues, but now he realized they were wrong. Some people wanted every place they visited to be another version of Chicago instead of appreciating what their new destination had to offer. So far, he liked what he saw of Atlanta.

The dinner meeting went well. Cynda was pleasant company, and once again shared her love for her hometown. It would be great working with her. They shared a chemistry that would go a long way toward getting things done and probably working through any problems that would crop up along the way. Thinking back on the conversation, he wondered if he might have said a few things that were inappropriate for a business conversation. Words slipped out of his mouth before he could stop them, but Cynda didn't seem to mind. Or she was ignoring them because of the deal. He'd call her tomorrow and apologize.

Darla and the dogs were waiting for him when he arrived. The dogs cavorted for his attention while Darla held the door open for him. He sat on the love seat and the dogs joined him. He had to admit he was getting used to them, but if it was his house he wouldn't let them sit on the furniture.

"So how did the meeting go?" Darla asked.

"Very good," he replied. "Urban Hits is nice."

"It is," Darla replied. "But it's not the place I think of when I imagine a business meeting. It's more of a date place."

"You know, it kind of felt like a date," Nelson said.

"Uh oh," Darla replied. "This Cynda. Is she attractive?"

"Yes," Nelson said. "But it's not just that. She's so easy to talk to. I've never met a person so comfortable with themselves, so laid back."

"Watch it, brother." Darla said. "She's a business associate, remember?"

"I know," Nelson replied. "Just making an observation."

"Okay, Mr. Observer. Remember what you came here for."

Nelson hugged her. "Don't worry about me, Darla. I know what I'm doing."

"This wouldn't have anything to do with you and Ronsie breaking up, would it?" Darla asked.

"No," Nelson replied.

"You sure? Because from what I remember she's the only woman you've been with."

Nelson's eyebrows rose. "You been checking on me?"

"I grew up with you, fool," Darla said. "It's been you and Ronsie forever. You and Daddy are so different.

"What are you talking about?" Nelson said.

"Mama and Daddy have been together forever, and I know he didn't cheat on her, did he?"

"Of course not," Darla replied. "But your perfect father was quite the dog when Mama met him. She tamed him."

"How do you know all this?" Nelson asked.

"Mama told me," Darla replied. "Women talk. Just around the time I became a teenager, Mama started telling me all sorts of things. She was preparing me."

"Daddy didn't tell me anything," Nelson replied. "Me and Ronsie were dating, so I guess he figured he didn't need to. He just kept saying, 'treat that young lady like I treat your mother and you'll never go wrong.' Yet here we are."

"If you want my opinion, it's the right thing," Darla said. "You've never dated anyone else. How do you know she's the right one when she's been the only one?"

"I've thought the same thing," Nelson said. "And apparently Ronsie has, too."

"Get out there," Darla said. "Play the field a bit, but don't be mean about it. Not Cynda, of course. She's business, and she should stay that way."

"You're right about both," Nelson replied. "Now let me get my ass in the bed."

They hugged.

"Night, sis."

"Night, bro."

Nelson went to his room and shut the door. He took a quick shower then took out his laptop to type a few more notes on the property. He paused for a moment, thinking about something funny that Cynda said then shook his head.

"Cynda's business," he said out loud. "Remember that."

* * *

They were late for Mama's doctor appointment. The twins got into a fight about breakfast and it took Cynda all her strength and wit to calm them down. After she dropped them off at daycare she rushed back home and helped Mama get ready.

Mama chose her purple track suit to wear to the doctor's office because it was comfortable and easy to take off. It was also her favorite color, and Cynda had the perfect jewelry to go with it.

"You alright Mama?" she asked as she guided her to the doctor's office door.

"I'm alright," Mama replied.

Only one patient sat in the waiting room. A nurse came from behind the door with a smile on her face.

"Mrs. Jones?"

"That's me," Mama replied.

The nurse smiled. "Perfect timing! You can follow me."

"Do you need my help?" Cynda asked.

"I'm alright baby," Mama said. "I'll be fine for a little while."

The nurse held out her arm to give Mama support then led her into the office. Cynda took a seat then pulled up her current read, a new romance novel by her favorite author Nicole

Givens Kurtz. As she read, her mind drifted to Nelson. It had been long time since she met a man like him, someone self-assured and confident in his work. Too bad it was business, otherwise she wouldn't mind learning more about him. She shrugged her shoulders.

"Girl, you have the worst luck," she whispered.

Cynda was so engrossed with her book that Dr. Reese had to call her twice before she heard him.

"I'm so sorry, Dr. Reese," she said.

"Must be a good book," the doctor replied.

Dr. Martin Reese as a stout middle-aged man with a brown copper complexion and infectious smile. He'd been Mama and daddy's doctor for years.

"How's Mama?" Cynda asked.

"That's what I wanted to talk to you about," Dr. Reese said.

Cynda felt a chill then braced herself.

"What's wrong," she asked.

Dr. Reese gestured for her to sit. He took a seat beside her.

"Your mother is doing fine," he said. "All her vitals are good, especially for someone her age."

"That's good to hear," Cynda said.

"I'll be honest with you," the doctor said. "There's no reason your mother shouldn't be getting around better on her own."

Cynda looked surprised. "I don't understand."

"Your mother does have some issues with her joints," Dr. Reese replied. "She's experiencing a good amount of pain, but nothing that couldn't be diminished by a good physical therapy program."

"Wait, are you saying Mama could walk?" Cynda asked.

"Yes," Dr. Reese replied. "I've told her this before, but she needs encouragement."

"I don't know, Dr. Reese. Mama's pretty stubborn. I'm not sure I can persuade her to do what she doesn't want to do."

Dr. Reese's expression became serious. "Let me put it this way. Time is running out on her mobility. If she doesn't start soon, what's a choice now might be a reality later. Use it or lose it, as they say."

"I'll do what I can," Cynda replied. "Lord knows it would make things easier for me. But most of all I want the best for her. It's times like this I wished Daddy was still alive."

"Your father was a good man," Dr. Reese said. "And he instilled everything he was in you. I'm sure you'll figure out a way."

The office door opened and Mama came out, supported by one of the nurses.

"Y'all talking about me?" she asked.

"Yes," Cynda said with a smile.

Mama huffed. "You can tell me about it when we get home." She patted the nurse practitioner's hand. "Thank you for walking me out, sweety."

"You're welcome, Miss Jones."

Cynda took Mama's hand. Mama waved at Dr. Reese with the other.

"You have a blessed day, Mrs. Jones."

"Thank you, doctor. You, too."

Cynda guided Mama to the car then helped her inside. She trotted over to the driver's side and climbed into the car.

"Where you want to go eat?" Cynda said. "No, let me guess. Krystals."

Mama laughed. "I don't even know why you asked me. Just hurry up."

Cynda pulled out of the parking lot. She turned on the radio, something she only did when Mama was in the car.

"Mama, Dr. Reese told me something interesting today," she said.

Mama gave her a side eye. "Oh really? What was that?"

"He said you could walk just fine if you wanted to."

"Baby, you know that's not true," Mama replied. "That hasn't been true for a long time."

"He said if you went to physical therapy, they could get you back on track."

"He just trying to get more of my money," Mama replied.

"I don't think so," Cynda said. "I think we should give it a shot."

"I tried, baby," Mama said. "After the accident I tried to keep moving like the doctors told me. I just hurt too bad."

"But you didn't go to the physical therapist like the doctors told you," Cynda said.

"Look at you, sounding like you the Mama."

Cynda took a breath. "Mama, I want the best for you. You know I do. I wouldn't be who I am if it wasn't for you and Daddy. You were there for me and Terrence. I want you to be there for the twins."

Mama smiled. "We used to have some good times, didn't we?"

"Yes, we did," Cynda replied.

"Even if I could get around better, I can't play with them babies like I did with you and Terrence. That was a long time ago."

"I'm not expecting that," Cynda replied. "But you could take them for walks, and you could watch them run around like the heathens they are."

Mama laughed. "That would be nice."

"And you could go to Paris with me," Cynda said.

"That would be really nice."

"So what do you say? Can I set up an appointment?"

Mama rubbed her chin. "I guess so. Not too early though. I have to get my sleep."

Cynda smiled. Getting Mama to change her mind was no easy feat. Now she just had to make sure she kept her promise.

They pulled into the Krystals drive through and orders a bag full of the diminutive sliders. Mama complained about how much they cost, remembering the days you could buy one for change. Cynda pulled out of the parking lot.

"Wait a minute," Mama said. "This ain't the way home."

"It's not," Cynda replied. "We're going to Grant Park. It's a nice day, so we're going to eat outside."

"That sounds good," Mama replied. "I need some sun. I'm tired of this light brown complexion."

"I can show you the building we're trying to buy too," Cynda said.

"How did your date go?" Mama asked.

Cynda looked puzzled. "What date?"

"The one you came from last night. You looked nice, by the way. Was that a new dress?"

Cynda laughed. "It was, but last night wasn't a date. It was a business meeting."

"So why were you all dressed up?"

"That was Miss Laura's idea," Cynda said. "I stopped by a place where she buys her clothes and they hooked me up."

"You should go to church dressed like that. Reverend Bowden would be impressed."

Cynda glared at Mama and Mama laughed.

"You a mess," Cynda said. "Curtis don't need any encouragement. I can tell that man no nine different ways and he'll be standing there waiting for the tenth. Got me thinking about changing churches."

"I don't see why you don't like him," Mama replied. "He's a nice-looking young man. Ambitious, too. I think y'all would make a good couple."

"Curtis wants a good woman that will stand behind him and have babies," Cynda said. "That's not me. You know that."

"Yes, I do. I'm still holding out for at least one grandbaby from you and Terrence."

"Put your money on Terrence," Cynda said. "Not that I don't want children. I just haven't found anyone I want to have children with. And I'm not about to be anybody's baby mama."

Mama frowned. "Baby Mama. I don't know where y'all get them damn words."

Cynda drove through the Summerhill district then to Grant Park. She parked by the recreation center, then helped Mama out of the car. There was a nice park bench not far away nestled under the canopies of three oaks. Mama eased onto the bench while Cynda set up the table.

"It's so pretty out here," Mama said.

"It is," Cynda agreed.

"We need to hurry up," Mama said. "Can't leave Terrence with the babies too long."

"Why not?" Cynda said. "He's their uncle. He'll be okay."

They took their time, enjoying their lunch, the weather, and the passersby. When they were done, Cynda cleaned the table then led Mama back to the car.

"That was nice," Mama said. "We should do this more often."

"We should," Cynda replied. "But I'm so busy."

"Won't be one day," Mama replied.

"Another reason you need to go to physical therapy," Cynda said. "Then we can go walking again."

"You don't need to keep convincing me," Mama said. "I said I'll do it."

Cynda kissed Mama's cheek.

"I love you."

Mama patted her hand. "I love you, too. Now let's get on home and rescue your brother."

Cyndal laughed. "If we have to."

They climbed into the car then headed back home.

MILTON J DAVIS

12

Nelson's flight arrived at O'Hare just before dark. He always returned from trips at night when possible to avoid the urge to go into the office. He didn't let anyone know when he was returning so he wouldn't be bothered. The terminal bustled with its mix of people arriving and departing. He took out his phone as he bypassed the luggage carousel and began dialing then stop, realizing that he was calling Ronsie. He smirked; old habits were hard to break. Instead, he contacted a rideshare through his app, went outside, and waited.

It didn't take long for the driver to arrive. Nelson jumped in and they were off to his condo, which luckily wasn't far from the airport. He was drained by the time he opened his door and stumbled inside. He unpacked and took a quick shower, which woke him up. Such a situation would usually mean more work, but instead he went to his refrigerator, took out a bottle of wine, then turned on his sound system. By the time he sat on his sofa, the room was filled with the sounds of Coltrane.

He thought about Atlanta as he sipped his wine. No, he actually thought about Cynda. She was attractive, smart, down to earth, and sexy in a girl next door kind of way. Working with her would be hard, and it would be all his fault. He was sure the reason he was interested in the deal was purely business, but he had to admit that he couldn't wait for his father to sign off so he could get back down to Atlanta and work with her. The music and the wine had the desired affect; Nelson dozed off on the sofa. He woke up long enough to put the wine away then stretched out on the couch and fell back to sleep.

His phone woke him the next day. Nelson felt around the couch until he found it. He looked at the time on the screen.

"Damn." It was 9:30 am. The call was from his father.

"Morning, Pops!" he said in his best attempt to sound like he was wide awake.

"I send you down South one week and this is how you act?"

"I got in late," Nelson replied. "I'll be there in a few."

"Are you sure? I wouldn't want to interfere with your rest."

"I'll be there in thirty minutes," Nelson said.

"Thank you," his father replied.

Nelson hung up his phone and ran into his room to change. He was out the door in ten minutes; it took another twenty minutes to reach the office. Darrell was typing at the receptionist's desk when he arrived.

"He's waiting for you in his office," he said without looking up.

"Thanks." Nelson dropped his backpack in his office before making his way to his father's office. The elder Carter stared at his monitor as he pinched his chin.

"Glad you could make it," he said.

"Sorry," Nelson replied.

His father grunted. "Interesting report."

"I'm glad you think so," Nelson replied. "I think this property has good possibilities."

"You sure about that?" his father said. "By the looks of the pictures and your notes, I'm not convinced this is a good move for us."

"Why not?" Nelson asked.

His father finally looked away from the monitor.

"You know that business always comes first," the elder Carter said. "While we do make sizable donations to various charities and nonprofits, profits take priority. I'm not sure this property fits our template."

Nelson placed his laptop on the desk and turned it on. It only took a few seconds to pull up the report his father read.

"I'll admit that the starting investment capital is higher than our norm, but the land and building have business and historical potential that exceeds any property we've invested in. I think the ROI will be significant."

"How significant?" his father asked.

"Four-fold," Nelson replied.

"That's a strong statement."

"I believe in this project," Nelson said.

His father leaned back into his plush leather chair.

"I need more before we pull the trigger on this one. I think you should do more research on existing properties and compare appreciation rates."

"Okay," Nelson said. "I'll fly down next week."

"That's something you can do from your desk."

"I don't think you get the full assessment for the Atlanta market from a distance."

"Sounds good," his father said. "Make sure you keep up with your other projects as well."

"I will," Nelson replied.

His father took off his glasses then intertwined his fingers.

"How's your sister?"

Nelson hesitated before answering. "She's fine."

Pops grunted.

"She's living with her partner in the Grant Park area. It's up and coming."

"That's your sister. More interested in trends than investments."

"It's a good area," Nelson said. "Solid growth and potential. Anyone interested in single family home investment would do well there."

"That's not our thing," Pops said. "I'm glad she's doing well. She could be doing better if she made the right decision about her future."

"She's doing what she wants and she's great at it."

"Of course she's good at it," Pops replied. "She's a Carter."

"She has a showing at a gallery. You and Mama should go see it."

"Something to consider," Pops said. He looked up from his screen then leaned back into his chair.

"What's this I hear about you and Veronica?"

Nelson lowered his head and pinched his nose bridge. "What did you hear?"

"Rashida and Omar were by the house this weekend. They said you two broke up."

Nelson lifted his head. "We didn't break up. We're taking a break."

"That's understandable," his father said.

Nelson was shocked. His parents loved Ronsie. "Really?"

"You two have been together since elementary school. You're both grown now out there seeing the world. You're bound to get curious. Best to get it out of your systems now before you tie the knot. If you tie the knot."

"You're quite calm about this," Nelson said.

His father smirked. "You know me and your mother love Ronsie and would love to see you two together. But it's your life. Besides, we wouldn't lose her. You would."

"I'm glad you feel that way," Nelson said.

"I do," his father replied. "Your mother might need a bit more explanation."

His father smiled for the first time since the meeting began.

Nelson nodded. "Anything else?"

"No, that's it," Pops said. "Let's make some money."

Nelson went back to his office with a smile on his face. The first thing he did was schedule a flight to Atlanta for next week. The second thing he did was call Darla.

"Hi Nelly! What's up?"

"I'm coming back next week."

"Excellent! Your room will be waiting. The dogs miss you. They keep wandering from room to room looking for you."

"I'm staying in a hotel this time. Got a lot of work to do. By the way, Pops said hi."

"Yeah right. I don't acknowledge it unless he tells me himself."

"That's gonna take a while. I also told him about your show. Suggested he and Mama check it out. Just giving you a heads up."

"That would be wonderful, but I'm not holding my breath. I'm happy you're coming back, though. I have so much more I want you to see!"

"This isn't a vacation. I'll be on the clock."

"Spending more time with the cute real estate lady?"

Nelson couldn't help but smile. "I doubt it. She was standing in for her boss."

"Okay, Nelly. See you in a week."

"See you, Red."

Nelson hung up. Working with Cynda's boss would be a better choice from a professional standpoint, but he'd miss working with her. He decided to make another call.

"Nelson!"

"Hi Ronsie."

"Back from Atlanta?"

"Yeah. I arrived last night. I'm in the office."

"So you came home and didn't call me?"

"I thought we weren't doing that anymore."

"We aren't, at least for right now. But you still could have called. I still care about you."

"I'll remember the next time. I'm heading back to Atlanta next week."

"Let's get together before then, okay?"

"Sounds like a plan. See you soon!"

"Bye!"

Nelson hung up. He wasn't sure if seeing Ronsie was a good idea. He might find himself sliding back into old habits, and that wasn't what they agreed on. It wouldn't help, but it wouldn't hurt, either. Even if they decided to stay apart, he didn't want to lose her as a friend. She was an important part of his life.

He decided to make one more call.

* * *

Cynda was sitting at her desk reviewing schedules when Laura entered the office. Her normally well-dressed boss wore a black warmup suit, baseball cap, and a large pair of designer shades.

"Welcome back!" Cynda said.

"Hey," Laura replied, her voice weak.

"Should you be here?" Cynda asked. "You sound terrible."

"My doctor cleared me to return to work, although she recommended I take another week to recuperate," Laura replied.

"By the look of it you should have taken her advice," Cynda said.

Laura waved her hand. "I'll be okay. Just going to do some light paperwork. Besides, I had to get out of that house. I was going stir crazy."

"I can imagine," Cynda said. "I'll handle all your calls."

"Thank you, Cynda. You're an angel."

Cynda watched Laura stagger into her office and shut the door before returning to her work.

"Some people don't know how to be sick," she said under her breath.

The phone rang and she answered.

"Benson Realtors."

"Hi Cynda. It's Nelson."

Cynda's face warmed. "Hi Nelson! How are you?"

"I'm fine."

"How can I help you?"

"Well, I met with my father this morning. While he hasn't approved the project yet, he is interested. I'm coming back next week to do more research."

"Very good!" Cynda said. "Miss Benson should be fully recovered by then."

"I was kinda hoping I could continue working with you," Nelson said.

Cynda hesitated before responding. "Unfortunately, that's not my call. I'll ask her and see what she says."

"That's all I can ask. Either way, I'm looking forward to seeing both of you next week."

"See you next week," Cynda said.

Nelson hung up. Cynda went at once to Laura's office.

"Nelson Carter just called," she said. "He's coming back next week for more research."

Laura's eyes brightened. "It's not a yes, but it's not a no. Dad probably wants more info on the market before making a final decision."

"One more thing," Cynda said. "He asked if he could continue working with me."

Laura grinned. "My diabolical plan worked! Of course he can. Y'all have the relationship."

"I don't know, Laura," Cynda said. "I'm not qualified for this work."

"Shoot girl, you're more qualified than anyone else in this office other than me. You work with realtors throughout the city, and you're a native Atlantan."

"I don't know," Cynda said.

"I do," Laura replied. "It's about time. I know you didn't expect to sit behind that desk the rest of your life, did you?"

She didn't, but she expected her move up to take place somewhere else.

"No," she replied.

"Excellent! I'm going to have to send you back to Justine's. Can't have you repping us like that."

"Here you go about my clothes again," Cynda fussed. "My clothes are fine."

"Yes, they are," Laura replied. "But this is our biggest deal. I can't have you looking just fine. You need to be spectacular, like me. Well, not me today, but you know what I mean."

"Uh . . . okay. But I'm gonna need you on standby."

"Of course!" Laura replied. "In the meantime, can you run out and get me some chicken soup? The Lovely Restaurant has the best. And get you something to eat, too."

Laura went into her purse, took out the company credit card, and handed it to Cynda.

"Don't come back with lobster," she said.

Cynda took the card then left Laura's office.

"I never do," Cynda replied.

"There's a first time for everything!" Laura said.

Cynda shut down her computer and walked to her car. The Lovely Restaurant was a decent drive from the job, so she pulled up her favorite playlist.

Nelson was coming back. She didn't know how to feel about that. It was a great opportunity for the business, but she had to admit she wasn't looking forward to seeing him again. It wasn't him; it was her feelings about him. She liked him in the wrong way. He was smart, charming, and handsome. How could a woman not be attracted to him, especially someone that hadn't been with a decent man for a long time. But this was business. Was his charm part of his sales pitch? What if his being so attentive was just a front? She knew how that worked. Most of their sales team were consummate charmers. Cynda sat up straight. Was that what he was doing? Charming her?

Cynda

Cynda exited the highway onto Grady Road. She couldn't get mad at him. That's exactly what Laura wanted her to do, dress up and look cute. According to her, it was part of the process, but to Cynda it felt cheap. But Laura was in charge. Dressing up wasn't' a big deal, especially since she could keep the clothes.

The line at The Lovely wasn't as long as usual, so it took her no time to place their order. She ordered chicken soup for Laura and a chicken sandwich for herself. She was back in the car heading back to the office in minutes. Her phone buzzed; it was Terrence.

"What?"

"I need to borrow some money."

"For what"

"I need to upgrade my laptop."

"Why? To play more games?"

"No. I need to increase my processing speed which will help me finish the game. I'm so close. Plus I have a company interested."

Cynda was skeptical. "Really, Tee?"

"Really? Who?"

"GenStar. They're one of the largest gaming companies in the world. They responded to my query and asked to see more."

Cynda sighed. "What about your credit card? Mama gives you an allowance."

"Yeah, about that. It's kinda topped out."

"Boy? Damn. I'll put five hundred on your card. And you have to pay me back."

"Just five hundred?"

"Negro, do you hear yourself?"

"Alright, alright. Five hundred."

"And don't ask Mama for it."

"I won't. Thanks, Cynda. Bye!"

Cynda hung up, clearly upset. It wasn't because she didn't have the money to give. She did. It was the fact that Terrence had to ask for it, and the only reason he wasn't going to ask Mama was because she gave it to him. She hoped this was a real job opportunity for him because it was past time for him to start taking care of himself.

Cynda returned to the office.

"I'm back!" she called out before entering Laura's office. Laura was slumped back in her chair, fast asleep. Cynda hit her table and Laura sprang upright.

"I'm awake! I'm awake!"

"You are now." Cynda sat the soup in front of her. "Eat this then go home, okay?"

Laura took the top off the soup, smelled it, then closed her eyes.

"Mmmm! I hope it tastes as good as it smells!"

"You know it will. It's from the Lovely," Cynda replied.

She was leaving the office when Laura called out.

"I made you an appointment at Justine's for tomorrow. They're going to measure you and create you a wardrobe for the week."

"Okay," Cynda replied.

"And do something about your hair."

Cynda touched her hair. "What's wrong with my hair?"

"Trust me," Laura said. "I have a place that can do wonders."

"That's alright," Cynda said. "I know somebody."

"I'm talking about a real style," Laura replied. "Not all that baby hair stuff."

Cynda laughed. "Stop worrying about me and get better. I have work to do."

Laura finished her soup while Cynda handled both of their duties. The realtors were having a great day, which kept her busy and made the time go much faster. When she finally got a chance to look up, Laura had left the office. Cynda went in with a mask and sanitizer, wiping down the desktop and chairs then spraying disinfectant. As the day ended, she looked at the card Laura gave her for a hairstylist. Like most people, she didn't just let anybody play in her hair. Ebony was her go-to, but it had been so long since she had her hair done, she wasn't sure if Ebony still did hair. She shrugged and dialed.

"Hair Flair, may I help you?"

"Uh, yes. This is Cynda Jones. I was given this number by Laura Benson."

"Oh Laura! How is she?"

"Better."

"You're the one she said would call to set up an appointment."

"Yes I am."

"We set aside this coming Saturday for you. Can you be here by eight a.m.?"

"Yes, I can."

"Good we'll see you then. Bye!"

Cynda hung up and headed out the door. She'd have to make arrangements for Terrence to watch Mama and the kids while she was at the shop. She'd probably be there most of the day if it was anything like she remembered. Maybe she would get a mani-pedi while she was there, too. If she was going to spend a day out, she might as well make the best of it. She sang as she got into her car and drove away.

13

Nelson's flight arrived Sunday night. He texted Darla, letting her know he landed. Thirty minutes later he was standing at baggage claim, watching people hunting for their bags on the carousel. Nelson didn't have that problem; his custom purple luggage was hard not to see. The bags tumbled onto the carousel and he pushed his way through the throng to claim them.

He called Darla on the way to the pickup area.

"Where you at?"

"Right behind you, big head."

He turned to see her pulling up to the curb. The trunk popped open and he tossed his bags inside. He jumped into the car and gave his little sister a hug.

"Thanks for picking me up."

"Don't mention it. You sure you don't want to stay at the house?"

"I'm sure. Your dogs are cute, but they're your dogs."

Darla frowned. "Just tell me you hate them."

"I said what I said."

Darla pulled into the traffic flow.

"I should have brought them with me."

Nelson rolled his eyes. "I would have called a ride share."

"So disrespectful!"

It didn't take them long to reach the highway.

"So how long are you here?"

"A week. I want to see the city in its entirety, every nook and cranny."

"You sure that's all?" Darla asked.

"Is there something else?"

"No. Someone else. Cynda."

"I keep telling you this is about business. I'm not going to lie, it will be nice seeing her again, but the main goal is to convince Pops that this is a good investment."

"That's going to be tough," Darla said. "He's a first impression kind of person. But if anybody can change his mind, it's you."

Darla followed the navigation to the W Hotel. She whistled.

"You fancy!"

"I deserve it," Nelson said. "They have great suites."

"Alright, big money. Promise that you'll come by the house at least one night for dinner."

"I promise."

"And bring Cynda with you."

"I won't promise that."

"Well, think about it. I'd like to meet her."

Nelson's eyes narrowed. "Why? So you can start some shit?"

Darla laughed. "I hope your trip is successful. Call me and let me know when you're coming through."

"I will. Love you, sis."

"Love you, bruh."

Nelson grabbed his bags from the trunk, bypassing the valet and heading directly to the desk. He checked in quickly and went to his room. The suite he rented overlooked the city and had an inspiring view of the skyline. It wasn't Chicago, but it was nice. He unpacked and put his clothes away, then set up his desk for business. He was walking to the bathroom to take a shower when his phone buzzed. He looked at it and smiled; it was Ronsie.

"Hey, girl!"

"Hey, boy! I haven't heard from you in a while."

"You know how it is. Always busy."

"Too busy for me?"

Nelson smirked. "What is this? I thought we were taking a break."

"We were . . . I mean are. But I miss you."

"I miss you, too. Wait a minute. Is this a booty call?"

"It's whatever you want it to be."

Nelson chuckled. "Wow. Unless you're willing to bring your booty to Atlanta, this is just a catch-up conversation."

"Atlanta?"

"Yes. Pops gave the go-ahead on the project. Well, not exactly. I'm doing more research before he'll make a final decision."

"What do you think?"

"It's promising. We'll have some gentrification issues to deal with, but the company we may partner with has some ideas to make both sides satisfied."

"I hope it works out."

"Me, too."

"How's Darla?"

"Crazy as always. She picked me up from the airport. I stayed with her the last time I was here, but I needed a break from her dogs."

"I'm happy she was finally able to get pets. She loved ours."

"She's living her life the way she wants and I love it for her. How about you? How are you doing?"

"I'm good. The world of finance is what it is, rocking and rolling from the emotions of greedy white people."

"You got it. You always have. How are other things?"

"I don't want to talk about that."

"Uh oh. Trouble in paradise?"

"You know that saying the grass is always greener on the other side? I'm feeling that right now."

"So you and your boy aren't together anymore?"

"No. I wanted a boyfriend, not a baby. The more I'm out here, the more I appreciate what you and I had."

Nelson's mood shifted from cavalier to serious. He sat on the edge of his bed.

"So what are you saying?"

"I don't know," Veronica replied. "If you were here, I'd ask you to come over and help me figure it out."

They'd split up because they both felt they needed to be sure about their relationship before they took the next step. While Ronsie's reasons were obvious, Nelson had yet to be with anyone else. The bottom line was he wasn't ready to get back together.

"Let's talk about it when I get back," he said.

"Okay," Veronica replied. "Love you."

"Love you, too."

He hung up. It was that last part. The words came out as natural as breathing. There was no doubt in his mind that he loved Veronica. The question was how. They'd been together since they were children; first as friends, then lovers. Everyone who knew them expected them to get married. But he had to be sure. For him, marriage would be a lifetime commitment. Once he was in it, he would be in it for good, and he wasn't willing to take that step until he was sure, no matter who it was.

Nelson fell back on his bed and sighed.

"Get it together, bruh," he said out loud. "First things first."

He was in Atlanta to take care of business, to close his first solo deal. Everything else would have to wait. He rolled off the bed and ambled into the spacious bathroom to shower. Afterwards, he sat on the edge of his bed, listening to his jazz playlist as he gazed at the

Atlanta skyline. His mind drifted to Cynda and the last time he saw her. He wanted to see the city the way she saw it, which would help his pitch to Pops. He went to the desk and turned on his laptop, working on an outline for his week. If all worked to plan, they'd be closing on the deal by the end of the month. Of that he had no doubt.

* * *

It had been years since Cynda went to a salon. Time and expense didn't allow for it, and she was pretty decent doing her own hair. It was at least good enough for work, and since she didn't go anywhere else it didn't matter. Hair Flair was a celebrity salon; Cynda was intimidated just looking at the place. But her boss was footing the bill, so she was going in. She parked her car in the crowded lot then walked to the doors as if she belonged. Once she stepped inside, she felt like a mutt at a dog show.

"Can I help you?"

Cynda was so distracted she didn't notice the receptionist.

"Oh, right. I have an appointment. Cynda Jones."

The receptionist browsed her screen and then frowned. "I don't see your name."

"Try Laura Benson."

Cynda

The receptionist searched then her eyes widened. "Here it is. Give me a few minutes to confirm."

The receptionist sent Laura a text. Seconds later she received a reply. The receptionist's demeanor changed in an instant from reserved to friendly.

"I apologize," she said. "I'm Mara. You have no idea how many people try to sneak in. It's ridiculous. Like we don't know our clientele."

"That is crazy," Cynda replied. "How many people want to go broke getting their hair done?"

Mara laughed. "I know, right? Come with me. I'll take you to your specialist."

"Specialist? Well now," Cynda replied.

Cynda followed Mara through the salon until they reached a small room with a chair, sink, and mirrors. Mara motioned her to enter.

"Wait right here," she said. "Chardonnay will be with you soon."

Cynda stepped inside then sat. Even when she was getting her hair done, it was never anywhere this elaborate. Her friends either did hair at their homes or in any place they could afford to rent. Hair Flair was built for one purpose only; hair.

Afrobeat music interrupted her musing. Chardonnay entered the room, her perfect white smile matching her hair, making her ebony skin shine. She wore a billowy blouse and a long skirt that gave a bohemian vibe. Her nails were so long Cynda wondered how she was going to get anything done.

"Hello, love!" Chardonnay chirped. Her voice was high pitched and cheerful. "Let's see what Laura sent me today."

Chardonnay assaulted Cynda's hair, touching, pulling, rolling, and smelling it. She stepped away just as Cynda was about to push her back. The stylist folded her arms.

"Not bad for someone that's been going commando," she said. "But I still have a lot of work to do. What kind of music do you like?"

"Ah . . . jazz?"

"Excellent!" Chardonnay pulled up her streaming service and linked to her jazz playlist.

"What's your favorite food?" she asked.

"Why?"

"Because we're going to be here for a while, love."

Cynda decided to indulge in the moment. "Vietnamese."

Chardonnay shrieked and clapped her hands.

"We're made for each other!"

Chardonnay handed Cynda a stylish apron.

"First thing we'll do is wash those chemicals out of your lovely hair."

Chardonnay went to work. Cynda relaxed as much as she could, entertained by Chardonnay's gossip and blatant flirting. She wasn't sure if she talked to all of her clients that way or if it was just her, but it didn't matter.

Between the music, the food, and the special treatment, this was the best hair appointment ever. It was well after dark when Chardonnay stepped away and admired her work.

"Now that I see what was hiding under all that, I'm even more in love. Look at yourself, love!"

Cynda looked at her hair. "Oh my goodness!" She teared up and Chardonnay smiled wider.

"She's crying! My work is done!"

"I'm afraid to move," Cynda said.

"Don't worry," Chardonnay said. "I'll wrap it so you won't disturb it until you're ready. I can't guarantee it will survive your paramour's eager hands, though."

"There's no paramour," Cynda said. "I have a very important business meeting , and Miss Laura wants me to look my best."

"Ms. Benson is meticulous that way," Chardonnay replied. She wrapped Cynda's hair then helped her from the seat.

"Thank you so much," Cynda said. She reached into her purse for a tip and Chardonnay shook her head.

"We don't do that here," she said. "Thank you for allowing me to transform you, love."

Chardonnay kissed her cheek. "Safe travels."

Cynda walked through the shop like a runway model and the other stylists and customers played along, clapping and whistling. She climbed into her car and then thought of un-wrapping her hair for another look.

"Nope," she said aloud as she lowered her hands. "Nelson Carter, I hope you're ready."

She started her car then drove into the late night Buckhead traffic.

14

Nelson woke to the sweet chirping of his cell alarm. He took a quick shower, dressed in his blue casual suit and walking loafers, then headed downstairs for breakfast. As he was eating his phone buzzed. It was Pops.

"Morning, Pops!"

"Morning, Son. You ready to get the day going?"

"Yes, sir. Finishing breakfast right now."

"I'm expecting a thorough evaluation. Not just where Atlanta is now, but where you think it will be ten years from now. I know our investment matures in five years but to reach five, the investment must be good for ten."

"Yes, sir." Nelson smiled as his father gave him the same pep talk he gave him every time before a deal. He listened patiently, knowing that interrupting him would just make it last longer.

"I hope you got all that," Pops finally said.

"I did, Pops. Thanks for the information."

His father was silent for a moment, then he laughed.

"You put up with me like your mother," he said. "I know you know all this, but it makes me feel good to say it. Have a good day, Son."

"You too, Pops."

He disconnected then checked the time before setting the phone on the table. He had thirty minutes before Benson Realty opened its doors, which meant he had time for another mushroom omelet. He wolfed down the delicious egg concoction then washed it down with orange juice and another cup of coffee. Afterwards he returned to his room to freshen up and grab his backpack. He called for rideshare then called Benson.

"Benson Realty," Cynda said. Her cheerful voice made him smile.

"Good morning, Cynda. It's Nelson."

"Of course it is. Are you on your way?"

"Waiting for my rideshare as we speak."

"Where are you?"

"The W, downtown."

"Stay right there. I'll come to you. That's where our tour begins."

"At the W?"

"No. Downtown. I'll be there in thirty minutes."

"Okay."

Nelson canceled the rideshare and returned to the restaurant for more coffee. He sat facing the entrance so he could see Cynda when she arrived. When she walked into the lobby, he almost spilled his coffee. She looked stunning in her form-fitting pantsuit, her hair perfect. Nelson signed for his bill then met her in the lobby.

"Good morning," he said. "You look amazing." Nelson admonished himself for those last three words.

"So do you," Cynda replied. "So are you ready for your tour?"

"I am," Nelson said.

They left the W and walked to Peachtree Street. The roads and sidewalks were as busy as one would expect on a Monday morning. A few blocks later they stood on Peachtree Street.

"The infamous Peachtree Street," Cynda said. "Contrary to popular belief, every street in Atlanta is not some form of Peachtree. Comedic exaggeration."

"It's funny though," Nelson said.

Cynda's eyes narrowed. "Don't get me started on The Bean."

"Watch it now!" Nelson said in mock anger. "That's a work of art."

"More like a work of a word that rhymes with art," Cynda replied.

"Oh! You got jokes!"

"All day. Let's walk."

They strolled by restaurants and offices buildings, Cynda giving a brief description of each one. She'd done her homework; Nelson had never met anyone so well versed on their own city, even if they lived there all their lives like Cynda.

They crossed over the 75/85 thoroughfare.

We're entering Midtown now," Cynda said. "This is the hospital where I was born. It was called Crawford Long back then, now it's a part of the Emory Health System."

"So you're not a Grady baby," Nelson said.

Cynda eyebrows rose. "What you know about Grady babies?"

"Only what I could find online."

Cynda smirked. "I'm not the only one that did their homework."

"You can only read words online," Nelson said. "You can't feel a city unless you walk its streets."

"Tell my brother that," Cynda replied. "According to him, he's been around the world many times. Only issue is that he's done it online and he thinks that counts."

"I'm sure that will change one day," Nelson said.

"I hope so. I'd be happy if I could get him to pay a bill. If Mama wasn't always taking up for him my life would be better." Cynda stopped then held up her hand. "I'm sorry. You didn't need to hear that."

"It's okay," Nelson replied. "I'm the same way when I get comfortable with people."

Cynda turned her attention back to the city. "This is Ponce De Leon," she said.

"What?" Nelson asked.

"Ponce De Leon," Cynda repeated.

"But it's spelled . . ."

"Don't start," Cynda said. "You're in the South now, so you're the one that talks funny."

Nelson chuckled. "True, true."

"Besides, every Black person in Chicago is only a generation or two removed from Mississippi. I can hear a little twang in your voice."

"Guilty," Nelson replied. "Except for me it's a little closer. Pops is a native Chicagoan, but Mama was born and raised in Nachez, Mississippi. We would visit every summer until I graduated from high school. Pops hated it, but I loved it."

"I've never been."

"Not many have. It's not exactly a destination spot."

"I haven't been anywhere."

"Not much of a traveler?"

Cynda sighed. "I've always wanted to. Just never found the time."

They crossed Ponce, took a left, and continued their walk. They took a stroll through the Georgia Tech campus, admiring the buildings of the urban campus. Afterwards they wound their way back to Peachtree Street and the Vortex Restaurant.

"Let's go here," Cynda said. "We can grab something to eat and rest our feet."

"I'm for that," Nelson replied.

"You like burgers?" Cynda asked.

"Who doesn't?"

"This place has some of the best burgers in the ATL."

They went inside and were seated quickly. Nelson studied the menu while Cynda excused herself to freshen up. She returned to the table then took the menu from Nelson.

"I'm ordering for you," she said.

Nelson laughed. "I might be vegan."

"You're not."

The waiter arrived and Cynda ordered. She left and Nelson found his eyes locked on Cynda's. They both looked away awkwardly.

"We got lucky," he said. "It's a nice day."

"It is," Cynda replied. "I had a Plan B if it turned out otherwise."

"Always prepared, I suspect."

"I have to be. I'm in charge of Ms. Benson's schedule and I'm my mother's caregiver. And the twins. And of course, Terrence."

"I see. What's up with Terrence if you don't mind me asking?"

Cynda took a sip of her water and then sighed. "My brother is working on a video game that will change our lives forever. At least that's what he says. To achieve that, he must focus all his time and effort on it."

"And does he?"

"All I hear is cursing and explosions coming from his room," Cynda said. "Whenever I call him on it, he says it's research. He has to know what the competition is up to. I'm like, 'What competition?' He doesn't even have a game yet."

"So Terrence is a dreamer," Nelson said.

"Terrence is a pain in the ass," Cynda said. "If Daddy were alive, he'd make him find a job. But I'm just his sister, and he's Mama's baby and we both live in her house."

"There must be a positive side to this," Nelson said.

"Really?" Cynda replied.

"There always is, if you look for it."

Cynda tilted her head and looked up in thought. *This woman looks good doing anything*, Nelson thought. Her eyes fell back on him.

"Well, he is around when I need him to babysit the twins or watch Mama, although he does it under protest."

"See? That's your positive side."

Cynda shrugged. "I guess."

The server arrived with the burgers. Nelson bit into his and smiled.

"This is a good burger. Good choice."

Cynda nodded as she chewed hers. They ate in silence, which is what happens when the meal is good. Nelson ordered a coffee and Cynda tea before they continued on their tour.

"I need a break from walking," Cynda said. "Let's take a rideshare to the High."

The High Museum was interesting, but not on the same level as the Chicago Art Institute. Afterward they walked down 14th Street to Piedmont Park. They toured the park then sat on a bench facing the lake.

"Wow," Nelson said. "I think I got my steps in for the week. Don't say we're walking back to the hotel."

"Lord no!" Cynda replied. "We're getting a rideshare back. Atlanta's not a walking city, but it can be done in certain places. The metro system doesn't compare to anything up north, but it works if you live inside the Perimeter."

"The Perimeter?"

"Yes, that's what we call I-285. It's the highway that circles the city. People here like to say, inside the Perimeter or outside the Perimeter. It meant more when most of the development was inside."

"This has been a great tour," Nelson said.
"What's next?"

"Dinner," Cynda replied.

"Let me treat you."

Cynda's eyes went wide. "And what do you have in mind?"

"The hotel restaurant is excellent. We can eat there."

"Okay."

Cynda called a rideshare and they strolled through the park while they waited. The driver arrived and they were on their way back to the W, the traffic so heavy that it took them longer to ride back than it did to walk. When they reached the hotel, they both hurried to the lounge area and sat.

"So, what do you think so far?" Cynda asked.

"I'm impressed," Nelson replied.

"No negative comparisons to Chicago?"

Nelson shook his head. "This isn't Chicago. It gets on my nerves when people do that. My job is to assess the value of developing the property to Atlanta and our investors. The main question to answer is how much will the value increase after purchase."

"There's that other angle too," Cynda said.

"The community affects," Nelson replied. "I know that's important to you and Ms. Benson, but to be honest, it's a secondary consideration for us."

"I think you'll see things differently after tomorrow," Cynda said.

"Really? How so?"

"You'll see."

"Well, I don't know about you, but I'm starving. Let's go to the restaurant and see what they have."

Nelson took Cynda's hand and she didn't let go. He smiled as he led her to the restaurant. The host greeted them then showed them to a table with a view of the city. Cynda ordered the salmon, while Nelson ordered the bone-in pork chops.

"So, is there someone special in your life?" Cynda asked.

Nelson eyes went wide. He wasn't expecting that question.

"I don't know," Nelson replied.

Cynda looked confused. "You don't know?"

"We're kind of in between," he said.

"What's her name?"

"Veronica, but I call her Ronsie. We've been together for as long as I can remember. Childhood sweethearts, high school couple, college, the whole thing. But we both realized we never knew what it was like to be with someone else. How could we be sure about us if we didn't know that?"

Cynda frowned. "Sounds like you came up with that."

Nelson laughed. "It was her. She met someone."

"Ouch," Cynda said.

Nelson shrugged. "Actually, I was cool with it. There's been quite a few times I've turned down invitations. It would be kind of cool to be able to say yes once in a while."

"Sounds like you're the loyal type," Cynda said.

"Why be in a serious relationship if you're not exclusive?"

"Y'all could have an open relationship."

Nelson shook his head. "We can do that without committing."

"You're kinda old school," Cynda said. "I like that."

Their meals arrived, interrupting a potentially awkward situation. Nelson bit into his pork chops and his eyebrows rose.

"This is pretty good!"

"Of course it is," Cynda replied. "It's the W."

"Just because the hotel is upscale doesn't mean the restaurant is. I've been disappointed quite a few times."

"Well, thank you for taking me to a restaurant you had no idea how the food would taste."

Nelson laughed. "You don't let anything slide, do you?"

Cynda nodded. "No I don't. The salmon is excellent, by the way."

"Thank goodness," Nelson said. "I have a feeling you would have given me a hard time if it wasn't."

Cynda smiled. "Of course!"

"What about you?" Nelson asked. "Who's the lucky man?"

"There isn't one," Cynda replied. "I don't have the time."

"There's always time from someone special."

"I haven't met him." Cynda said. "At least not yet."

"Well, when that man comes along, he'll be very lucky."

Cynda looked at Nelson and smiled. "I'm glad you think so."

Nelson ate a little more. "So what does Cynda Jones do for fun?"

"Fun? What's that?"

"Come on now. You must have some hobbies?"

"I do," Cynda replied. "Resting and sleeping."

"Seriously, what do you do when you're not working?"

Cynda put down her fork. "And here I was thinking you were listening to me. I don't have time. There's always something to do."

"Everybody has time," Nelson said. "You just have to claim it."

"That easy for you to say, Richie Rich."

"Ouch," Nelson said.

"I'm sorry," Cynda said. "It just came out."

"It's good," Nelson replied. "I know what everyone thinks about us 'rich' kids. And some of it is true. I hate seeing you not taking time for yourself."

"I'll have time one day," Cynda said. "And when I do, I know exactly where I'm going."

"Where is that?"

"Paris. I've been taking French lessons for two years. I heard the French are nicer to you if you can speak the language or at least try."

Nelson nodded. "Good choice. It's a beautiful city."

"Of course you've been there."

"I have, on business," Nelson said. "It's different from being on vacation. I see things on my way to business meetings. Plus, you're there with people you don't want to be with. It's not like experiencing with someone you like."

Nelson let his eyes linger on Cynda. Yes, he was flirting. Cynda grinned then looked away.

"Well, I hope you get to check it out the right way one day. With the right person."

Nelson lifted his glass. "I hope so, too."

They finished dinner in silence, passing glances at each other. When they finished the server collected their plates then shared the dessert menu with them. Nelson waved his hand.

"I surrender," he said.

Cynda glanced at the menu. "I'll pass."

"Don't stop because of me," he said. "I saw the way you were looking at that menu."

"Well, that chocolate lasagna looks decadent."

"Go for it."

"I can't eat all that alone," Cynda said.

"We'll split it." Nelson gave his menu back to the server. "We'll get the chocolate lasagna with two forks."

"I thought you were full," Cynda said.

Nelson smiled. "I can make a little room to share."

The server excused himself to put in their dessert order.

"So where are you off to after Atlanta?" Cynda asked.

"Portugal," Nelson replied. "It's up and coming. A very popular vacation and retirement country for Europeans and Americans."

"Really? I never considered visiting."

"You should, after Paris of course," Nelson replied.

"Okay, now you're teasing me," Cynda said.

"No I'm not. You'll make it," Nelson said.

The server returned with the chocolate lasagna, which was delicious. Cynda looked at her phone.

"Wow. It's late. I have to go. Early start tomorrow."

"Really?" Nelson said.

Cynda nodded. "Yep. Wear something casual."

"How casual?"

"Jeans if you have a pair."

"Actually, I do."

Cynda stood. "Good. See you tomorrow."

"See you."

Nelson watched Cynda as she walked away. He ordered a coffee and lingered at the table, thinking about the day. He liked what he saw, but what he enjoyed most was Cynda's company. He couldn't wait until tomorrow.

* * *

Cynda gazed out the window of the rideshare as she returned to the office. The first day had gone well. Nelson was noticeably impressed. She'd have good things to say when she talked to Laura tonight. But then there were the other things that happened that made her heart race. The way he looked at her. The way he complimented her. How he listened to her talk about her personal issues that she had no business sharing with him. And the way he held her hand as if he'd been doing it for years.

"No you don't, Cynda Jones. No you don't!"

"Excuse me," the rideshare driver said.

"Nothing," Cynda said. "Just talking to myself."

"I don't need to be worried, do I?"

Cynda laughed. "No. I'm not crazy. At least not today."

The driver glanced at her in the rear-view mirror.

It was dark when they arrived at the office. The parking lot was almost empty, the only cars belonging to her, Laura, and Ray. She rolled her eyes.

"Why doesn't that old man go home like everyone else?"

She opened the front door with her keys; the door was always locked after hours. As she turned off the alarm, Ray emerged from his office.

"Hello there, Cynda! My, you look amazing!"

"Hi, Ray," she replied as emotionlessly as she could muster.

"So you're selling real estate now?"

Cynda sat at her desk to review her emails.

"No. Just handling this one thing while Laura recovers."

"And what is that?"

Cynda looked at Ray, clearly annoyed. "Look Ray, I got work to do. Don't you have some woman your age you'd like to spend time with?"

"Ouch," Ray said. "I'm just trying to be friendly. I happened to be on my way to a date. And yes, she is much younger than me. Some people appreciate vintage wine."

Ray brushed by her on his way to the door. "Good luck with your little project."

Laura emerged from her office as Ray walked out. Cynda glared at her.

"You should fire that man," she said.

"If his closings keep dropping, I will," Laura replied. "How did the first day go?"

"Excellent," Cynda replied. "We spent the day downtown. We walked from the W to Midtown then took a rideshare to the High and Peidmont Park."

Laura's eyes bulged. "What!"

"Yeah, I thought the same thing. But it was great. We kept walking and talking and the next thing I know, we were there."

"And he was fine with that?"

"Yes. I expected the usual Chicago/Atlanta comparisons, but he didn't do that. It seems he was seriously evaluating the city on its own merits."

Laura leaned against the wall. "So what's planned for tomorrow?"

Cynda smiled. "Tomorrow, we're tourists. We'll hit the landmarks and eat at the icons."

"You're not taking him to the Varsity, are you?"

"Yes I am."

"Girl, if you get that man sick, I'll never forgive you!"

"What? The Varsity is great. And can't say you've visited Atlanta until you've been there."

Laura waved her hand and shook her head. "I ate at that place one time and my food ran out of me faster than it went in."

"Eeww! Too much information!"

"I'm just saying, you might want to take that off your list."

"I'll think about it."

"And go home," Laura said. "You had a long day today and it looks like you're going to have a long one tomorrow."

"What about you? You're still officially sick."

"I'll be right behind you."

"Okay."

Cynda turned off her computer then walked to her car. Her phone buzzed; it was Terrence.

"What?"

"When you coming home?"

"I'm on my way now. Is something wrong?"

"No. I'm tired of playing with the twins. I have some serious work to get done."

Cynda was about to say something mean but stopped.

"Okay. I'll be there in a few."

"Cool."

She drove out of the parking lot then made a detour on the way home, stopping by the local K-dog restaurant to pick up two dogs. The twins met her at the door, hugging her legs.

"Auntie Cee!" they yelled.

"Hey babies! Let me put this stuff down and we'll get y'all ready for bed."

Terrence walked up, his annoyed expression changing when he saw the bag.

"Yes!"

Cynda grinned. "Your reward."

Cynda peeked into Mama's room. She was fast asleep, and the TV was on the home improvement channel. Cynda knew better than to shut it off; Mama would wake up as soon as the talking stopped. She got comfortable before making sure the twins bathed then read them a story before leaving them on their own to sleep. Then she took her shower and prepared her clothes for the next day.

She was exhausted, but she had one more thing to do. She went to Terrence's room. He munched on his K-dog as he studied his monitor.

"How's the dog?" she asked.

"It's great! Thanks! I'm surprised you remembered the one I like."

"I pay attention," Cynda replied.

"You do."

She sat on the edge of his bed.

"What are you doing?"

"Cleaning up some of the code for the game," he replied. "Some unnecessary stuff that will slow it down."

"Editing."

"Exactly."

"I just wanted to stop by and thank you for watching Mama and the twins. I'm going to be late coming home this week."

"No worries. Big deal?"

"Very big."

"Good luck with it."

"Thanks. Good luck with your game, too."

Terrence turned and then stared at her. "I thought you thought this was a waste of my time."

"I'm not gonna lie, I don't understand what you do, but it's important to you," Cynda said. "To make a living doing exactly what you want is a dream most people don't achieve. Go for it while you can."

Terrence lunged at her, wrapping her in a hug while managing not to drop his k-dog.

"Thank you, Cynda!"

"If you get k-dog juice on my jammies I'm gonna be so mad at you."

"Oh . . . right. Sorry."

"G'night, Terrence."

"Good night, sis."

Cynda trudged back to her room. Tomorrow would be a long day, but more relaxed. She was looking forward to it in more ways than one.

15

Cynda woke up before her alarm went off and hurried into the kitchen. She turned on the stove eyes and then covered them with pots and pans. This morning was going to be a big breakfast morning for everyone. She had a long day ahead, and she was in a good mood. Part of it was because of how things went with Nelson the day before. The other part was that she was spending the day with him again.

Terrence appeared from his room bleary-eyed.

"What's up, sis?"

"Good morning!" Cynda sang.

Terrence rubbed his eyes as he entered the kitchen. He froze.

"Wait. You cooking breakfast? On a weekday?"

"Yep," Cynda replied. "You got a problem with that?"

"Not at all!" Terrence replied. "I think it's wonderful! But isn't that gonna make you late for work?"

"I'm not going into the office today," she replied. "I'm meeting the client at his hotel."

"Oh, okay. That makes sense. What about the twins?"

"That's why I'm up early. What's your excuse?"

"I never went to sleep. Just finished up with the coding. I'm sending the demo to the company later today after me and the crew playtest it."

"Baby Girl?"

Cynda wiped her hands with the hand towel.

"Watch this while I talk to Mama," she said.

"You know I don't know how to cook," Terrence said.

"Just tell me when the water's boiling," Cynda replied.

Mama was sitting up when Cynda entered the room. They shared a smile.

"Morning, Mama."

"Morning, baby. You cooking breakfast?"

"Yes, ma'am."

"Can you make me some sausage? I haven't had sausage in a long time."

"I sure can!"

"Thank you, baby."

"You make sure Terrence helps you."

"I will, Mama."

"I'll be in there in a minute."

Cynda looked concerned. "You sure?"

"Yes," Mama replied. "I feel good today, and I'm tired of laying in this bed."

"Okay. I'm going to get back to cooking."

When she returned to the kitchen the water for the grits was still heating. Terrence looked at her with relief.

"You cut it close."

Cynda went to the freezer and took out the frozen sausage. "Look in the drawer and get a teaspoon measure."

"What?"

"Get a teaspoon measure."

Terrence opened the drawer and took out the measure.

"Now fill it with salt and add it to the water."

Terrence followed her instructions.

"What are we doing?" he asked.

"Teaching you how to make grits."

"Oh!" Terrence smiled. "I love grits. What next?"

"Get a stick of butter out of the refrigerator. Cut off about a quarter stick and add it to the water. I know you know where the butter is. You put it on everything."

Terrence took the butter out of the refrigerator, cut off a chunk, then dropped it into the water.

"Good," Cynda said as she opened the box of frozen sausage patties. Terrence's eyes widened.

"Sausages, too? Oh snap!"

"Calm down, greedy boy. Now when the water starts boiling, slowly add that cup of grits I measured out. Stir it with the spoon as you add it so it won't clump."

Terrence watched the water as Cynda added the sausage to the hot pan. She left the kitchen and went into the twins' room.

"Time to wake up sleepy heads!"

The twins groaned as they stirred.

"I need y'all to dress yourselves today like big kids. Auntie's making a big breakfast this morning."

Malon lifted his head then sniffed. "I smell sausage!"

"Yes, you do."

He threw his covers aside then grabbed his clothes off the dresser. Sha'kwon barely stirred.

"Get up Sha'kwon," Cynda said. "If Malon gets dressed before you do, I'm giving him your sausage."

Sha'kwon popped from under his sheets and ran for his clothes. Cynda left the room with a smirk on her face.

"These boys and their food," she whispered.

Terrence had taken it upon himself to flip the sausage and had added the grits to the water.

"The grits are almost boiling," Cynda said. "Turn them down to simmer then put a lid on the pot. Let them simmer and stir them now and then until they thicken up right."

"Okay," Terrence said. "What can I do now?"

"Go check on the twins and make sure they're putting their clothes on right. I'm gonna start on the biscuits."

By the time Cynda finished breakfast, the family sat at the kitchen table. Terrence helped her make everyone's plate, proudly telling Mama and the twins he made the grits. They ate together, talking and laughing in a way that was usually reserved for weekends. When they were done, she put the plates in the dishwasher and then went to her room to get ready. We she emerged, the twins were waiting. The three of them said goodbye then hurried out of the door and to the car. After dropping them off at school she headed for the W.

Fifteen minutes later she pulled into the hotel entrance roundabout and called Nelson.

"I'll be right down," he said.

Cynda began checking her makeup then stopped.

"Not a date, girl. Not a date," she whispered.

Nelson walked out moments later, wearing a short-sleeved shirt and khakis. He smiled as he entered the car.

"Good morning!"

"Morning," Cynda replied. "Have you had breakfast?"

"Yes."

"Good. That means I don't have to eat twice."

Cynda pulled out of the hotel roundabout and into traffic.

"So where are we headed?" Nelson asked.

"The King Center," Cynda replied.

"Great! I've never been there."

"You're getting the tourist tour today," Cynda said. "I'm showing you everything that makes Atlanta special. We don't have the grand buildings and deep history like Chicago or New York. Our history is in our people."

"Let's do it," Nelson said.

The drive to the King Center wasn't far, but the early morning traffic made it challenging. They arrived a few minutes before opening, joining the line of tourists waiting to enter. Once inside, they explored the images and displays of the movement. Nelson was engrossed with everything. Cynda had visited the center a number of times on school field trips and with visiting relatives. Nelson seemed really interested, which made her smile.

They left the center, leaving a sizable donation.

"That was amazing," Nelson said. "You grow up thinking you know the whole story, but to see it in front of your eyes is on another level."

"It is," Cynda replied.

"You're privileged to have grown up here."

"Let's go visit his home," Cynda said.

The walk to the home of Dr. Martin Luther King didn't take long. The house had been restored to its original condition, as were the nearby homes.

"Can you imagine growing up in this neighborhood?" Cynda said. "How empowering it must have been?"

"Especially back then," Nelson replied.

"I see you appreciate history," Cynda said.

"Very much," Nelson replied. "I'm a history nerd."

"In that case, I'm making a slight change in our tour."

They returned to the car. "We're going to the AU Center."

It was a short ride to the cluster of historically black colleges. Cynda found a parking spot across the street from Clark Atlanta University.

"This is where I was attending school," she said. "I hope to come back one day."

They took a walking tour, visiting the various buildings and stopping faculty members who were more than gracious sharing their experiences. After the tour, they went to lunch.

"This great," Nelson said. "I knew all this was here, but to actually visit these places brings it home."

"That's why I love Atlanta," Cynda said. "I don't think I could feel comfortable anywhere but here."

"I think you'd like Chicago," Nelson said.

"Really?"

"Yes. If this deal goes through, you should come up. I'll return the favor and give you the grand tour."

Cynda's smile betrayed her feelings. "I would like that. Very much."

They were quiet for a moment, their eyes locked. Nelson cleared his throat before looking at his phone.

"Wow. It's almost noon. Time flew by." He smiled. "So what's for lunch?"

"It's a surprise," Cynda said.

They returned to the car and were on their way. Cynda worked through the lunch rush traffic, choosing the surface streets to the highway. She described the neighborhoods along the way, adding personal anecdotes. Nelson tried his best to pay attention, but all of it was going through his ears. Everything Cynda said was drowned out by her face and her emotions. He liked her . . . a lot. This was going to be a tough working relationship.

The neighborhoods were replaced by high rises and businesses.

"Welcome to Buckhead," Cynda said.

"Nice," Nelson replied.

Cynda drove to Lenox Square Mall valet parking. She handed over the key pod to the young valet and they entered the mall.

"Lenox Square Mall has been a shopping destination since the 60s," Cynda said. "It began as an open-air shopping center but transformed into an enclosed mall during the 70s."

"Kind of like the Magnificent Mile in Chicago," Nelson said.

"I wouldn't know," Cynda replied.

"You should put it on your list. And let me know when you do."

Cynda glanced at Nelson and their eyes met. They smiled.

"I'll think about it," she finally said.

"Think about it? You just hurt my feelings. I thought we were friends."

"We're business associates," Cynda corrected him. "We'll be friends if this deal goes through."

Nelson laughed. "Okay. I see how you roll."

Cynda nodded. They strolled the mall in silence. Cynda snuck a look at Nelson as he window shopped. She wouldn't mind being his friend. In reality, she could see herself being much more. It was just her luck that the only man she'd found interesting in a while was the one man she couldn't touch. She sighed.

"Everything okay?" Nelson asked.

"I'm fine," Cynda replied. "Just thinking."

"About what?"

"An impossible situation."

"Nothing's impossible," Nelson replied. "At least that's what my father says. It's just a matter of patience and persistence."

"Good advice I guess," Cynda said.

"This is a great mall," Nelson said. "But I'm really getting hungry now. What's for lunch?"

Cynda grinned. "Follow me."

Cynda led him through the mall to the escalator. They rode it down to the busy food court, working through the crowd until they reached a cafeteria style restaurant with a long line. Nelson smirked.

"What's this? Tight budget?"

Cynda laughed. "Of course not. These folks have the best teriyaki chicken in the city. Trust me. You get us a table."

Nelson nodded then walked away. Cynda waited patiently until it was her turn. She ordered chicken for both of them with rice and steamed vegetables on the side. It took a few minutes to prepare the meals, the cook shoveling the food into the Styrofoam to go boxes. As she walked to the table, Nelson looked at her suspiciously. She sat the meals on the table. Nelson studied his food before taking a taste. His eyes widened.

"This is good!"

Cynda grinned. "Told you."

Nelson took another bite. "Not the best teriyaki chicken I've had, but the freshness of the vegetables makes up for it."

"It's a great spot for a quick, healthy meal," Cynda said.

They finished their food and then left the mall.

"So how are you holding up?" Cynda asked Nelson.

"This has been great, but I need to head back to the hotel."

"There's a lot more to see," Cynda said.

"I think I've seen enough," Nelson replied.

"And?"

Nelson smiled. "It's very positive, but I'm not the final say so."

"I understand," Cynda said. "I don't think you can go wrong with this investment."

"I can't promise anything," Nelson replied. "But I can tell you that I'm for the deal."

"Squee!" Cynda lunged for Nelson, throwing her arms around his neck and hugging him. Nelson hugged her back, and they relaxed in each other's arms. A minute later Cynda realized what they were doing and let go. She retreated to her side of the car.

"I'm so sorry," she said.

"Don't be," Nelson replied. "It's not often I meet someone so passionate about their project."

It wasn't just the project she was passionate about, she thought.

"Let's get you back to the hotel," she said.

They made it back to the hotel just before the after work traffic jam. Cynda pulled up to the hotel.

"So what next?" she asked.

"I'm heading back tomorrow," Nelson said. "I'll meet with my father and we'll come up with a decision."

"How long will that take?" she asked.

"I'm not sure, but not long," Nelson said. "It's just a matter of crunching numbers."

"All we can do is wait," Cynda replied.

Nelson began walking away then turned around."

"So, what are you doing for dinner tonight?"

"Ah . . . I have no plans, actually."

"How about letting me treat you again."

"That's not necessary," Cynda said.

"I know it's not, but I want to. I have a place in mind. I've already made reservations. It would be ashamed to waste them."

Cynda fell silent. She could see in Nelson's eyes that this would not be a business dinner. This would be a date, which meant this was not good. Always keep business and personal separate. But on the other hand, a deal had not been made, so technically they weren't partners. And she knew she wanted to see him again even if the deal fell through, especially if the deal fell through.

"Okay," she said.

"Cool!" Nelson replied. "You can text me your address. I'll get a rideshare and pick you up."

"Okay." Cynda texted him her address. Nelson checked his phone.

"See you tonight." Nelson flashed his amazing smile then sauntered away. Cynda watched him for a moment then shook her head.

"Cynda Ella Jones, what are you getting yourself into?

She pulled away from the hotel and merged into traffic.

* * *

Nelson ambled to the hotel elevator, a wide smile on his face. He couldn't remember the last time he had such a good time on a business meeting. But he knew it had nothing to do with business, and everything to do with Cynda. She was amazing. He was ready to pen the deal just because she wanted it. But this was business first, which was why he was happy that buying the hotel made business sense. He liked the project, he liked Atlanta, but most of all, he liked Cynda.

He entered his room and headed straight to the bathroom to freshen up for dinner. He took a quick shower then decided to shave. As he was applying shaving cream, his phone rang with a familiar tune. He wiped his face then answered.

"Hey, Pops."

"Nelson. There's been a change in plans."

Nelson stiffened. "What's going on?"

"An amazing opportunity has become available in Sao Paulo," his father replied. "I need you to get there as soon as possible. My contacts are waiting for you."

"But what about Atlanta and Portugal?" he asked.

"We'll have to put them on the back burner for now. This deal takes precedent."

"What do I tell Cynda . . . I mean Ms. Benson?"

"Tell her the truth. She'll understand."

"Yes sir. I'll work on my report and send it to you tomorrow. I think you'll like it."

"Excellent. Let me know as soon as you arrive in Sao Paulo. Safe travels."

"Thanks, Pops. G'night."

"G'night."

Nelson ended the call. He finished shaving, a twinge of worry in his gut. His father was losing interest in the Atlanta project. He never gave him a new project until the preceding project was completed. That or he was trusting him with more responsibility, but that didn't usually happen without a serious meeting. His father loved big pronouncements.

After shaving he turned on his laptop and pulled up his report. After a quick review, he emailed it to his father's assistant. If all went well, he'd have approval before he returned from Brazil and could share the good news with Ms. Benson and Cynda. He smiled; he couldn't wait to see the look on Cynda's face when they got the good news. He wanted to see her happy. She deserved it.

Nelson shut down his laptop, grabbed his jacket then headed downstairs. The rideshare was waiting, and in a few minutes, it pulled into Cynda's driveway. Nelson went to the door and rang the doorbell.

"Bye everybody!"

The door opened and Cynda stepped out. She looked amazing.

"Wow," he said.

"Thank you," she replied. "Ready?"

"Yes. Where are we going?"

"I heard of this place called Bones. The hotel concierge recommended it."

"Wow. That's way out of my budget!"

"I told you it's on me," Nelson said.

"I can't let you do that," Cynda replied. "You're the client."

"Let me spend some of this expense account money," Nelson said.

Cynda shrugged. "It's your money."

Nelson smiled. "Exactly. Let's go."

It didn't take long for them to reach the restaurant. Nelson paid for the rideshare then played the gentleman, opening Cynda's door as they entered the restaurant. They were welcomed by the greeter, who took them to their table. Their waiter arrived immediately, a tall man with perfect hair and an engaging smile.

"Welcome to Bones! I'm Raphael, your server. Is this your first time here?"

"Yes, it is," Nelson said.

"Then you are in store for a treat. We have the best steaks in Atlanta. If you ask our owners, we have the best steaks in the U.S."

"Hold on now," Nelson said. "I'm from Chicago. We might have something to say about that."

Raphael smirked. "I guess we'll find out tonight."

The server turned his attention to Cynda. "Are you from Chicago as well?"

"No," Cynda said. "Born and raised in the A."

"Well at least I have one person on my side.
Let's get started with your drinks."

They ordered their drinks then took a look at
the menu.

"Mm," Cynda said.

"What?" Nelson asked.

"You know a place is expensive when they
don't have prices on the menu."

Nelson laughed. "Yeah. But it's on me, remember?"

"I know," Cynda replied. "But I can't help but
notice. I run a tight ship."

"I can imagine," Nelson said.

Cynda gave Nelson a skeptical look. "Can
you?"

"My family hasn't always been successful,"
Nelson replied. "This is first generation wealth.
Mama and Daddy built the business from the
ground up. Mama paid the bills with her nursing
job while Pops searched for clients. Once it took
off, Mama quit nursing and helped him manage
the office. And here we are."

"I'm happy for y'all," Cynda said. "You seem
to be a nice person."

"Seem?"

"All this is business," Cynda said. "I don't
know who the real Nelson is."

"I could say the same about you," Nelson replied.

"Facts," Cynda replied.

"But I have a feeling that you're a genuine
person," Nelson said.

"What you see is what you get," Cynda said.
"Wait, no, I didn't mean it like that."

Nelson grinned. "Like what?"

Cynda looked away. "Here comes the waiter."

They placed their orders then sipped on their drinks.

"I have something to tell you," Nelson said.

Cynda sat up straight, her eyes wide. "We have the deal?"

"No," Nelson replied. "Although I'm optimistic. I'm leaving tomorrow for Brazil. I have a prospect I need to take a look at."

Cynda slumped in her seat and Nelson felt bad.

"I'll still be working on your deal," he added quickly. "Honestly, it's just a matter of details."

Cynda brightened, and he felt better. He did want to do the deal, but most of all, he didn't want to disappoint her.

"That's great to hear," she said. "Thank you."

"Don't thank me yet," Nelson said. "A deal isn't done until the papers are signed."

Their meal arrived, and they were delicious. Nelson shook his head as he savored the bite of ribeye in his mouth. Their server arrived with a smile.

"So, how is everything?"

Nelson nodded. "I have to admit, this is a damn good steak."

The waiter grinned as he turned his attention to Cynda.

"Miss?"

Cynda held up her hand as she finished chewing her filet mignon. She put down her fork and knife before answering.

"Oh. My. Goodness! I'm ruined. I won't eat steak again unless it's here." She gave Nelson a mock glare. "I hate you."

Nelson and the waiter laughed.

"Then our work is done," the waiter said. He handed them a wine menu. Cynda waved her hand in surrender.

"I can't," she said. "I have to work in the morning."

"The check please," Nelson asked.

The waiter nodded then walked away.

"This was amazing," Cynda said.

"I'm happy you enjoyed it," Nelson replied.

Cynda's smile faded, her expression becoming serious.

"Nelson, we need to talk," she said.

"About what?"

"I'm a pretty straight forward person," she replied. "I like to keep things one hundred. Less confusion and pain that way."

Nelson became concerned. "What's wrong?"

"Nothing's wrong," Cynda replied. "Everything's great. And that's the problem. There's something between us, and it's not just about business."

"I don't know . . ."

Cynda cut him off with a skeptical stare. Nelson grinned. He liked this woman. A lot.

"Okay, I'll admit I do like you," Nelson confessed. "If circumstances were different this would be a date. But I believe in keeping business professional. I think you do, too."

"I do," Cynda replied.

"So that means we'll both behave ourselves."

"We will."

"At least until this project is complete."

Cynda shook her head. "Until then."

They raised their glasses and made a toast to seal the deal.

"Friends until then," Cynda said.

"Friends until then," Nelson repeated.

Nelson and Cynda took a rideshare to her home. Nelson walked Cynda to the door.

"Thank you for a great evening," she said. "I hope your trip to Brazil is successful."

"You're welcome, and thank you," Nelson replied. "I'll get things wrapped up so I can get back to you . . . I mean this project."

Cynda reached out and placed her hand on his shoulder. She leaned in and he leaned toward her.

"Cynda baby? Is that you?"

"That's my Mama. I have to go. Thank you for a wonderful evening." Cynda gave him a peck on the cheek.

"The pleasure was mine," Nelson replied.

Nelson watched as she unlocked the door then went inside her home, glancing over her shoulder and sharing a smile before closing the door.

Nelson lingered, savoring the moment. So this was what it felt like to like someone else. He couldn't wait for this deal to be over. He strolled back to the ride share, humming a tune along the way.

16

Cynda woke to a light drizzle pattering her bedroom window. She stretched, then fell back onto her pillow. Last night was wonderful. But it shouldn't have been. She was falling for Nelson, but she shouldn't be. Was she so desperate that she couldn't help but like the first man that had been nice to her in years?

But he wasn't the first. There were others that vied for her attention, including Reverend Bowden, but it was easy to avoid them. Family was first. Her time with Nelson was necessary.

She finally climbed out of bed and searched for her house coat. At least she wasn't alone with her feelings. Nelson liked her, too. He'd admitted it. But it wasn't proper, at least for the moment. Now she had another reason for her to want the deal to be successful. She wanted to get to know him so much more.

The morning routine was the same. Cynda woke the boys and got them ready for school, then knocked on Terrence's door to wake him. Although she teased him often, she really hoped video games would work out for him. At least somebody would fulfill their dream.

"Stop that, Cynda," she said to herself out loud. "You're doing the right thing. Your time will come."

But would it?

She walked into Mama's room. Mama opened her eyes and barely smiled at her. Something wasn't right.

"Mama?"

Mama opened her mouth to speak, but nothing came out.

"Mama!"

Cynda ran to Mama, gripping her shoulders. Mama slowly raised her arms and barely held her. Cynda ran to her room for her phone and then called 911.

"911. What is your emergency?"

"Something's wrong with my Mama!" she said. "I think she had a stroke."

"What is your address?"

"445 Morning Glory Road, Jonesboro, GA 30339."

"We'll dispatch an ambulance right away."

Cynda ran back to Mama's room then cradled her in her arms."

"Terrence!"

Terrence stumbled into Mama's room rubbing his eyes.

"What . . ."

His eyes went wide when he looked at Mama. He fell to his knees beside the bed.

"I think it's a stroke," Cynda said, her voice surprisingly calm. "I called the ambulance and they're on the way. I need you to help the twins get ready. When the ambulance arrives, I need you to get the twins in the car and follow us."

"Okay."

Terrence held Mama's hand then squeezed it before leaving the room.

"It's gonna be alright, Mama," Cynda whispered. "It's gonna be alright."

The ambulance arrived five minutes later. Terrence let the paramedics in and they rushed to their job, getting Mama onto the stretcher and into the ambulance. Cynda got inside, holding Mama's hand the entire time. She looked around inside the vehicle as it sped to the hospital. This must have been how it was when Daddy had his heart attack. She remembered how guilty she felt for not being there, and how she made a promise that she would always be present if Daddy survived. He didn't, but she kept her promise to her family.

The ambulance arrived at the emergency room and Mama was rushed inside. Cynda filled out the paperwork as Terrence and the twins arrived. Terrence had grabbed a few books and toys. He walked them to the chairs, keeping them occupied while Cynda finished the forms. Once she was done, she walked to her family.

"What's wrong with Grandma?" Malon asked.

"Grandma is not feeling good," Cynda replied. "The doctors are going to check her out and let us know."

"She needs some chicken soup," Sha'kwon said.

"We'll fix her some when she comes home," Cynda replied.

She sat beside Sha'kwon and hugged him. She and Terrence played with the twins, but the worry was clear on both of their faces. After an hour, a doctor entered the emergency room.

"Cynda Jones?" she said.

Cynda jumped to her feet and hurried to the doctor.

"Yes?"

The doctor extended her hand. "I'm Dr. Camille Robertson. Your mother has had a mild stroke. The good thing is that she's already responding well, but she'll have to spend a few days here as we evaluate her and find out the extent of the damage."

"Can we see her?"

"We're getting her settled into a room now. As soon as we're done a nurse will come get you."

"Thank you, Dr. Robertson," Cynda said. She walked back to Terrence and the twins.

"What did the doctor say?" Terrence asked.

"Mama had a mild stroke," Cynda answered. "The doctor said there doesn't seem to be any serious damage, but only time will tell."

Terrence dropped his head. "Thank goodness."

"We still don't know how things will be," Cynda said.

Terrence raised his head. "Yeah, but Mama's alive."

That was one of the things she loved about her brother. He was always finding the positive in almost any situation. She hugged him.

"You're right," she said. Cynda looked at the twins.

"I need you to do me a favor," she said to Terrence. "Take the twins to daycare. I'll stay here and wait."

"Okay," Terrence replied. "I'll come back after I drop them off. When you calling Feenee?"

"As soon as I get y'all going," Cynda replied.

"She's gonna have a fit."

"I know."

Cynda and Terrence went to the twins.

"Hey boys, Uncle Terrence is taking y'all to daycare this morning. I'm staying here with Grandma."

"Okay," Malon said. "Give her a kiss for me."

"Me, too," Sha'kwon said.

"I will," Cynda replied. As rambunctious as they were, they were also sweethearts. She walked with them to the car then waved as Terrence drove away. Cynda returned to the emergency room waiting area, sat and punched in Tiffany's number. Tiffany answered immediately.

"Hey sis! This is an odd time to call."

Cynda took a breath. "Feenee, I'm at the hospital. Mama had a stroke."

Cynda closed her eyes as Fenee wailed then cried. She'd always been emotional.

"I'm coming home," she finally said.

"Can you?" Cynda asked.

"Yes. I'll request emergency leave."

"What if they don't grant it? You know how the army can be."

"Then I'm coming anyway."

"Look, don't get in trouble," Cynda said. "We can handle things until you get approval."

"I'll be there in a few days. Tell Mama and the babies I'll see them soon."

Tiffany disconnected. Cynda didn't try to call her back because she knew she couldn't stop her from doing whatever she was planning to do. All she could do was prepare for the fallout. She hoped it didn't come to that.

Cynda texted Reverend Bowden because she knew Mama would want her to. She also knew he would use it as an opportunity to ask her on a date, but she would have to suffer through it. The man didn't know how to take no for an answer. She guessed sometimes praying for something could be annoying to the person you're praying for.

Next, she called Laura. It was early for her boss, but she wanted to leave a message so Laura could plan for the office. After the call, she put her phone away and waited.

After an hour, Dr. Robertson returned. Cynda jumped to her feet.

"How is she?" Cynda asked.

"She's okay for now," the doctor replied. "We're still running tests, but from what I can see it doesn't seem like the damage was severe. We're already seeing movement on her right side. Give us some more time then you can see her."

"Thank you, doctor."

Dr. Robertson nodded and smiled before walking away. Cynda was walking to sit down when Laura rushed through the emergency room doors, her arms outstretched. Cynda fell into the hug.

"Oh, Cynda!" Laura said. "I'm so sorry! How is Mama Jones?"

"I'm not sure," Cynda replied. "The doctor said it could have been worse, but they're still running tests. I hope they'll let me see her soon."

"Whatever you need, let me know," Laura said. "I mean it."

"Thank you, Laura," Cynda replied.

They both sat. Laura looked at her for a minute the spoke.

"I know this isn't the best time to ask, but . . ."

"You want to know how things went with Nelson yesterday," Cynda said. "It's okay. They went well. As a matter of fact, if it was up to him, we'd have a deal. I'm sure of it."

"Great!" Laura said. "Did he give you any idea of when they'll make a decision?"

Cynda shook her head. "He's on his way to Sao Paulo. A business opportunity came up. He said he'll come back to make a final decision after he's done."

"When did he tell you that?" Laura asked.

"Yesterday after dinner."

Laura eyebrows rose as she smirked. "Dinner again?"

"Yes. He insisted."

"Where did you go?"

Cynda hesitated before answering. "Bones."

Laura's mouth fell open. "So y'all went on a date. A very expensive date."

"It wasn't a date," Cynda said.

"Yes it was," Laura replied. Laura placed her hand on Cynda's shoulder. "Look, Cynda. I'm not surprised. He's a good looking man and you're a beautiful woman. Y'all been spending a lot of time together. Back in the day I had a few business situations that became . . . interesting. All I'm asking you to do is to keep it professional."

Cynda didn't have the energy to defend herself from something that was true.

"Okay," she said.

Laura nodded. "On the other hand, if Nelson is on our side because he likes how you look in a tight skirt, I'm not going to complain."

Cynda's eyes went wide. "Laura!"

"That's my name." Laura phone buzzed. She checked it then stood.

"I got to go open the office. Let me know how she's doing, and I mean it when I said if you need anything, let me know. Anything."

Cynda and Laura hugged again.

"It's gonna be awkward when you have to fire me one day," Cynda said.

"Shoot girl, ain't nobody getting fired around here. As long as I have a business, you'll have a job. What's going to be sad is when you turn in your resignation. You deserved better, and one day you'll have it."

Cynda squeezed Laura a little tighter. Knowing she didn't have to worry about employment was a salve and knowing that Laura understood she'd have to move on one day was a relief. But would she ever? It was hard to see beyond caring for her family.

"Thank you, Laura. You're a good friend."

"Yes, I am," Laura replied. "Now let me go."

Laura kissed her on the cheek then strode out of the emergency room. As she walked through the sliding doors, Revend Bowden entered. He was dressed for Sunday morning in a fitted blue suit with matching shoes. Cynda couldn't remember seeing him any other way, even at casual church functions. She imagined him sleeping standing up fully dressed like a robot, waiting for sunlight to switch him on. She smiled at the thought, an expression that probably gave the young pastor the impression that she was happy to see him. She was, but not in the way he most likely imagined.

"Cynda. I came as soon as I got your message. How is your mother?"

He extended his right hand and Cynda took it.

"I'm not sure, Reverend."

The reverend smiled. "Curtis."

Cynda grinned. "Curtis. The doctor said they're still running tests."

"Let's pray," Curtis replied.

Cynda bowed her head and closed her eyes, taking in Curtis's words. When he was done, she felt better.

"Thank you, Curtis."

"I can sit with you for a while if you'd like," he said. "I don't have any pressing appointments."

They went to the chairs and sat.

"What does a pastor do during the week?" she asked.

You'd be surprised," Curtis said. "I'm pretty busy, but I leave my schedule flexible for emergencies like this."

"Thank you," she replied. "You're a good man."

"It comes with the job," Curtis joked.

"Not really," Cynda replied. "I watch reality TV."

Curtis chuckled. "Pastors are human, too."

Curtis took her hand again. "I'd love to get to know you better, Cynda."

Cynda closed her eyes. She knew it was coming, but she hoped the situation would prevent it. She pulled her hand away. It was time to be blunt.

"Curtis, I meant it when I said you're a good man, but you're not the man for me."

Curtis continued to smile. "I think I could change your mind if I had a chance."

"I don't think so," Cynda replied. "For that to happen, there has to be something there in the beginning. I like you as a friend, and I respect you as a pastor and a person. But that's as far as it goes."

Curtis nodded, his smile diminished. "I understand. Your mother will be disappointed, though."

Cynda smiled. "I'm sure she will."

Curtis stood and straightened his suit. "I'll be praying for your mother and your family all day. Please contact me if you need me."

"I will," Cynda replied. "Thank you so much for coming."

"You're welcome. Goodbye, Cynda."

"Bye, Curtis."

Curtis left the emergency room. Cynda closed her eyes and said a silent prayer for Mama.

MILTON J DAVIS

17

The Sao Paulo trip was a whirlwind of activity. The investment team was waiting for Nelson when his plane landed and whisked him to the property. When he saw the building and its location, he knew why Pops wanted to move fast. This was prime real estate, and with the current exchange rate, practically a steal. But his father was not the type of person to take advantage of a situation. He would negotiate a fair price for both parties in order to instill goodwill and create an opportunity for future business. It was his secret sauce, and it was very successful.

Mauricio Santos, their now partner, took off his shades and tucked them into his shirt pocket before speaking. He was a dark brown man with intense eyes and a narrow smile. Mauricio was born in the favelas, but with determination and intellect managed to earn a stellar education and start his own real estate business. Like Nelson's father, the color of his skin limited his opportunities, but just like Pops, he persevered.

"It's beautiful, isn't it?" he said.

"It will be," Nelson replied.

"You have to see into the future, amigo."

"I do. That's why I'm here."

Mauricio tugged his arm. "Come. I have something else to show you."

They went to Mauricio's car then drove to the nearby favelas.

"This is my home," he said. "Since your father was so generous, I'm able to invest a part of my profits into a project I've been working on for years. Your father wasn't interested in investing, but I thought you might be."

Nelson was taken off guard. "Me? Why?"

"Because you are young like me," Mauricio said. "More willing to take a risk, I think."

"I've never done a deal outside of our company," Nelson said.

Mauricio grinned. "Maybe you should. You have your own money, no?"

"I do."

"That's all it takes."

This was an unexpected opportunity. Nelson had never imagined making any deals on his own until Pops thought he was ready. Personally, he thought he was, but it was the validation he looked for.

Their journey ended in front of an abandoned building near the favelas. Mauricio parked and they exited the car. It was a three-story structure, the outside walls covered with graffiti. Nelson was not impressed.

"What are we looking at?" he asked.

"The future," Mauricio replied. "The impression is that people in the favelas have no money. They do, but they are careful how they spend it. If they see something that will benefit them, they will support it."

Mauricio and Nelson around the building. "There's no decent food market in the area. I want to make this a market where people can shop in peace and local farmers can sell their goods. It will have state of the art amenities and the best security. We'll hire local people to police the grounds, people respected by the community. I've also worked out an agreement with the local gangs to designate the area a neutral zone."

They entered the building. The smell was unpleasant but bearable.

"Since the market is outside the community, it will attract customers from the city as well. The best of both worlds."

They walked back out on the street.

"And here's the best part," Mauricio said. "As the market becomes popular, other businesses will want to set up nearby. If we purchase the surrounding land, our investment will grow with the market."

They returned to the car. "Most of all, the market will be a catalyst for growth and improvement in the favelas. That's most important to me."

"It sounds interesting," Nelson said. "Give me few weeks to think about it."

"Take all the time you need," Mauricio replied. "And if it's not a go for you, that's okay, too. It's not like there's a line of people waiting to buy this property."

They stopped by a local restaurant for a delicious lunch. The conversation was light, but Nelson wasn't paying much attention. He was thinking about Cynda. While the business in Sao Paulo was significant, he couldn't wait to get back to Atlanta to see her. He'd get the approval for the project from his father, then move to Atlanta to personally supervise it. He'd stay with Darla and Simone until he could find a decent condo for the duration of the project.

"Nelson, are you with me?" Mauricio asked.

Nelson looked up from his plate. "Yes, of course."

Mauricio smirked. "I don't think so. What's her name?"

"What are you talking about?"

Mauricio wiped his mouth with his napkin then leaned back into his chair. "I know that look. I've had it a few times myself when on a business trip. You're missing someone."

Nelson chuckled. "It's complicated and I'm not going to waste your time with my personal issues. I'm here to buy a building."

"It's okay to talk to me. I don't know anyone in your personal life, so who am I going to tell?"

"True. The reason it's complicated is because it's a client."

"Ah. That can be complex. You have to be careful important decisions are not clouded by lust."

"That's just it," Nelson replied. "If it was just lust, I could handle that. It's deeper."

"Then you have to take yourself off the account," Mauricio said.

"Can't. There's no one else."

"Do you have a picture of her?"

"I don't . . . wait."

Nelson took out his phone the searched for Benson Realty images. He found a picture of

Cynda and Ms. Benson, then enlarged the picture.

"This is her. Her name is Cynda Jones."

Mauricio looked at the picture and his eyebrows rose. "She's lovely."

"It's not just her looks," Nelson replied. "It's everything. She's so down to earth, smart, and honest. Fun, too."

"Are you sure she's not just being a savvy salesperson?"

"I'm sure. I can feel it."

"And does she know how you feel about her?"

"Yes. We had a conversation about it before I came here. The feeling is mutual."

"Then it seems you do have a dilemma."

Mauricio took a sip of his drink. "Life is short, my friend. We don't get bonus points for denying ourselves its pleasures. We end up with regrets on our deathbed. If you both feel this way, you should pursue it."

"That sounds nice, but like I said, it's complicated."

Mauricio's eyes narrowed. "Is there someone else?"

"For me? No . . . yes . . . maybe. Ronsie. We've been together since childhood. Our parents arc bcst fricnds and everyone assumed we were going to get married. Even us. A few months ago we decided to take a break to make sure we were ready for the next step. Neither of us had ever dated anyone else, and Ronsie had met someone."

"How did you feel about that?"

Nelson shrugged. "I wasn't sure. I'm still not. I figured I'd wait until she came to her senses. But then I met Cynda."

Nelson's throat went dry, and he took a sip of water. "I love Ronsie in a familiar sort of way, but I've never felt for her like I do for Cynda."

"It's called passion," Mauricio said. "The heart has made its choice. It would be foolish not to pursue it."

"If it was only that easy."

"Sometimes the obvious choice is hard to make. Always trust your heart. Whatever complications happen, it will be worth working though. Thus says Mauricio."

"I'll remember that," Nelson said.

They finished lunch then Mauricio took Nelson back to his hotel. Nelson took a shower then sat down with his laptop to update his notes. He opened his documents, saw the Benson file, and smiled. He looked at the time on his phone. It was noon in Atlanta.

"Not too early," he said aloud. He punched Cynda's number.

"Hi Nelson," Cynda said.

"Hi! How are you?"

"Not good," Cynda replied. "My mother had a stroke. I'm at the hospital."

"Oh no! How is she?"

"The doctor says it's not as bad as it could be, but they're still running tests."

"How can I help?"

"Pray," Cynda said.

"I will. I'll let you go."

"No," Cynda said. "It's good to talk. I'm going crazy sitting here. How's Sao Paulo?"

"It's good," Nelson replied. "The deal is going well. I should be returning in a couple of days."

"Are you coming to Atlanta?"

"Of course."

"Good news, I hope."

"Me, too."

They talked for an hour about little things. Nelson could sense Cynda needed to, so he gave her his full attention. But he was enjoying it as well. He didn't realize he desired a distraction from work until that moment. He recalled Mauricio's words and grinned.

"Wait," Cynda said.

There was a pause, then she returned to the phone.

"It's the doctor. I'll have to call you back."

"That's okay. Do what you need to do. We'll talk later."

"Promise?"

"I promise."

Nelson ended the call then sat for a moment, staring at his phone. He knew it wasn't his place, but he had to go back to Atlanta. He had a feeling that Cynda would like it if he did. He'd wrap up his work in Sao Paulo and change his flight first thing in the morning.

MILTON J DAVIS

18

Cynda sat by Mama's bed, her eyes on her peaceful face. The doctor's prognosis was as good as it could be considering the situation. There was no sign of serious damage, but she would have to remain in the hospital for a few days. Part of her recovery from the stroke would be physical therapy, and that would include walking. But there would have to be mental therapy as well. She had work to do.

"How's my big sister?"

Cynda jerked around. Tiffany stood in the doorway in her fatigues, a bright smile on her face. Terrence was behind her, holding the twins' hand. Cynda jumped to her feet and met her baby sister halfway. They hugged and cried.

"Feenee!" she squealed.

"Ceecee!"

Cynda stepped aside to let Tiffany go to Mama. She touched Mama's hair then looked at Cynda.

"Go ahead," she said.

"Mama? It's Feenee."

Mama stirred and her eyes opened.

"Is that my baby?" Mama slurred.

"Yes, it is!"

Mama tried to sit up, but Tiffany placed a gentle hand on her shoulder, before leaning over and hugging her."

"Baby, what you doing here?"

"I got a flight when Cynda told me what happened."

"She shouldn't have said nothing. I'm alright."

"No you're not, Mama," Cynda said. "But you will be."

"Help me sit up," Mama said.

"Mama, I don't think . . ."

"It's okay."

Dr. Robertson entered the room with her pad and a smile. "It's good to see the family here."

"This is my sister, Tiffany," Cynda said. "You know the rest of the crew."

Dr. Robertson shook Tiffany's hand. "Hi Tiffany. Thank you for your service."

Cynda and everyone made room for the doctor. She checked the instruments as she punched her pad, then sat beside the bed.

"How are you feeling, Mrs. Jones?"

"I feel just fine," Mama replied. "Good enough to go home."

"We're going to need you to stay with us a little bit longer before we send you home," the doctor said. "Would you like to go walking with your family?"

"I'm not so good at walking," Mama replied. "It's been like that since my husband died."

"Why don't you give it a try?" the doctor said. "It will help with your recovery."

"We got you Mama," Terrence said. "Just like we do at home."

Mama worked her jaw a bit before answering. "I guess it won't hurt to take a few steps. I got all my babies here. Somebody will catch me or fall with me."

Cynda laughed. A nurse entered the room with a walker and they helped Mama out the bed and to the walker. The six of them made their way out of the room and into the hallway, the doctor trailing behind.

"Don't try to do too much," she said. "When you get tired, let us know. We have a wheelchair to take you back."

"I don't want no wheelchair," Mama said.

Cynda, Terrence, and Tiffany looked at each other and smirked. They knew that was coming.

The six of them walked out into the corridor.

"Take it easy this time," the doctor said. "If you can make it to the elevator and back, that's a good day."

Mama looked at her grandkids. "Okay babies, let's race!"

The twins took her seriously, of course, sprinting down to the elevator.

"We win!" they shouted.

"Y'all sure did," Mama replied as she struggled down the corridor.

"You got here fast," Cynda said to Tiffany.

"I had good timing. Caught a ride on a cargo plane that just happened to be leaving when I needed." Tiffany touched her shoulder. "I need to tell you something."

"What's that?"

"I'm taking the twins back with me."

Cynda froze. "Are you serious?"

"What?" Terrence asked.

"Nothing," Tiffany replied.

"Terrence, can you finish walking Mama down the hall?" Cynda asked.

"Uh oh, woman talk," Terrence said. He took Mama's arm. "Come on, Mama. Ceecee and Feenee got some lies to tell."

Cynda waited for them to make some space before talking again.

"You can't take care of the twins by yourself," Cynda said. "That's why they're here with me."

"And you can't take care of them with Mama like this," Tiffany replied. "We both know that as much as we love him, Terrence ain't much help."

"He's been better, and I could hire babysitters. You'll have to send more money."

"I'm taking them back with me," Tiffany said. "I missed them so much, and I can't stand being away from them any longer. There's one more thing."

"What?"

"Malcolm is coming to Germany."

Cynda felt heat flash in her face. "I know you ain't about to let this . . ."

"Ceecee, we've been talking for months now. His engineering firm had an opening come up in Frankfurt. He asked for it and got it."

"You two weren't good together, Feenee."

"We were young and made a lot of mistakes," Tiffany confessed. "You know that. We've been working things out, but I didn't want to tell you until I felt sure."

Cynda looked into Tiffany's eyes and saw her resolve. She hugged her.

"Okay. But you know where to find me."

Tiffany laughed. "Yes I do."

"So when are you going to tell the twins?"

"A few days before we leave."

"Good. That way we won't have to deal with all that wild energy."

"I know, right?"

Cynda hugged Tiffany again. "I just want what's good for you," Cynda said.

"I know, and I love you for that."

They hurried and caught up with Mama and Terrence. They turned around and walked Mama back to the room where the nurse was waiting.

"Hello everyone. I'm Nadine. I'll be looking after your mother."

"Hi Nadine," Cynda said. "I'm Cynda. This is my sister Tiffany and my brother Terrence. And these are the twins, Malon, and Sha'kwon."

"Such a lovely family!" Nadine moved closer to Mama. "Mrs. Jones, let's get you settled so I can take your vitals."

Nadine led Mama into the room.

"I'll stay," Terrence said.

Cynda was surprised. "Are you sure?"

"Yes. I brought my laptop. It's in the car."

Cynda frowned. "So you're going to play gamcs?"

"It's alright," Mama said. "You go on with your sister."

"You sure, Mama?"

"I'm sure. I'm gonna be sleep anyway."

"Okay," Cynda said. "But you call us if you need us."

"You know I will," Terrence replied.

"Malon, Sha'kwon, y'all come give grandma some sugar."

The twins rushed over and kissed Mama on the cheek. Cynda and Tiffany did the same.

"Don't worry," Nadine said. "She's in good hands."

"Thank you," Cynda replied.

They left the hospital and went to the parking lot. Tiffany had rented an SUV; after securing the twins in the back seat she and Cynda climbed into the car and they were on their way back to the house.

"It's so good to be home," Tiffany said.

"It's good to have you here," Cynda replied. "How long can you stay?"

"I have a month," Tiffany replied. "Longer if needed."

"As much as I'd love you to be here longer, I hope you don't have to be."

"Me, too."

"I thought about getting takeout for dinner, but I'm making a homecooked meal."

Tiffany's eyes went wide. "Fried chicken, rice, and collards?"

"Your favorite."

"I'm officially home!"

"What did you bring me from Germany?"

"You'll see when we get to the house."

Cynda relaxed in her seat. She was still worried for Mama, but with Tiffany home, things wouldn't be as stressful. Her thoughts went to Nelson. It would be nice to see him too, but she had to put those feelings aside for now. Family first.

MILTON J DAVIS

19

Nelson's phone buzzed as he waited for his morning flight to Chicago. It was his father.

"Morning, Pops."

"Good morning, son. I read your report. Excellent work. Putting together the investment portfolio now."

"Excellent. Mauricio and I took a look at some additional property as well."

"Excellent," his father replied. "We think the same way. Are you on your way back to Chicago?"

"Yes. I have a layover in Atlanta. I want to do a little more research on the hotel property there."

"That won't be necessary," his father said.

"What?"

"I'm pulling the plug on the Atlanta project."

The bottom dropped out of Nelson's stomach.

"But why? It's a good deal."

"It is, but it's not right now. I think our money will be better invested in Brazil."

"I don't think we should walk away from Atlanta," Nelson said. "It's more than just money. It's an opportunity to revive a community the right way."

"Son, you know I understand that more than anyone. But sometimes profit has to take priority. The investors we're representing at the moment are more concerned with that."

"Maybe we can present the property to other investors."

Nelson heard his father sigh.

"Looks like this project has become personal to you. Is there something else I need to know?"

"No Pops," Nelson said. "It's just that it's a great opportunity. I'd hate to lose out on it. It won't be on the market forever."

"I'm sure it won't, but this isn't the one for us right now. Atlanta's a good market. There will be others. I'll have Darrell contact Miss Benson and let her know."

"No, I'll do it." Nelson replied. "I can't change my flight, so I might as well handle it. Besides, I'll visit Darla while I'm there."

"Tell her I said hello."

"You tell her," Nelson said. "She'd love to hear from you."

"I just might. I'll see you when you get back," his father said.

"Bye, Pops."

Nelson ended the call. This would not be a good day. He did think the hotel was a great deal, but most of all he didn't want to disappoint Cynda, especially now. She was dealing with enough with her mother's condition and now this. But it had to be done. Once his father made up his mind there was no changing it. He put in his earbuds and listened to his jazz playlist. He needed a few minutes of calm before he did what he had to do.

His flight landed at Hartsfield-Jackson Airport that night. Nelson waited for the other passengers to exit before getting his bag from the overhead bin. As he exited the plane, he considered various ways to break the news but wasn't satisfied with any of them. He'd put if off for another time. At the moment he was hungry.

He called Darla.

"Hey boy!"

"Hey sis!"

"Where are you?"

"My plane just landed in Atlanta."

"You're here? Why didn't you tell me you were coming?"

"I wasn't planning to. I made a detour, and now I wish I hadn't."

"I'll come pick you up."

"You don't have to."

"Yes I do. I have a great place I want to take you for dinner, then you can tell me why you don't' want to be here."

"Cool. I'll meet you curbside."

"See you in a few."

Nelson took his time through the airport, reaching baggage claim about twenty minutes after leaving the plane. His phone buzzed. It was Darla.

"Where are you?"

"On my way."

When Nelson exited the airport, he saw Darla in a serious discussion with a policeman. She looked over the policeman's shoulder and pointed at him. The officer turned his head, then put away his ticket book. By the time Nelson reached the car he'd driven away.

"You're paying for dinner," Darla said. "Get in."

Darla sped away from the airport.

"So what's up?"

"Pops killed the Atlanta deal."

"That's too bad. I know you liked that project, and I was looking forward to seeing more of you."

"That's how it goes. I really feel bad for Benson Realty, though. This is their dream project."

Darla cut her eye at Nelson. "Do you feel bad for Benson, or for Cynda?"

Nelson chuckled. "You don't miss anything do you, detective?"

"Nope."

"We talked yesterday. Her mother suffered a stroke. I'm going to see her while I'm here. I also need to let them know the deal is off."

"Not the best time to share bad news."

"No it's not."

Carla exited off the highway to Moreland Avenue.

"Where are we going?"

"A Mexican restaurant I've wanted to go to for months."

"Let me guess, Simone won't go."

"Bingo! She's not a fan of Mexican food, and I know you'll eat anything."

Nelson laughed. "Almost anything."

They drove a few miles to a nondescript building with a small parking lot that filled quickly as they parked.

"Looks popular," Nelson said.

"It is," Darla said. "It's not your usual Mexican restaurant. All they serve is chicken, but it's the best chicken."

They entered the restaurant then stood in line to place their order. They were lucky; there was a table available in the small dining area. After they sat Darla rested her chin in her hand.

"So, what are you going to do about this deal?"

"What do you mean what am I going to do? Nothing."

"So you must not care that much about it."

"Of course I do, but once Pops makes up his mind it's done deal."

Darla sucked her teeth. "You're such a wuss."

"What are you talking about?"

"Giving up like that. You know you can disagree with the old man."

"For what good that will do."

"Have you ever tried?"

Nelson hesitated. "No. I haven't."

"See? You need to start living your own life. You just go along with things. Just like Ronsie."

"Darla!" the food server called out.

Their food was ready. Nelson got their trays and plastic ware and returned to the table. He tasted his taco and grinned.

"This is good," he replied.

"And don't say almost as good as Chicago."

Nelson laughed as he indulged.

"So what are you going to do?" Darla asked.

"About what?"

"If I didn't have this fork in my hand I'd pop you upside your head. The building!"

"For now, nothing. Pops always makes good decisions. I follow his lead."

Darla shrugged. "A missed opportunity."

"Maybe. Maybe not."

"Well, the one good thing that could come from this is that you can start dating Cynda."

Nelson thought on Darla's words as he ate his second taco. Cynda aside, he really did believe in the project. But to disagree with his father? He wasn't sure he was ready for that. As far as he was concerned, he was still learning, still an apprentice. Maybe in a few more years, but not now.

They finished their meal then headed for the car.

"Hey, can you take me to get a rental?"

"Use my car," Darla replied.

"Really? I don't want to leave you stranded."

"I'll be at the house. No need for you to spend the money if you're flying out tomorrow. I can drop you off at the hotel unless you want to spend the night with us."

"I'd prefer the hotel. I'm not in a dog shmoozing mood."

"Ha. Ha."

They drove to Darla's house. After a brief love session with the dogs, Nelson headed for the hotel. He called Cynda on his way.

"Hi Nelson."

"Hi Cynda. How's your mother?"

"As well as can be expected. She's still in the hospital. We don't know for how long. My brother is with her. I'm going later."

"Do you and Laura have time for a meeting tomorrow morning?"

"Of course! I'll call her tonight."

"Okay. See you tomorrow."

Guilt settled on Nelson as soon as he disconnected. He should have given her some kind of warning. He also hoped he would just be meeting with Cynda, but he should have known better. This was an important project for both of them so it made sense that Miss Benson would be present.

Nelson arrived at the hotel, the long flight finally catching up with them. He checked into his room, took a quick shower, then collapsed on his bed. He'd deal with the situation the next day. He yawned, closed his eyes, and fell asleep on top of the sheets.

* * *

Morning arrived sooner than he hoped. Nelson dragged himself out of bed then washed up before donning his casual business suit. He ate a light breakfast, picked up his car, then headed for Benson Realty. The drive wasn't as long as he thought it would be; he grimaced as he pulled into the parking lot anticipating the reaction to grave news he was about to deliver. As Nelson entered the building, Cynda was walking to the door.

"Welcome back," she said.

Her voice made him smile. He put out his hand but she hugged him instead.

"How's your mother?" he asked.

"As good as can be expected. Thank you for asking." She gestured with her hand. "Come on back. Miss Benson is waiting."

The walk down the hall to the meeting room felt like a death march. He was about to ruin these women's dreams. This wasn't the first time he'd turned down a deal, but it was the first time he'd told someone he liked he wasn't going to help them. He mentally shook his head. This was business; nothing more, nothing less. And like Darla said, with the deal out of the way he could pursue Cynda properly. If she was still interested.

Miss Benson stood as he entered the room. She was a full figured, attractive woman with an engaging smile. Nelson could tell she was a heartbreaker back in the day.

Miss Benson walked around the table and gave him a firm handshake.

"Mr. Carter," she said. "It's good to finally meet you. I hope Cynda's been taking good care of you."

Nelson glanced at Cynda and they both smiled.

"She has," he replied. "Call me Nelson, Miss Benson."

"And you can call me Laura," she replied. "Have a seat."

Laura motioned at the seat at the head of the table. As Nelson sat, he felt as if a stone was placed on his shoulders. Laura and Cynda sat opposite each other to the left and right of him, their eyes on him.

"Thank you for meeting with me at such short notice," he began. "Let me start by wishing your mother a quick and speedy recover, Cynda. I'll be praying for her."

"Thank you," Cynda replied. Laura glanced at Cynda with a raised eyebrow.

"Let's get down to business," Nelson continued. "Thank you for giving us the opportunity to partner with you on this project. The building has a lot of potential, and Cynda's tour of Atlanta proved to me that this is a market well worth investment."

"It's a hidden gem," Laura said. "Just standing there waiting for someone to recognize its value. I was sure your company would."

Nelson's throat tightened. "Could I have some water, please?"

"Of course." Cynda left the table and returned with a bottled water.

"Thanks." Nelson opened the bottle and took sip. "I spoke with my father this morning, and we've come to a decision."

Nelson looked at Cynda and Laura.

"We've decided to partner with you on the project."

Laura jumped to her feet. "Yes!"

Cynda lowered her head and closed her eyes. Nelson's heart dropped as he watched them celebrate. He'd said what he wanted to say. He lied to them. He stood quickly.

"I should have the papers ready to sign in a few weeks," he said. "I wish I could celebrate with you, but I have to make my flight to Chicago this afternoon. I hope you understand."

"Of course we do," Laura said. She shook Nelson's hand. "I'm looking forward to working with you. It's a dream come true."

"I'll walk you out," Cynda said.

Nelson did his best not to show his nervousness. Cynda touched his arm.

"Thank you so much," she said.

"You don't need to thank me. You and Laura did all the work. Now it's time for me to do my part."

"Do you have to go back to Chicago today?" Cynda asked.

"Yes," Nelson replied. "I need to hit the ground running on this one. Between Atlanta and Sao Paulo, I'm going to be slammed."

Cynda walked him to his car. He turned to face her They gazed at each other, the desire clear in their eyes.

"Well . . . I should go," Nelson said. He was about to get in the car when Cynda grabbed his hand. She pulled him into a hug, then kissed his cheek. Nelson touched her chin, then walked away.

He got in his car then watched Cynda enter the building. As soon as she was gone, he slammed his hand against the steering wheel.

"Stupid, stupid, stupid! Why did you say that? Why?"

As he drove away, he answered his own question. He couldn't sit there and disappoint them like that. This project had become as personal to him as it was to them. When he got back to Chicago, he would use everything in his power to convince his father to greenlight the deal. But what if he wasn't able to do it? Then he'd be right back where he started.

"It's going to happen," he said out. "This is going to happen."

It took him thirty minutes to get back to Darla's house. She met him at the door with the dogs, and they went to her studio. The dogs hovered around him for a bit as Darla sat before her canvas and continued painting.

"So how did it go? Did they take it well?" she asked.

"It went great," Nelson replied. "I told them we were taking the deal."

Darla dropped her paintbrush as her mouth dropped open. "What!?! Nelson, you didn't!"

"I couldn't do it, sis. I just couldn't."

"So what are you going to do now?"

"I'm going to try to convince Pops one more time."

"Good luck with that," Darla said. She picked up her brush and started back painting. "And what if that doesn't work?"

Nelson leaned back in his chair. "I don't know."

20

Cynda peeked out the office window, watching Nelson drive away. Once he was out of sight, turned and leaned against the door. Laura stood in the conference room door, a wide smile on her face, her eyes glistening with tears of joy. They screamed then ran toward each other, meeting in the middle of the hall then hugging and hopping.

"We did it!" Cynda said.

"No baby, you did it," Laura replied.

Cynda wiped her eyes. "I can't take credit for this. This is your dream. You had this in your heart way before I started working here."

"Yes, that's true," Laura replied. "But you made it real. The best thing that ever happened was me getting sick that day. I don't think I could have pulled it off. But you did."

"Well, if you insist on giving me the credit, I'll take it."

They laughed as they went to Laura's office. Laura fell into her chair and sighed.

"This is only the beginning. Once we announce this deal, the other commercial realtors will start taking us seriously. Not only will it open up more opportunities, but it will also open us up to financing."

"Sounds like you're ready to build an empire," Cynda said.

Laura smiled. "I am. And I can't do it by myself." She sat up, placing her elbows on her desk and intertwining her fingers. "I want you to do it with me."

Cynda smiled back. "I'm here as long as I can be. You know I plan to go back to school to finish my degree once things settle down around my house."

"I know, and you should. But you don't understand. I don't want you to continue working for me. I want you to work with me. How does Benson and Jones Realty sound?"

Cynda was stunned. "Wait, what?"

"I've been thinking about it for a long time. The only reason I've been able to grow this business over the last five years is because of you. You've kept this place humming while I focused on landing the big deals. And now this. Plus, I like you. I can't think of anyone better to go into the future with."

"Wow, I'm flattered," Cynda replied.

"One more thing," Laura said.

"What's that?"

"At my age you start to think about your legacy. With me not having any children, if something was to happen to me, I'd want this place to continue to thrive. I can't think of anyone better to make sure that happens than you."

Cynda's mind reeled. So much was happening in such a short time.

"I'm gonna need some time to think about this," she finally said.

Laura's glow dimmed a bit. "Take your time, Cynda. I know this is a lot, especially with what your mother is going through. In fact, why don't you take the rest of the day off and see about her."

"Okay. What are you going to do?"

Laura stood and opened the cabinet behind her desk. She turned around with a bottle of wine and two glasses.

"I'm going to sit here and celebrate," Laura said. "And you can't leave until you have at least one glass with me."

"Of course!"

Laura popped the cork and poured the wine. They lifted their glasses together.

"Cheers!"

Cynda sipped the wine and smiled. It was excellent, just like the moment. She finished her glass and Laura picked up the bottle to pour her another. Cynda shook her head.

"That's it for me. I have to drive to the hospital, remember?"

"More for me, then," Laura said.

Cynda shook her head as she stood. "Please don't sit there and get drunk in this office. You know the realtors will be coming through later."

"I'll just close the door. It wouldn't be the first time. You have to celebrate your victories, Cynda."

"You're a mess," Cynda said.

Laura stood, shuffled around the desk, and gave Cynda a hug.

"And you're an angel."

Cynda left Laura's office, walking down the hall like a medal winning gymnast. It had been a long time since she had something to celebrate. A partnership! She never imagined Laura offering her something like this. It never occurred to her to ask. The realty company was just a job to her, something to pay the bills until she was able to go back to school and finish her degree. She did like the work, especially since Laura let her take on more responsibilities. But did she like it enough to make it a career? She'd have to think about it.

It was late afternoon when she arrived at the hospital. Tiffany and the twins were in the room with Mama. Tiffany and Mama smiled at her while the twins ran to her with their usual exuberance.

"Auntie Cynda! Mama's taking us to Germany!" Sha'kwon shouted.

"Yay!" Malon said.

"You told them, I see."

"Yes," Tiffany replied. "I set everything up. I also talked my commander into letting me stay another week."

"You don't need to do that," Mama said.

"I want to," Tiffany replied. "I need to get everything together for the babies. They need passports and a big box to put them in."

"Noooo!" the twins said, as they hid behind Cynda's legs.

Tiffany stood and Cynda took her place in the chair. "Well, I have great news. We got the deal!"

"Congratulations!" Tiffany said.

"That's wonderful, baby," Mama replied.

"Thank y'all. Nelson is sending us the contract soon. And Miss Benson offered me a partnership at the company."

"That's amazing!" Tiffany said.

"It's about time," Mama said. "You been doing all that woman's work for years."

"I've been doing my job," Cynda replied. "Working hard just like y'all taught me."

"You gonna take it?" Tiffany asked. "I know you want to go back to college."

"I don't know. It's not exactly my dream, but it is a good opportunity and I like working there."

"You can always do your art in your spare time."

Cynda laughed. "Spare time? What's that?"

"Something you'll have once I take the twins back with me."

Cynda looked at the little ones as they played their games. She would miss them, the good and the bad. But it would be great to have some more time to herself.

"I might just do that," she said.

"Good." Tiffany extended her hands and wiggled her fingers. "Come on, babies! Time to go home!"

The twins grabbed her hands and they walked toward the door.

"See you later," she said.

Cynda waved. "Bye!"

She turned her attention to Mama.

"How you feeling?"

"I feel better. I'm ready to go home."

"The doctor will have to tell us that."

"What she waiting on?"

Cynda laughed. "For you to get better. You feel like walking?"

"Yes. I can't walk with Feenee and them boys. They walk too fast, and Feenee talks too much."

Cynda laughed. "She's happy to be home. If I'd been gone a year I'd talk your head off, too."

Mama patted her hand. "No you wouldn't. You know my moods."

"That I do."

"Now help me out of this bed."

Cynda helped Mama out of the bed and put on her housecoat. They walked into the hallway and toward the elevators, the nurses waving and speaking along the way. She was walking without the walker now, which was progress.

"You should take that job," Mama said. "You deserve it."

"We could use the money," Cynda replied.

"It ain't about the money. It's about you having something of your own."

They met Dr. Robertson on their way back to the room.

"Hello! This is good. This is very good."

"Hi, Dr. Robertson."

"Helly Cynda. Hi Mama Jones. I'm glad you're here. I have your latest test results."

They followed the doctor back into the room. Cynda helped Mama into the bed then sat beside her.

"We've confirmed a stroke," the doctor began, "but there was little brain damage. I think with good physical therapy Mama Jones should be close to normal. There's going to be some changes in diet, and you'll have to make sure you move around more. There's no reason you shouldn't."

"I don't know if I can do all that, doctor," Mama said.

"She'll do it," Cynda replied. "We'll make sure she does."

"So y'all going to be telling me what to do?" Mama asked.

"No, Mama. We'll ask you and you'll do it because you love us."

Mama chuckled. "I guess I will."

"That was easy," Dr. Robertson said. "We'll keep you here another day, then it's home for you."

"That's great!" Cynda said.

"Thank you, Jesus!" Mama replied.

"I'll give you a list of things to do while she's home," Dr. Robertson said. "You also need to schedule a physical therapist to come by to work with her until she's well . . . or as well as she can get."

The doctor came closer to the bed and placed her hand on Mama's shoulder. "I'm not going to lie to you, Mama Jones. You may not recover completely. But we're going to do the best we can to get you as close as possible."

Mama held Dr. Robertson's hand. "I understand, baby. I'm just thankful I'm still here with my children and can do what I can. I thank the Lord for that."

"We do too," Cynda said.

"I'll leave you two alone," Dr. Robertson said. "Be sure to buzz the nurses if you need anything."

"Can they bring an extra bed?" Cynda asked. "I'd like to stay the night if I can."

"I'll send Nadine," Dr. Robertson said.

"Baby, you don't have to stay," Mama said.

"I know, but I want to."

"You gonna miss your bed. I know I miss mine."

"It can do without me for a night. Besides, I've been dying to taste some of this wonderful hospital food."

"Ain't no need for you to be lying up in here."

They both laughed.

21

Nelson was on an early plane to Chicago. He had to make up for his mistake. Darla was right. If he believed in the Atlanta project, he needed to fight for it. If Pops respected him, he would listen to him.

But what if he still said no? He would have no choice but to tell Cynda and Laura the truth. It would crush them.

"That's not going to happen," he said to himself. "This will work. It will work."

Two hours later he landed. He was walking to baggage claim when his phone buzzed. It was Ronsie.

"Hi!"

"Where are you?"

"Just landed at home."

"You got time to see a cute friend today?"

"Of course I do, and you're much more than a cute friend."

"I'm glad you said that."

"What does that mean?"

"I'll tell you when I see you."

"Okay."

"Let's have lunch."

"That sounds perfect."

"Love you."

"Love you, too."

Nelson took a ride share to the office. Darrell greeted him with his smiling face.

"Welcome back!"

"Good morning, Darrell. Is my father in?"

"As always."

Nelson went straight to his father's office. Pops sat at his desk, eyes fixed on his monitor as the sounds of Al Jarreau melodic scatting filled the space.

"Morning, Pops."

His father looked up with a smile.

"Morning, Prince."

Nelson couldn't help but grin as he sat. His mother and father were the only people that called him by his first name.

"Congratulations again on Sao Paulo," his father said.

"Thanks. Pops, I think you should reconsider Atlanta."

His father put his computer to sleep and swiveled his seat around.

"Is there some new information?"

"No. I just think it would be a good deal."

"I didn't say it was a bad deal. I don't think it's right for us now, especially with what's going on in Brazil and the current exchange rate. We can't do both."

"What about the effect on the community? That's always been our priority."

"True. But there are times we have to focus on the bottom line. This is one of those times."

Nelson fell silent. He stared at his father, studying his face. There was no flexibility in his expression. The deal was dead. He would have to tell Cynda and Laura.

"You seem to be taking this one personally," his father said.

"I am," Nelson replied.

"That happens sometimes. But we have to move on."

Nelson went back to his office. He sat then looked at his phone, dreading the call he'd have to make. Instead of doing it, he called Ronsie.

"There you are," she answered.

"Lunch at Tony's?"

"You read my mind. See you there!"

Nelson spent the rest of the morning absently catching up on his paperwork. He was still trying to think of ways to change his father's mind on the Atlanta deal. He also thought of Cynda and how the news of the deal tanking would affect her. Not only that, how it would affect them. He lied to her and Laura. He could have told them the truth, but he was sure he would be able to convince his father to move forward. That was a lie, too.

He was relieved when lunch time came. He rushed out of his office to meet Ronsie.

"Hey!"

He turned to see his father standing in the doorway of the office.

"Want to grab something to eat?"

"I have a lunch date with Ronsie, actually."

"Really? You two back together?"

"No, but we're still friends."

"Tell her I said hello."

"I will."

Tony's was a three block walk down the street from the office. The line extended out the door as always. Nelson was about to call Ronsie when his phone buzzed. It was her.

"Hey. This line is terrible."

"I'm already inside. Got us a great table. I ordered for you, too."

"Perfect!"

Nelson made his way by the line. Veronica sat in the far corner, greeting him with a wide smile. She wore a cute top and jeans, meaning she was working from home that day. She stood to greet him and they hugged. He was about to kiss her cheek, but she turned her head and their lips met. Nelson was surprised.

"It's great to see you," she said.

"Likewise."

She pointed at his Italian Beef sandwich. "I hope I got it right."

Nelson inspected it and smiled. "How could you get it wrong? We've eaten here a thousand times."

"At least. So what happened with Atlanta?"

Nelson bit into his sandwich before answering. He needed the tasty distraction.

"Something terrible. Pops changed his mind. He killed the Atlanta deal in favor of the Sao Paulo project."

"It doesn't seem that bad," Ronsie replied. "I'm sure they'll be disappointed, but I'm also sure this isn't the first time that's happened."

"Yeah, but I told them the deal was approved after I knew it wasn't."

Veronica's eyes went wide. "Why did you do that?"

"Cynda showed me the real Atlanta. She introduced me to the people and the community. I felt a connection there."

Ronsie's eyes narrowed. "To the city, the project, or to her?"

Nelson grinned. "All three."

Veronica's smile faded. "Well, that complicates things."

"What are you talking about?"

"The reason I asked you to lunch is because I wanted to talk about us."

Nelson put down his sandwich. "Us?"

"Yes."

Nelson wasn't hungry anymore. "I thought we were taking a break."

"We were . . . I mean are."

"Let me guess. Things didn't work out between you and that dude."

"Kevin," Veronica replied. "No, they didn't. But that's not why I wanted to talk about us."

Ronsie reached out her hand and Nelson took it in reflex.

"The more I'm out here single, the more I appreciate you. Our love wasn't a firestorm, but it was comfortable and safe. I know you better than almost anyone else. I didn't appreciate how important that is to a relationship until now."

"It takes time to get to know someone," Nelson replied. "We had all our lives. And Lord knows I ain't perfect."

Ronsie laughed. "I know that's right! Me, either. But like I said, I know you, and you know me."

"So what are you saying? You want to get back together?"

Ronsie gave him an innocent grin. "If you want to."

Nelson didn't answer. He had strong feelings for Cynda, but he couldn't deny the fact that getting back with Ronsie wouldn't be so bad. Like she said, they knew each other. Besides, his parents and her parents would be ecstatic.

"I understand if you have to think about it," Ronsie continued. "This whole thing was my idea. If I hadn't said anything we wouldn't be having this conversation. So take your time. I'm not going anywhere."

"You sure?"

Ronsie smiled. "I'm sure. Now eat the rest of that sandwich before I do."

It was a leisurely lunch. They ate each other's fries like they always did and although their conversation was light and playful, Nelson felt the tension. He wasn't sure he wanted to get back together, but he felt like he had to give her a chance. This was Ronsie. He couldn't just say no.

They finished lunch. Nelson paid the check, and Ronsie walked with him back to the office.

"What are you doing later?" she asked.

"Catching up on paperwork," Nelson replied.

"Just like your daddy. If you change your mind and want to hang out, give me a call."

"I will."

"Bye."

This time they kissed on the cheek. Ronsie walked backwards for a moment waving at him then turned and walked away. Nelson watched then went back to the office. He couldn't give Ronsie an answer until he spoke to Cynda again. He'd have to clear the air with her about the deal going bad and find out for sure how she felt about him. And he'd have to do that face to face. When he returned to his office, he booked a flight to Atlanta.

MILTON J DAVIS

22

Cynda was busier than she'd been in a long time. In addition to keeping up with Mama's physical therapy, she was lining up contractors for the upcoming project with Nelson. The deal hadn't been officially closed, but Nelson assured them it was going to happen.

She was interrupted by a phone call.

"Benson Realty."

"Hello, this is Thomas Carter. May speak to Laura Benson?"

"Yes, of course! I'll transfer you right away!"

Cynda buzzed Laura.

"Yes?"

"It's him! Mr. Carter!"

"Yes! Transfer him!"

Cynda transferred the call then hurried down the hall to Laura's office. The conversation had started by the time she entered. Laura's face was serious . . . and concerned.

"I understand. No need to apologize. It was an honor just for the opportunity. Thank you. You have a blessed day."

Laura hung up the phone. She stared at it for a moment, then looked at Cynda with glistening eyes.

"What happened?" Cynda said.

"More like what didn't," Laura replied. "There is no deal."

"What!?! Wait, Nelson said . . ."

MILTON J DAVIS

"Nelson lied. I just got off the phone with the man himself and he called to apologize, which he didn't have to do. I'll give him credit for that."

Anger welled up in Cynda. She spun and stomped out of the room.

"I'm calling him," she said.

"Why? It won't do any good."

"Because I want to know why he lied to us." She grabbed her phone off the desk and punched his number. There was no answer.

Laura showed up a few minutes later.

"Let it go, Cynda," she said. "Maybe this wasn't meant to be."

"No. You've dreamed for this too long. We'll find someone else."

"Who? I've talked to everyone in this city. No one's interested, at least not interested in doing it with me." She placed her hand on Cynda's shoulder. "We have a good thing here. And if you're worried about the partnership deal, don't be. I was sincere. I want you to be my partner. It's just going to take a little longer to make it happen."

"I appreciate that," Cynda replied.

"C'mon," Laura said. "Let's go say goodbye to our dream."

Laura walked out of the office door. Cynda grabbed her things and followed.

* * *

Nelson trudged off the plane at Harts-field/Jackson airport in a somber mood. He had no baggage to carry or claim, so headed straight to the rental car shuttle. In a few moments he had his car and was driving to the Benson Realty office. He could have done this over the phone, but he had to do it in person. He'd have some explaining to do to Laura and Cynda, but especially to Cynda.

When he reached the office, it was closed. Nelson thought it was unusual for the time of day. He went to his car then called Cynda's personal number. She answered.

"Yes?"

"It's me."

"I know. What do you want?"

"We need to talk. Where are you?"

"At the building."

"I'll be right there."

Nelson put the phone back in his pocket. This was going to be worse than he imagined.

* * *

Cynda put her phone back into her back pocket then sipped her tea.

"That was Nelson," she said to Laura. "He's on his way here."

"Then maybe I should leave," Laura said.

"Why? He lied to both of us."

Laura chuckled. "This isn't about the building. It's about you and him. There's nothing for him to say to me. The conversation with his father was my closure."

"So you're going to leave me stranded here?"

"No. I'm just going to go sit in the car. I'll still be able to hear the yelling."

"I don't yell," Cynda replied.

"We'll see."

Laura walked to her car then got inside. A few minutes later a red SUV pulled up and parked on the side of the road. Nelson stepped out and Cynda's resolve wavered. Her feelings for him stepped forward, but she reminded herself that she was angry with him for good reason.

"Cynda," he said. "I have something to tell you."

"I already know. Your father called the office this morning. There is no deal. What I want to know is why did you lie to us? Why did you lie to me?"

Nelson looked away. "It wasn't a lie, at least I didn't think so."

"What? Your father had already told you the deal was dead, and yet you sat in front of both of us and said we had a deal."

"I didn't tell you the truth because I thought I could change his mind and I didn't want to disappoint you and Laura. Especially you."

Cynda rolled her eyes. "You could have told us exactly what you just said and we would have understood. Instead you chose to lie. And I hate liars."

"I'm sorry. Please forgive me."

Cynda fell silent. She wanted to forgive him. He was the closest she'd been to a real relationship in years. But she wasn't desperate. If he lied about this, what would be next?

"I can't," Cynda finally said. She extended her hand. Nelson stared at it, then looked into her eyes.

"So that's it?"

"That's it. I have too much going on in my life right now, Nelson. If you had been straight with us, there might have been something between us after the deal. But now? I need solid people around me, people I can trust to do what they say they can do."

"I made a mistake," Nelson said. "I won't do it again."

"No, you won't."

Nelson's face sagged and Cynda could see his pain. He took her hand, holding it gently for a minute before it became a firm handshake.

"Goodbye, Cynda Jones. It was wonderful meeting you, and a joy working with you. I hope I get the opportunity again."

"Goodbye, Nelson." It was all she could manage to say. She watched him walk back to the SUV and drive away. She was still watching when Laura pulled up in front of her.

"Well, you didn't yell," Laura said.

"Because I wanted to cry," Cynda replied. "I liked him. I really liked him."

"Get in," Laura said. "Let's go to our spot and get shrimp and grits. And maybe a few shots of bourbon. It's been that kind of day."

Cynda got inside, tears staining her cheeks. "Let's go."

They ended up at McCormick and Schmick, eating and drinking in silence. Afterwards they returned to the office.

"Go home," Laura told Cynda. "I can handle things."

"I'm alright," Cynda replied.

"No you're not. Go home. I'll see you tomorrow."

Cynda wasn't going to argue. "Okay. Thank you."

They hugged and Cynda went to her car and drove home. She arrived to see Tiffany and the twins playing in the front yard. Mama sat in her wheelchair, a smile on her face. The scene lifted her spirits.

The twins ran to her as she got out of the car.

"Auntie Cynda!" Malon shouted. "Come play with us!"

They grabbed her hands and pulled her into the grass.

"You're back early," Tiffany said.

"Laura gave me the rest of the day off. We learned today that the deal didn't go through."

"Oh no! I'm sorry!"

Cynda shrugged. "The worst thing is that there was never a deal. Nelson lied to us."

"That's terrible," Tiffany said.

"Auntie Cynda, catch!" Sha'kwon shouted. Cynda saw the orange ball just in time. She caught it then tossed it back to Sha'kwon. They threw it back and forth as she and Tiffany walked to Mama.

"He said he didn't mean to lie, that he was trying to convince his father to reconsider. But Mr. Carter called Laura to apologize for turning down the deal."

"Sounds like he was trying to work things out," Tiffany said.

"All he had to do was be honest," Cynda replied. "You know how much I hate liars."

She stopped beside Mama and kissed her cheek. "I'm happy to see you outside."

"I'm happy to be outside," Mama replied. "I spend too much time in that room. Feenee, tell her what we talked about."

"I told Mama it would be nice if we took a trip up north. Maybe visit Helen. It's been a long time since we took a trip."

"I said it was a good idea," Mama said.

Cynda smiled as memories of visiting the Bavarian inspired town came to mind.

"It's been a long time since I had a fresh funnel cake."

"Then let's do it!" Tiffany said. "It will be a fun getaway before we go to Germany."

Cynda could feel the stress falling away. "Yes, let's do it."

MILTON J DAVIS

23

It had been a decade since the Jones family visited Helen, Georgia. Daddy was still alive and Cynda was in high school. The town was much more crowded these days, but they'd chosen a slower time of the year, plus they were leaving early to avoid the afternoon crush. Tiffany and Terrence carried the still sleeping twins and fastened them into their seats while Cynda helped Mama. She needed less assistance these days; the physical therapy had her walking better than before the stroke. Dr. Sullivan, her primary care doctor, always said that part of Mama's problem was that she wouldn't do the exercise he'd given her. It was Dr. Robertson who finally convinced her. Now she was working out with gusto. Cynda thought it had something to do with all her children being back home, although that was temporary. Tiffany and the twins would be leaving next week, which would leave the house a little emptier. Cynda looked forward to being relieved of babysitting duties, but she had to admit she would miss them.

They made it as far as Dawsonville when the twins woke up feisty and hungry. They were ahead of schedule so they stopped at a local breakfast restaurant and ate. As they walked back to the van, Terrence came up to Cynda with his hand out.

"I'll drive."

"I got it."

"You always got it. Stop being the big sister all the time."

Cynda gave him the side eye. "Do you know the way?"

"No, but the navigation system does."

Cynda gave him the keys.

They continued, Cynda in the back with Tiffany and the twins. She was glad Terrence asked to drive. Laura gave her a few days off to recover from the news of their plans falling through. Cynda told her she didn't need it, but Laura insisted. She was glad she did. It had been a while since she took time off, and with Tiffany in town this was the perfect time to do it. Cynda was upset about the deal, but she was more upset about Nelson. How could he lie to them like that? It didn't matter that he was stalling to see if he could salvage the deal; all he had to do was to be honest with them.

But it was more than just the deal. She felt like she was dealing with a breakup, the end of a relationship that never was. She didn't realize how much she cared for him until she didn't want to see him anymore. It didn't make any sense, but emotions rarely do, at least for her. She shook her head to clear it.

"What's wrong, Auntie?" Shakwon asked.

"She got a bug on her head," Malon answered.

Cynda grinned. "I do, and I'm going to put it in your mouth!"

Cynda pretended to take a big bug from her hair and the twins squealed and laughed.

"Hey, keep it down!" Terrence said.

"Keep your eye on the road, little brother," Tiffany said. "We clowning back here."

"Don't make me pull over," Terrence replied in mock anger.

They all laughed at that, even Mama. This was going to be a great trip.

They arrived too early to check in, so they went to the town. Mainstreet Helen divided the quaint Bavarian style buildings, the morning pedestrian traffic light. It would be very different in a few hours.

"So what's first?" Terrence asked.

"I want to go tubing," Tiffany said, "but the twins are too small."

"We'll split up," Cynda replied. "You and Terrence can go first while I watch Mama and the kids. I'll go when y'all get back."

"You sure?" Tiffany asked.

"Yep. If I remember correctly, there's a park with a playground not far from the tubing docks."

"But you'll have to do it by yourself," Terrence said.

"That fine. It's not like we're going to be holding hands on the way down the river."

Cynda looked at Mama and grinned. "You want to try it, Mama?"

"Goodness, no!" Mama replied. "I don't feel that good."

"Then let's do it!" Tiffany said.

Terrence set the navigation for the tubing business just outside the town to the north. The business was opening as they arrived, so the line was short. The owners set Terrence and Tiffany up with their tubes and poles, gave them a few instructions, then launched them into the Chattahoochee River. This far north, the river was a lazy stream, perfect for drifting.

Cynda walked Mama and the twins to the empty playground and the twins reveled in not having to share the swings and other equipment. Cynda and Mama strolled around park holding hands.

"I'm sorry about your business," Mama said.

"Thank you, Mama. It's done now. Have to move on."

"Have you talked to that boy you were working with?"

"Nelson? Oh no. No reason to."

"I don't know about that."

Cynda glanced at Mama. "What do you mean?"

"I think you kinda liked him. And I think he liked you, too."

"That doesn't matter," Cynda said. "Whatever was happening between us is over."

"That's sad to hear," Mama said. "You been living for everybody else. It's time you start living for yourself."

"I'm doing what I have to do. I'm doing what Daddy would have done."

Mama squeezed her hand. "Your daddy and I had a whole lot of years together before we had to start worrying about y'all. We had a bag full of memories to keep us going. You don't have that."

"So what you want me to do, Mama?"

"Tiffany done come to take the babies back
with her. That will give you more time to yourself. Terrence is a grown man. He may not act
like it, but he is. He'll be moving on soon
enough. And Miss Laura don't need you as much
as she says she does. She got along fine before
you started working with her. You have to stop
being everybody's crutch."

"What about you, Mama?"

Mama smiled. "I love you taking care of me,
but it doesn't have to be you all the time. We can
always hire somebody when you need time to
yourself."

"I don't trust just anybody looking over you,
Mama."

"I don't either. But you need to live your life."

"I'll think about it."

Mama squeezed her hand. "You do that."

The tubing bus returned with Terrence and
Tiffany. The two of them ran to the playground
like exuberant children.

"That was so cool!" Terrence said.

"I haven't been that relaxed in years," Tiffany
agreed. I want to go again!"

"Oh no you don't," Terrence replied. "You're
not leaving those little tornados with me."

Tiffany scowled. "You ain't right."

"Yes I am."

"My turn." Cynda walked by them, crossing
the street to the tubes. One of the workers, a
young pink faced boy with red hair and freckles
smiled at her.

"Hi, ma'am, I'm Luke."

"I'm Cynda."

Luke led her to the riverbank. "So it's really simple. Just sit in the center and let the current take you. We give you this staff so you can push off any rocks or the shore. And stay in the shallows near the bank. The deeper the water, the slower you'll go."

"Got it."

The young man helped Cynda onto the tube and pushed her on her way. Cynda laid back and fell into the moment. She closed her eyes and drifted, the sound of chirping birds and gurgling water as it flowed over the rocks soothing her mind. She didn't realize she dozed off until she woke up. She looked around; she was in the deep water, her tube floating as slow as a snail creeping uphill. She stuck her pole down; the river was too deep. Cynda was a good swimmer, but she had no intention of getting wet.

"Oh well," she said, then settled in. She closed her eyes and dreamed of Paris, of visiting the Eiffel Tower, of walking the Champs-Élysées, marveling over the art of The Louvre, and then taking a detour to the south of France before returning home rested . . . and married.

She opened her eyes. Marriage was not a requirement for happiness for her. She could imagine a single life, of traveling the world alone. But she would love someone to experience it with, someone who loved her and took care of her like she did for so many others. Mama was right. It was time for her to start living her life for herself.

But how do you do that when you're the one everyone else depends on?

She finally reached shallow water then used her steering pole and worked her way to the landing. When she finally returned to the tubing shop she was met with glares.

"What took you so long?" Terrence asked.

"I hit the deep water."

"We've been waiting forever. It's getting hot out here."

"It wasn't that bad," Tiffany said.

"I know," Cynda replied. "Terrence will always be a drama queen."

Terrence tossed his head back. "I have no idea what you're talking about!"

They laughed and the twins joined in.

"That's what I like to see," Mama said as he walked up to them. "But Terrence is right. It's getting warm."

Cynda checked her phone. "And it's early check in time. Let's go to the condo. Terrence, give me the keys."

The condo Cynda rented was a few miles outside the city in the mountains. Laura gave her a bonus a few months ago and she stashed it away for a special occasion. Their destination was a large cabin shadowed by towering oaks, with a spectacular view of the river. As she pulled into the driveway, Mama gasped.

"Oh my goodness! Baby, where did you get the money for this?"

"Don't worry about it, Mama. Just enjoy."

They got out of the van and walked to the front door. Cynda punched in the code and opened the door to reveal an open space updated with the latest home enhancements.

"Oh wow!" Tiffany said.

"Yay!" the twins replied. They invaded the home with enthusiasm, jumping on every chair and sofa, and running their hands across the granite countertops.

"I'm going to find my room," Terrence said.

"Stay away from the main bedroom on the first floor," Cynda replied. "That's Mama's. The one upstairs is mine."

"No baby, you take it," Mama said to Terrence. "I don't need all that space."

"You haven't seen it," Cynda replied.

"I don't need to."

"I'm okay, Mama. I just need a little space," Terrence said.

Cynda walked Mama to the room. "See? The ensuite is design for people with special needs."

Mama inspected the room then smiled. "It is nice. I'll take it."

"Good." Cynda looked at Tiffany. "Your room and the kids' room are on the main floor on the other side of the kitchen. Terrence, your room is upstairs with mine."

The family settled in. While Mama napped and Tiffany played with the kids, Cynda went out on the back patio from her second floor room. The expansive space overlooked the river winding through the trees, the sound calming. Just beyond the trees she spotted more mountains rising in the distance, displaying the bluish haze that gave the region its moniker, the Blue Ridge Mountains. She could imagine sitting in this same spot with Nelson, sipping coffee or wine, whichever the situation required.

"Stop, girl," she said. "That's done. Move your ass on."

"Who you talking to?"

Terrence came out onto the terrace, laptop under his arm.

"Myself as always," Cynda replied. "The only person with good sense that I know."

"Ha. Ha."

Terrence sat on the seat next to her and opened his laptop.

"No. Uh Uh. This is an electronics free zone. Relaxation only."

"I have something to show you."

Cynda heard a serious tone in Terrence 's voice, which was rare. "What's wrong?"

Terrence turned on the laptop then ran his fingers over the keyboard.

"Look at this." He set the laptop on her lap. There was an open email. "Read it."

Cynda scanned the formal letter and her eyes went wide.

"Tee! This is amazing!"

Terrence 's face was neutral. "Is it?"

"What's wrong with you, boy? This is what you wanted!"

"I'm not so sure now." Terrence stood and walked to the balcony railing. "I've worked so hard on this game. I was so deep into making it work that I barely considered what would happen if it did blow up. Yeah, I talked about it, but honestly, I didn't really believe it."

"But it has," Cynda said.

"That's a lot of money, Cynda. A LOT of money. I don't want to become one of those rich assholes."

Cynda joined her brother and hugged him. "Slow down, brother. You haven't accepted the deal yet. And the fact that you're worried about becoming an ass tells me that you won't. You got me and Feenee to keep you grounded, big head."

"I know that's right." Terrence turned to her. "There's something else."

"What's that?"

"They sent me first class tickets to fly out to meet them next week in San Franciso."

"That's amazing!"

"Cynda, I've never flown on a plane!"

"You'll be fine."

"Can you go with me?"

"Of course not! I have to stay here with Mama."

"She can come, too. They asked if I needed more tickets. They think I have a team."

Cynda laughed. "No she can't."

"Why not? She's feeling better, and the doctor didn't say she couldn't travel."

He was right. Mama was doing better, and it might do them some good to go on a real vacation. Plus she needed some time off. Even Laura said so. But there was another issue.

"And whose going to pay for all this?"

Terrence grinned. "My potential new partners."

"Let's talk to Mama to see if she's willing to go. If you can get us tickets and rooms, I'll put in for the time off."

Terrence lunged at her and hugged her tight. Cynda laughed as she hugged him back.

"Calm down, boy. Let's make sure we can do this."

They sat on the balcony, Terrence rambling about the details of his game while Cynda listened. She didn't understand most of what he said, but his passion riveted her. She'd never seen him so engaged. She wished Daddy could be there; she knew he would be proud. He always encouraged them to pursue their passions. He would say that if you loved what you did, you'd make a good living doing it because your love would show in your work.

Cynda liked working for Laura, but she didn't love it. She gave up her passion to take care of the family, which was the right thing to do. But she gave up her dreams in return, and that would always be on her mind until she had the chance to pursue them again or let them go completely. And she wasn't ready to give up.

"Let's go inside and share the news," Cynda said. She hugged Terrence again then kissed his cheek. "I'm so proud you. Daddy would be, too."

"That means a lot, Cynda. You're the G.O.A.T."

"Let's go, boy. You're about to make me cry."

MILTON J DAVIS

24

Nelson sat at the nightclub table, ignoring the pulsing music, throbbing lights, and dancing people around him. He swirled his drink then took a sip, wincing as the vodka announced its presence to his inexperienced throat. Mauricio was on the dance floor, holding his own with two women, one who kept gesturing for Nelson to join them. He wasn't in the mood. His mind was cloudy like a stormy sky, his thoughts spinning around Ronsie and Cynda. Although he and Ronsie agreed to give things another try, he knew the only reason he agreed was because he'd blown it with Cynda. He lied to her, and it didn't matter if he did it for a good reason.

Mauricio sambaed his way back to the table.

"Amigo, you're killing my vibe," he said. "We should be celebrating!"

"You're doing enough for both of us."

Mauricio sighed then sat. He turned to glance at the women he danced with and shrugged. They frowned then disappeared into the other dancers.

"Just call her," Mauricio said. "Beg her forgiveness."

"I can't go to her empty-handed," Nelson replied. "I promised her a deal and didn't deliver."

"If the only reason she was interested in you was because you were a potential investor, you should forget about her. It will be about the money from now on."

"That's not Cynda," Nelson replied. "She doesn't care about the money. She's all about character. If I can make this thing work, it will be a start. It will show her how much I care about what she cares about."

"Let me see it," Mauricio said.

"See what?"

"The building."

Nelson pulled up the photos on his phone then handed it to Mauricio. Mauricio studied them then gave the phone back to Nelson. He folded his arms.

"Pitch me."

Nelson looked confused. "What?"

"Pitch me," Mauricio repeated. "I told you when we first met that I was interested in real estate investments in America. Convince me that this is the one I should start with."

"Are you serious?"

"As a heart attack. I trust you, amigo. If you think this building is worth the investment, I believe you. But you have to give me something to convince my business partners. They don't like you like I do. So pitch me."

Nelson lit up. He told Mauricio everything, backed up by the pictures on his phone. When he was done, he leaned back in his chair then sipped on his drink.

"So, what do you think?"

Mauricio smiled. "I'm impressed. To invest in a building that has not only commercial value but historical significance would be very inviting for my people. In fact, if you can stay around for a few more days, I'll set up a meeting."

"I'll stay as long as I need to if it will help seal this deal."

"Good." Mauricio stood. "Now let's get on the dance floor. I refused to let you come to Brazil and not learn to samba."

Nelson stood. "Okay. But let me warn you, I'm a better than average dancer."

Mauricio laughed. "That might be true, but you're not Brazilian."

"Challenge accepted!"

Nelson and Mauricio sambaed their way to the dance floor, engaging the women Mauricio danced with earlier. Nelson's dance partner, Fernanda, was tall and dark brown, her afro reminding him of a seventies supermodel. She spoke fluent English and was a patient teacher, and after a few songs he was dancing good enough to enjoy himself.

"Not bad for a gringo," Mauricio said.

"Told you," Nelson replied.

They danced for the rest of the night. Fernanda let him know her interests went beyond dancing, but Nelson couldn't muster up the same feeling. All he could think about was Cynda.

They left the nightclub at midnight. As they drove back to the hotel, Mauricio patted his shoulder.

"You got it bad, amigo," he said. "Fernanda really liked you. And she's an amazing woman."

"I'm sure she is, but the heart wants what it wants," Nelson replied.

"Then talk to her."

"I've tried. She won't take my calls."

Mauricio laughed. "So your love life depends on my investors."

"Sort of."

"You can't go on that, amigo. What if my associates decide not to invest? Then what will you do?"

"I guess I'll give up."

Mauricio shook his head. "No. If you love her, you fight for her. Find a way to plead your case. If she doesn't want anything to do with you after that, you move on."

"I guess I need to get a flight home."

"Yes, you do. But first, I have one more stop for us."

"This late?"

"For me, this is early. Come on, I'm sure you'll love it. It's more laid back."

"Okay. Lead the way."

"Excellent!"

Mauricio pressed the gas and they were on their way to their next destination. Nelson hoped they wouldn't be out too late because he was exhausted. He would stay a few more days to meet Mauricio's partners and then he would go home.

25

Delta Flight 631 from Atlanta circled San Fransico in time for its 12pm arrival. Cynda watched the descent from her window seat, excited to be on the West Coast for the first time. Mama sat beside her fast asleep, Cynda thankful that she rested the entire flight. Terrence occupied the aisle seat, his eyes still closed. Flying terrified him.

"You can open your eyes now," Cynda said. "We've arrived."

"Thank God!" Terrence exclaimed.

Some of the other passengers looked his way, their expressions ranging from irritated to amused. Cynda laughed.

"This is it. Are you ready?"

"As ready as I can be," Terrence replied. "Thank you for doing this, Cynda."

"You don't need to thank me," Cynda replied. "It's good to get out of town."

"Too bad we won't have time to sightsee," Terrence said. "You missing the twins?"

"I missed them the minute they boarded the plane to Germany," Cynda replied. "It's good they're back with their mama, though. They can make up for lost time."

Terrence smirked. "They're gonna drive Feenee crazy."

"I know that's right!" Cynda replied.

Mama stirred then opened her eyes. "Y'all need to be praying for your sister instead of making fun of her."

"We're doing both, Mama," Cynda replied. "We always do."

The landing was smooth. An attendant with a wheelchair met them at the door of the plane and help them with Mama. As they walked through the airport to baggage claim, Cynda's mind drifted to her dream of visiting Paris. She imagined walking through Charles de Gaulle Airport with one full bag and five empty ones, hoping to return home with the latest fashions. She sighed; that was a dream that might never happen and if it did, it was a long way off.

"What's wrong baby?" Mama asked.

"Nothing, Mama," she replied. "Just daydreaming."

Someone caught her attention ahead. It was a fashionably dressed petite woman holding a sign with Terrence 's name.

"Uh, Terrence, I think someone's looking for you?"

"What? Oh, Oh!"

The woman smiled when Terrence met her gaze.

"Welcome to San Francisco, Terrence!"

"Hi Fantasia!" Terrence replied.

They shook hands and laughed. Cynda eyes narrowed.

"This woman is flirting with my brother," she said under her breath.

"She sure is," Mama replied. "It's cute."

"Your son is about to be wealthy," Cynda said. "He needs to be careful. Terrence isn't that experienced when it comes to women."

"How do you know?" Mama replied. "Leave that boy alone."

"Y'all talking about me?" Terrence asked.

"No," Cynda said.

"Yes," Mama said.

"Well whichever, y'all about to get left. Come on."

They picked up their baggage and Fantasia led them to a waiting limousine. Terrence and Cynda helped Mama into the car; Cynda sat in the back while Terrence rode in the front with Fantasia.

"I'm so excited to finally meet you!" she said. "I've been studying your game ever since you shared it with us. You're a genius!"

Terrence blushed. "Not a genius, but I am very smart."

"You are!"

Terrence's smiled faded. "Wait. You said you've been studying my game. Y'all aren't trying to rip me off, are you?"

"No!" Fantasia replied. "We're an ethical organization. The agreement you signed is very specific about technology. You have read the agreement, haven't you?"

"Ah . . . yes. I have."

"That sounds like a no," Fantasia said. "Make sure you do before the meeting tomorrow."

"Are you saying your bosses are not to be trusted?" Cynda asked.

"I've been with the company for a long time and I've never seen them do anything under-handed. But it's always different when it comes to us."

Fantasia gave Cynda and Terrence that look. "What you have is truly unique, Terrence. That's why you're here. They're pulling out all the stops."

"I'll be sure to read the contract before tomor-row," Terrence said.

"One more thing," Fantasia said. "Our com-pany isn't the only game in town. There are other companies that would be interested in looking at your design. Whatever happens tomorrow, don't feel like you have to make a decision. Take your time and do what's best for you."

"Wow. Thank you, Fantasia!" Terrence said. "I really appreciate this."

"You're welcome. I wanted to tell you this be-fore we arrived. That's why I'm driving."

"We really appreciate it, Fantasia," Cynda said. "You're one of the good ones."

Fantasia smiled at Cynda. "I try to be."

The drive from the San Francisco airport to Palo Alto took just over thirty minutes. Fantasia and Terrence chatted the entire drive. Mama slept, and Cynda enjoyed the scenery. She couldn't remember the last time she was in a car without intention. She could get used to this, but she knew she shouldn't. Work and stress were only a few days away, but she would make the most of the time.

Cynda

The Palo Alto Four Seasons Hotel was amazing. The concierge greeted them at the limo, expecting their arrival. They whisked through check-in and were on the elevator in minutes on their way to the Presidential suite. Like Fantasia said, her employers spared no expense.

"So what do you think?" Fantasia asked.

"It's amazing!" Cynda replied.

"We booked additional rooms for you and your mother, although there's plenty of room for you to stay here if you like."

"We'll give Terrence his own space," Cynda said. "Were you able to book a handicap room for out mother?"

Fantasia smiled. "Of course!"

"I'll stay with her," Cynda said.

"Oh no you won't," Mama replied.

"What?"

"I want some privacy too," Mama said. "You can help me get settled then I'll be just fine."

Cynda was surprised. "You sure?"

"Yes," Mama said.

"Okay then. We'll see you for dinner, Tee."

"Okay. Fantasia, do we have dinner plans?"

"Of course. The hotel has a great restaurant, but I have a place that I'd like to take y'all, if you're interested."

"Of course I . . . I mean, we are," Terrence replied.

"Y'all young folks go on," Mama said. "I'm tired from the flight. I'm going to order dinner from room service and get me some rest."

"Great!" Fantasia said. "I'll get you and your mother settled in your rooms. Terrence, I'll be back to help you get acquainted with your room. I've been in your shoes before. All this can be a bit much."

Terrence grinned like a lottery winner.

"Okay."

Cynda and Mama followed Fantasia back to the elevator. They descended to the next floor. Fantasia took them to their rooms, two adjoining suites with more than enough room. Fantasia gave Cynda her number.

"I'll contact you an hour before dinner," she said.

"Sounds good," Cynda replied.

The bellhops had delivered their bags. Cynda help Mama unpack, then channel surfed as Mama put on something more comfortable. A few minutes later Mama came out of the bedroom wrapped in a hotel bathrobe and sat beside her.

"This is nice," she said.

"It is," Cynda replied. "You sure you're going to be alright tonight?"

"I'll be fine, Cynda. Don't worry about me. There's a whole hotel to do that."

"Okay. I'm going to get settled in my room. I put the TV on the channel that you like. We're three hours behind Atlanta so the showtimes are funky."

Cynda went to her room and got comfortable before calling the office. Laura answered.

"Cynda? What are doing calling here?"

"Just checking on things."

"Girl, you're on vacation!"

"Not really. I'm here as moral support for Terrence."

"Are you attending any meetings with him?"

"No."

"Are you taking any notes?"

"No."

"Then honey, you're on vacation. So don't be calling the office. Have some fun. Go see the Golden Gate Bridge. Ride down that crooked street. Visit Chinatown. But don't call here."

Cynda laughed. "Y'all gonna be okay?"

"Of course not!" Laura replied. "But we'll survive. Have fun and tell your Mama and them I said hello."

"I will. Bye!"

Cynda hung up the phone. As she lay back on the bed, she thought about Nelson. She wondered if he'd ever been to San Francisco, and if he had, what places he would show her. And then she remembered how he lied to her and Laura, how he raised their hopes then let them down. It wasn't so much the fact that he lied, but that he didn't come forward to them with the truth. She would have been disappointed of course, but she would have been able to get through that and continue to see him . . . if his feelings for her were real.

"Stop it, Cynda," she said to herself. "You're on vacation. Don't spend your time pining over some man."

Cynda's quick nap was interrupted by her pinging phone.

"Hi Cynda! It's Fantasia! I got your number from Terrence. I hope you don't mind."

"Not at all."

"Great! We're meeting in the lobby for dinner in about an hour. See you then!"

"Okay."

Cynda got up and dressed for the evening. She checked in on Mama before catching the elevator to the lobby. Terrence and Fantasia waited in the lobby, chatting and laughing. Terrence saw her first and waved.

"Hey Cynda!" He trotted to her and gave her a hug.

"It's only been an hour," she said.

"What? I can't hug my sister?"

"You usually don't."

Cynda looked at Fantasia. "You got any of these?"

"Four," Fantasia replied. "I love them all, but I was so ready to get away from them. It was like having four extra fathers."

Cynda laughed. She was beginning to like this woman. It still didn't mean she trusted her. Fantasia looked at her phone.

"The car is here! You're gonna love this restaurant. I picked it just for you."

A driverless rideshare waited for them. Terrence's eyes lit up!"

"Nice! I always wanted to try these!"

Cynda was not amused.

"Y'all go ahead. I'll get a rideshare with a driver."

Cynda

"Don't worry," Fantasia assured her. "These things have been here for years. They don't always take the most direct route, but they'll get you there in one piece. I take them all the time when I'm not driving."

Terrence took her hand. "Come on, sis. You only live once."

"Exactly."

They got in the car, and it whisked them to their destination, an elegant restaurant that served Cajun/Creole food. It was surprisingly good. Terrence and Fantasia were chatting and laughing, and Cynda began to get suspicious.

"So Fantasia, where are you from?" she asked.

"Seattle," she replied.

"A West Coast girl."

"Born and raised. I graduated from Stanford and began working for GenStar right out of college."

"So how did you meet Terrence?"

Fantasia's eyes went wide. "Excuse me?"

"How did you meet my brother? Y'all ain't fooling me. Y'all are too familiar with each other to have just met. I'm figuring y'all have been online dating for a minute."

Fantasia and Terrence looked at each other like kids caught in a lie. They smiled, then held hands.

"I met her gaming online," Terrence confessed. "We would tease each other while we played. Our team got annoyed so we started texting and stuff."

"You mean sexting," Cynda said.

"Cynda!" Terrence exclaimed.

Cynda tilted her head. "Am I wrong?"

Fantasia and Terrence were silent. Cynda's eyes shifted to Fantasia.

"So I guess you gave him a great tour of his room. Probably didn't miss a spot."

Fantasia smirked and Cynda burst out laughing.

"My baby brother. Mama said y'all looked cute together."

"Fantasia helped me work out the details of my game," Terrence said. "She's been in the industry long enough to know what they're looking for. We were able to change the game without giving up the vision."

"So that's why you're so confident in GenStar picking up the game?"

"Not just GenStar. Everybody," Fantasia replied. "To be honest, Terrence isn't here to get a job. He's here to start a business."

Cynda leaned back in her seat. "Okay, hold up. That's a whole 'nother level. I'm not a business owner but I've worked for Laura for a long time. Starting a business takes a lot of time and money."

"That's why I'm meeting GenStar," Terrence replied. "I'm looking for investors. Fantasia has lined up a series of meetings with different companies and individuals. I'm going to be here for two weeks."

"Two weeks? I can't stay that long. I have to get back to work."

"You don't have to," Fantasia replied. "Terrence asked to you come because you needed the break."

Terrence placed his hand on Cynda's. "Despite what you think, I've been paying attention, and I've appreciated everything you've done for me and the family. You've been the glue since daddy died. Now it's payback time."

Cynda's eyes glistened. "You're going to make me cry."

"We also made arrangements for your mother," Fantasia said. "She's staying here until we land a deal."

"So she was in on this, too?"

Terrence nodded. "Tiffany, too. We felt you needed a break. After our meeting here we're moving to a rental condo in Napa."

Cynda sighed. "Napa Valley? I've always wanted to visit Napa Valley." Her eyes narrowed. "Wait. Where is all this money coming from?"

"I have a little savings I'm using," Fantasia said.

"You're spending your savings on my brother?"

It was then that Cynda saw it. They were in love, and they believed in each other. Cynda was happy for them and jealous of them at the same time.

"Let me know what I can do," she finally said.

"Pray for us," Terrence said.

"You know I will."

"Thank you so much, Cynda," Fantasia said. You're everything Terrence said you were and more."

"Now I'm going to cry," Cynda said.

"Not before we finish this gumbo," Terrence replied.

Cynda laughed. They finished their meal, Cynda taking the time to get to know Fantasia. They ordered an extra meal for Mama and a dessert for each of them to take back to the hotel. The ride share they called this time had a human driver, to Cynda's relief. The trip back to the hotel was peaceful and pleasant. For the first time in a long time, Cynda felt things were moving forward.

26

Nelson was happy to be back in Chicago. Brazil was fun, but there was nothing like home. As he strolled through the airport with his luggage, he thought about his situation. He worked for his family business, travelling the world and having amazing experiences. His future was almost certain. He thought about how so many people would be content—no, happy— to be in his shoes. But somehow, he wasn't.

His phone buzzed; it was his father.

"What's up, Pops?"

"Come see me as soon as you're here." He hung up.

Nelson stared at his phone a moment before putting it back in his pocket. His father could be short, especially when he was busy, but this seemed colder than usual. Nelson shrugged. Whatever it was, he'd find out when he got to the office.

Nelson took a rideshare to the office. He put his bags in his office then went to see Pops. His father sat at his desk, the surface cleared, his fingers intertwined. This was serious. Nelson sat.

"What's up, Pops?"

"Running a business is hard work," his father began. "It's especially hard when the people who work for you don't do what you ask."

Nelson tensed. He sat straighter in the chair. Like his father, he wasn't one to dance around an issue.

"Pops, what is this about?"

"It's about Atlanta. I thought I told you that deal was dead."

"You did."

"Then why did I get a call yesterday from Paul Jennings questioning my decision to go through with the deal?"

Nelson dropped his head. When Mauricio said he had friends, he didn't think it involved anyone his father was dealing with outside of Brazil.

"I told Mauricio about the opportunity," Nelson began. "He said he and a few others were looking for a property to invest in America, and he thought the Atlanta hotel was a good deal."

His father stood and paced.

"When I make a decision, it's not an opinion. When it's done, it's done. I thought you understood that."

"I do."

"Apparently you don't." His father sat back down. "Do you have any idea how I felt on that call? I had to dance around, talking to him as if I knew what was going on."

"I didn't mean to get you involved."

"But you did. Nelson, it took me a long time to build my support network. There are few people on this level, hell, on any level, that will work with a Black man, no matter how successful I am. I have to be extremely confident in an investment before I bring a deal to them. I have very little room for error."

"It shouldn't be that way," Nelson said.

"But it is," his father replied. "My contacts see you and I in harmony. When you say something, they assume I feel the same way. I don't feel the same as you do about Atlanta. You know this."

"Then tell them the truth," Nelson said. "Tell them you have nothing to do with this. Tell them that this is my first solo project. I don't need your help."

His father's eye went wide. "Don't be ridiculous."

"I'm serious. I've been ready for some time. I don't know how many of your friends are involved in this, but I know they'll drop out if you tell them to. I have my own reserves. I can make up the difference."

"I pay you," his father said. "Whatever you have might not be enough."

"I'll make it work."

His father tilted his head. "You're not doing this because of that woman, are you?"

"Her name is Cynda. And yes, she's part of the reason. Not because of my feelings for her, but because of her passion for the project. I have no doubt that she and her boss will make this work. But they can't do it without my help."

"Son, you can't make business decisions based on your feelings. It's all about the numbers and the risks."

"You're telling me you never made a business decision just because it felt right?"

His father glanced away. "I have, in my early days. I was lucky they worked out. But I'm trying to teach you better. I want you to learn from my mistakes."

"I'm sure it was more than luck, Pops. And I'm doing this," Nelson said.

His father sighed. "You're too much like me." He sat. "So, do it. I won't give you my endorsement, but I won't recommend against it, either. And you won't get a dime of my money."

"That's fair," Nelson replied. "If you'll excuse me, I have work to do."

Nelson left his father's office. He wasn't angry with him; he had gone against his advice so it was on him. He would have told him once the deal went through, but it was what it was.

The first thing he did when he got back to his office was review his savings and investments. He had enough to cover a quarter of the cost of the property, but zero for renovations. That would have to come from the other investors. He'd have to see what Mauricio and the others could do, and he would have to meet again with Laura and Cynda to see what they could bring to the table. If they still wanted to do the deal.

"They would if it's not me," he said aloud.

His phone buzzed. It was Ronsie.

"Hey, Ronsie."

"Hey, Prince."

Nelson laughed. "So we're going by first names today?"

"No, just calling it like I see it. You are a prince."

Nelson cooled. He and Ronsie had agreed to give it another try, but if he was being real, his feelings weren't the same for her. It wasn't her; it was Cynda.

"And you are a queen," he replied. "What's up?"

"You got time for dinner tonight?" Ronsie asked.

"I do. You pick the place."

"Excellent. I'll make reservations."

"See you then."

Nelson hung up. It had come to this again. He should have said something on the phone. But he had to be sure. Seeing her was different from talking to her. Tonight would decide everything.

* * *

Nelson grinned as he pulled up to Gino's Pizza. The old pizzeria had occupied the corner for decades, long before Nelson was born. Ronsie wasn't playing games; Gino's was the site of their first date and their first kiss. This was where they went from being friends to much more. Their parents were ecstatic when they heard the news; it was as if they had announced they were engaged.

Nelson entered the restaurant. The greeter, a young man with an electric smile approached him. Nelson saw Ronsie at their favorite booth over his shoulder, smiling and waving.

"Welcome to Gino's," the man said. "Would you like a table or booth?"

"Someone's waiting for me," Nelson said. He walked by the greeter to the table. Ronsie stood and they hugged. He was relieved she didn't try to kiss him.

"Hey you," she said.

"Hey you," he replied. They sat on opposite sides of the table. The waiter arrived and they ordered a large pizza with everything and two beers.

"So how long are you home?" Ronsie asked.

"For a while. Sao Paulo is in good hands. It's the new project that's gonna take up my time for a while."

"Where is that?"

"Atlanta."

Ronsie's eyes widened. "I thought your father killed that deal."

"He did. This is all me, for better or worse."

Ronsie finished her beer. "Speaking of better or worse, I've been thinking again. About us."

"Ronsie . . ."

"No, let me get this out. I said this before. I've loved you for as long as I can remember. And when we became boyfriend and girlfriend, it wasn't a surprise. But then I got out a bit and wondered what it would be like to be with someone else. So I did. And I broke your heart in the process."

"Ronsie . . ."

"No. I'm not finished yet. So I got out there, and I discovered that it wasn't all that. I realized that you were special, and maybe I screwed up. Which is why I wanted to get back together."

Nelson was about to take a swig. He placed the mug on the table.

"Wanted?"

"I know, I know. You're thinking, here she goes, changing her mind again. But this time is the last time. I realized that I can't give up because of one bad relationship. And I can't get in your way if you're interested in someone else. You're my best friend, Nelson, and I want what's best for you. And if that's Cynda, then so be it."

"Well, that's not an issue anymore," Nelson said.

"What do you mean?"

Nelson explained the situation while Ronsie ate a slice of pizza. She took a minute before answering.

"You screwed that up," she said.

"Blame it on a lack of experience," Nelson replied.

"Based on what you've told me, I think she would give you another chance if you were sincere."

"You sound like Mauricio."

"Who's Mauricio?"

"Our business partner in Sao Paulo. I talked him into taking a look at the property and possibly investing in it. Which pissed Pops off because he'd told me no. So now I'm investing my own money to make it happen."

Ronsie whistled. "When you go, you go big."

Nelson raised his beer. "Always have!"

They both laughed and ate more pizza.

"I still think you should talk to her," Ronsie said. "If she's that special to you, it's worth a shot. And if it doesn't work out, you know how to find me."

"Are you serious?"

"Of course not. We've had our time. Our parents will get over it. But I must admit, I probably won't like her when I finally meet her."

"That's fair," Nelson replied.

"Now that that's settled, let's finish this pizza before it gets cold."

"Ronsie, are you sure you're good with this?"

Ronsie smiled. "I'm sure."

"I love you," Nelson said.

"I love you too," Ronsie replied. "Now shut up and eat."

They finished their meal, then took a stroll on the nearby streets. Nelson felt some sadness about this final decision; being married to Ronsie wouldn't have been so bad. But there was something missing, something that he felt when he was with Cynda. He hoped he could have that feeling again, if not with Cynda, with someone else. It was all he could ask for.

27

Cynda was home. Terrence, Fantasia, and Mama had come with her to the airport, staying with her as long as they could before she had to report to the gate. She was still surprised that Mama was staying, and yet she was happy. Mama had barely been out of the house since Daddy died, and she hadn't left the city at all. Now she was on the other side of the country living her best life. Cynda couldn't be anything but happy for her.

She arrived at Hartsfield in the late afternoon, enough time to pop into the office before she went home but decided not to. Laura would probably fuss at her as she pushed her out of the door. Laura played as hard as she worked, and she thought everyone else should. She picked up her car from parking then drove home. That's when the strange feeling surfaced. With the exception of driving to and from work, she was rarely in the car alone. She stopped and picked up Chinese takeout, chatting a bit with the owners who knew her well because she ordered from them so much. It was early evening by the time she reached the house; the motion detector lights came on as she pulled into the garage.

It was when she opened the door and stepped over the threshold when it hit her. The house was completely silent. She couldn't remember any time in her life it had been this way. She sat her meal on the kitchen table then walked slowly through the house, visiting each room. It was unnerving to be alone, something she'd prayed for at times but never thought would actually happen.

Cynda rolled her luggage into her bedroom; she would unpack later. Instead she took a tray table from the pantry and set in front of the loveseat before the television. Her food was still warm, so she turned on her favorite streaming service and watched while she ate. She kept expecting one of the twins or both of them to interrupt her show with a silly question or a sillier argument. She also waited for Mama to call out to her for something she needed or one of the long lists of pills she took.

Pills. Did she leave the pills? Were they enough?

Cynda got her cell and punched the numbers. Mama answered.

"Hey baby!" Mama said. "I see you made it home alright."

"I did. Hey Mama, do you have all your pills?"

"I do, baby. You packed them with my toiletry bag. You don't remember?"

"I do, but I was just making sure. How are you doing?"

"I'm wonderful," Mama said. "Sitting up here in this fancy room running up the room service bill."

Cynda laughed. "Be careful. We don't want Terrence to lose his deal over astronomical add on charges."

"I ain't worrying about those folks," Mama said. "If they can pay for all these rooms, they can pay a little more for my spa session."

"How's Terrence doing?" Cynda asked.

"Oh my goodness!" Mama said. "You ain't been home a whole day and you're already missing us!"

"I'm not, not really," Cynda said weakly.

"It's okay," Mama replied. "We all a big part of your life. Just enjoy the quiet and call me whenever you get the urge. Okay?"

"Okay, Mama. I need to hang up now. My food is getting cold."

"What did you get?"

"Mongolian Beef and Hot and Sour soup."

"The usual."

"Yes, ma'am."

"You enjoy your meal, baby. I'll talk to you tomorrow, okay?"

"Okay, Mama. I love you."

"Love you too, CeeCee."

Cynda felt better after talking to Mama. She thought about calling Tiffany, but it was much later in Germany and the last thing she wanted to do was wake up the twins. She knew firsthand how hard it was to get them back to sleep. Instead she finished her meal then did a little channel surfing before stopping on an old romance she'd seen a thousand times. It took place in Paris. She watched until she fell asleep, visions of the Eiffel

Tower and a mysterious man swirling in her head. When she woke up the movie had long since ended. She cleaned up, took a shower, and went to bed.

* * *

"Look who's back!"
Laura greeted her at the door, a big smile on her face and two cups of coffee in her hands.
"Good morning, Laura!"
"It's a better morning than you think. Follow me."
Cynda took a cup and followed, waving at the sales reps as they made their way to Laura's office.
"Close the door," Laura said.
"Uh oh," Cynda replied. She sat in the guest chair.
"So what's up?"
"I got a call last week while you were away. A man by the name of Mauricio Santos. He represents a group of international investors, and they're interested in our property."
Cynda jumped to her feet. "You lyin'!"
"I'm not. Cynda, we got investors!"
Cynda pressed her hand to her chest as she sat. "That's so . . . wait. How did a group of international real estate investors hear about our project?"
"Nelson told them."
A chill swept through Cynda. "And you trust him?"

"Nelson didn't back out on the deal. His father did. If I'm upset with anyone, it's him."

"But he lied to us."

"Because he didn't want to disappoint you," Laura said. She gave Cynda that look and Cynda looked away. Did everyone know how they felt about each other?

"Still, I'm skeptical. How do we know this won't happen again?"

"It might," Laura said. "No deal is certain. But at least this time they're coming based on a recommendation. Besides, this is our last shot."

"So when is this meeting taking place?"

Laura smiled. "Today."

Cynda's eyes bulged. "Today! We're not ready! I'm not dressed!"

Laura laughed. "You look fine, and we've been ready. Mauricio Santos will not leave this building without signing an agreement."

"We have to set up the conference room!"

Cynda rushed from Laura's office to the conference room. When she entered, she was surprised. Everything was in perfect order; the coffee machine, water dispenser, fresh pastries from Big Tarts, and computer projector with the first image from their presentation on the screen. Cynda turned her head as Laura enter the room, a grin on her face.

"You did all this?" Cynda said.

"I didn't always have Atlanta's best assistant working for me," Laura replied. You forget I started this business out of my house. Well, actually it's still in my house, but you know what I mean."

"I guess we're ready then," Cynda said.

"As ready as we can be. Now take your ass up front and look cute when our guest arrives."

Cynda sashayed to her desk and grinned when Laura laughed. She sat, drinking her coffee and nervously waited for Mauricio to arrive. The sales reps stopped on their way out, letting her know where they would be working for the day. Cynda updated their schedules and gave them a pleasant goodbye. She was even nice to Ray, which caught him completely off guard.

Cynda busied herself with inventory updates as time passed. It was a few minutes before lunch when the front door opened and a handsome, brown-skinned man with an infectious smile entered the building. Cynda stood and extended her hand.

"Mauricio Santos?"

"Yes." Mauricio took her hand and kissed it. "And you must be Cynda Jones."

Cynda pulled her hand away slowly. "I am."

"Nelson's description doesn't do you justice. Excuse me if I'm being forward. It is not my intention."

"It's okay. Let me show you to our conference room."

Cynda led Mauricio to the conference room. "Would you like coffee?"

"I would."

Cynda was going to the coffee maker but Mauricio stopped her.

"I'm a modern man. I can make it myself."

"Oh. Okay. I'll get Laura."

Cynda hurried to Laura's office.

"He's here!"

Laura stood then adjusted her dress. "Okay. Let's do this."

They walked to the conference room. Cynda entered first and Mauricio stood with his coffee. Laura followed and they shook hands.

"Hi, Mr. Santos," she said. "I'm Laura Benson."

"Pleased to meet you, Miss Benson. And please, call me Mauricio. May I call you Laura?"

"Of course."

Everyone sat at the conference table.

"I'm happy you came all this way to meet with us," Laura said.

"Nelson spoke very highly of the project and of you," Mauricio replied. "And I never miss an opportunity to visit the US, although this is my first visit to Atlanta."

"We've set up the presentation," Cynda said.

Mauricio waved his hand. "No need for that. Nelson was very thorough, and I've done my own homework. All I need to do now is see the property."

"Oh, okay," Laura said. "Then let's go."

"I'll drive," Cynda added.

They left the office and got into Cynda's SUV. The drive to the property was fast since morning rush had subsided. They parked in the parking lot opposite the building then crossed the street to the property.

"It can use some work," Laura commented. "But the location is ideal. When you figure in the community impact, the value is enhanced."

Mauricio continued walking around the building, Laren and Cynda following.

"I'm very interested in investing in properties that will improve the community without negatively affecting the existing neighborhood. I grew up in the Sao Paolo favelas, so I understand the need and caution."

"That's always been our goal," Laura replied. "There's also the opportunity to develop the surrounding property for local businesses and neighborhood support."

Mauricio turned to them and smiled.

"I've seen enough," he said. "Let's make a deal."

"Really?" Laura said. "That's it?"

"That's it. I'm satisfied with what I've seen. Let's go back to the office and get the process started."

They returned to the office and the conference room. Mauricio gave Laura his card.

"Send your preliminary contract to my office. We'll take a look at it and make any changes we feel necessary. Once we reach an agreement, we'll need your financial information so we can make the money transfer. I'll be the main contact, so I'll travel here periodically to keep up on progress."

"Thank you so much," Laura said.

"I'm looking forward to working with you," Mauricio said.

"I'll walk you out," Cynda said.

Cynda and Mauricio walked into the parking lot to his waiting car.

"I was hoping we would have some time alone," Mauricio said.

"Oh really," Cynda replied.

"Yes. Cynda, I've only known Nelson for a short time, but even I could tell he's crazy about you. He worked hard to set up this deal. He even invested his own money."

"It still doesn't make up for the fact that he lied to us. He lied to me."

"People make mistakes. And when it comes to mistakes, this one was not so bad. I'll say to you what I said to him. Life is short and love does not come often. Don't let a misunderstanding keep you from happiness."

Cynda was done talking about Nelson. "It was nice meeting you, Mauricio. I'm looking forward to working with you."

Mauricio smiled. "You are a tough one. We'll talk soon."

Cynda stayed in the parking lot until Mauricio drove away. Laura was waiting for her when she came back.

"It's crunch time!" Laura said. "You and I are going to work this contract until we get this deal. You ready, sister?"

"I'm always ready," Cynda replied.

"Then let's do this!"

The next week was slammed. Cynda and Laura worked together on the contract, meeting virtually with Mauricio's team daily to create an agreement everyone was satisfied with. She talked to Mama, Terrence, and Tiffany in her spare time. Everyone was enjoying themselves and it made Cynda felt good that they were getting along without her help. She knew Mama would be returning soon and be back under her care, but it would be easier without having to watch the twins and support Terrence. Though he hadn't said it officially, Cynda had a feeling that her brother wouldn't be returning to Atlanta any time soon, even if he didn't get the deal with GenStar.

It was a late Friday night when they finally finished the contract. Laura looked over the document while chewing on a piece of cold pizza, while Cynda sipped on her third cup of coffee.

"I think this is it," Laura said. "Except for one thing."

Laura's fingers danced across the keyboard. "There, now it's perfect. Take a look."

Cynda scooted over to look at the screen.

"What did you add?"

"Something at the end."

Cynda took a look at contract. At the end was the list of partner names. She hesitated when she saw Nelson's name, then laughed.

"His first name is Prince?"

"I thought that was funny, too," Laura said. "Keep reading."

Cynda continued reading until she got to the last names. She saw Laura's name . . . and then she saw hers. Spelled out under both of their names was Benson and Jones.

"So it's real," Cynda said.

"Yes it is, partner."

"I don't know what to say."

"You don't have to say anything. You earned it."

Cynda jumped out of her seat and hugged Laura.

Laura hugged her back. "I don't have any children, but if I did, I'd be blessed if they were anything like you, Cynda."

"Now you're going to make me cry."

"Let's sign this contract and send it on its way before all that," Laura said.

Cynda gave Laura one more squeeze. "Let's do that!"

It didn't take long for Mauricio and his partners to return the signed agreement. Cynda received the email and was hit for another loop. She ran into Laura's office.

"They want us to come to Sao Paulo!"

"I figured they would," Laura replied. "We'll meet the other partners."

"I've never been out of the country before!" Cynda said.

"Do you have a passport?"

"Actually, I do," Cynda replied. "I always dreamed of going to Paris, so I kept a passport just in case."

"I'll make the arrangements," Laura said. "Give me a few minutes."

Cynda bounced on her toes back to her desk. Everything was happening at once. She'd have to check with Terrence to see if Mama could stay in

California for a few more weeks. Otherwise she'd have to plan for someone to look out for her while she was out of the country. There were a few church members that would be happy to do it.

"Okay, we're all set!" Laura said. "Check your email."

Cynda pulled up her email. "No. No!" She ran into Laura's office.

"These are tickets to Paris!"

Laura grinned. "Surprise!"

"Wait, I don't understand all this."

"It's simple," Laura replied. "You don't think I haven't been paying attention to all you do, not listening to everything you say? You've been a blessing to so many people, so now it's time for someone to be a blessing to you. I can handle Sao Paulo. You go get you some rest and have some fun."

Cynda couldn't hold back. She dropped her face in her hands and cried. All the mental weight she'd carried for years was released in one moment. She felt Laura's arm rest on her shoulders.

"Your flight leaves in two days. You don't even need to pack if you don't want to. I'm going to give you a few minutes alone."

Laura kissed her on the forehead then left the room. Cynda sat alone until her joy subsided. She wiped her eyes, took a deep breath, then look up.

"Daddy, I never thought this day would come. I dreamed about it, but I figured I'd keep working and supporting everyone until I couldn't do it anymore. But now I'm here with almost everything

I ever wanted right in front of me and I don't feel like I deserve it."

She stood up and began walking toward the door.

"Thank you for showing me how to be strong. I don't know how things are going to work, but I know whatever it is, I can handle it because of you. I love you."

Cynda walked out of the room and into her new future.

MILTON J DAVIS

28

Nelson waited nervously in the lobby of Mauricio's hotel, glancing at the time on his phone. The meeting should have been over at least an hour ago, but Mauricio still had not returned. His fingers drummed on the granite surface of the table where he sat, his coffee long gone cold. He had no doubt about Mauricio; he was almost convinced from what Nelson shared with him in Sao Paulo. His uncertainty was with Laura and Cynda. He'd done wrong by them, and they might not be in a forgiving mood.

He didn't want them to know he was one of the major investors for the same reason. Mauricio told him it would be a bad move; his name would be on the final contract, and withholding his information would make them trust him even less.

Mauricio finally strolled into the hotel. Nelson was on his feet and fast walking toward him before he noticed.

"So how did it go?" Nelson asked.

Mauricio smiled. "Hello, Nelson! Didn't expect to see you here. We have a deal. It's all about the details now."

"Have they seen the contract?"

Mauricio shook his head. "They will eventually."

"So we're not in the clear yet."

Mauricio put a comforting hand on his shoulder. "Don't worry, amigo. Everything will be fine. I explained to them the reason for your loss of judgement, and they seemed to be satisfied."

"What about Cynda?"

Mauricio sat. "Ah, Cynda. A beautiful woman. Bright, too. You can see it in her eyes. No wonder you're in love."

"I'm not in love," Nelson replied.

"Well, that's something you both have in common," Mauricio said.

"What's that?"

"Lying about how you feel about each other," Mauricio replied.

Nelson was getting annoyed. "What makes you an expert?"

"I'm Brazilian," Mauricio said.

Nelson laughed. "Thank you for this."

"I should thank you," Mauricio said. "If it wasn't for your broken heart, I would have never had the opportunity to be a part of this deal. Let's hope it's the salve you hope it will be. Now let's have a drink to celebrate."

"It's a little early," Nelson said.

"I'm sure the bourbon will forgive us for violating its curfew. Oh, wait. It doesn't care."

Nelson followed Mauricio to the bar. Maybe a drink or two would do him some good. They were on their third glass when Mauricio spoke.

"You know, she's right here."

Nelson put down his glass. "I can't just walk up on her. I should call first."

Mauricio shook his head. "And give her the chance to hang up on you? Meet her face to face. Plead your case. It's harder to refuse someone when they're standing right in front of you."

"That sounds aggressive," Nelson said.

"It is. You're fighting for your love. This is not the time to be soft."

Nelson finished his drink. "No. I think I'll wait. Let's see if the deal goes through. If it does, I'll give it a few months then talk to her."

"A few months?" Mauricio laughed. "If you wait that long she'll be with me. She's beautiful, and I'd love to show her Sao Paulo."

"Quit playing," Nelson said. "You are playing, right?"

Mauricio shrugged. "That's enough for me. I'm going upstairs. Think about what I said."

"You are playing about Cynda, right?" Nelson called out.

"Goodbye, Nelson!"

Nelson watched Mauricio walk toward the elevator. Although he knew Mauricio was joking with him, he made a good point. A woman like Cynda wouldn't be single forever, especially with her life changing this way. He wasn't sure, but he had to say something. He paid for the tab and headed for his rental. He did a search for the nearest flower shop and bought a dozen roses, then he headed for their office. The closer he was, the less nervous he was. This was the right thing to do. It was all or nothing.

As he pulled into the parking lot, Cynda walked out of the office. She was smiling, looking radiant. He reached for the door latch then stopped. She was happy; his presence would probably ruin the moment. Instead, he watched her walk to her SUV, climb inside and drive away. He waited until she was gone before walking to the office door and leaving the flowers. He went back to his car, then headed to the airport.

* * *

The airplane wheels touched the O'Hare Airport tarmac, jolting Nelson awake. He yawned and stretched as the husky voice of the flight attendant thanked everyone for choosing their airline, then he waited patiently as the other passengers stood then trickled out. He was exhausted. Physically he was fine but mentally was another issue. He was about to risk his entire life savings on a project and a woman he believed in. At least he had a chance with the project. Cynda was another matter.

As he went to pick up his bags, he decided to stop by the gym before going to his condo. A good workout always cleared his mind and energized him.

His phone rang as he waited for his rideshare. It was Mama.

"Hey Mama!"

"Hey Prince! I hope your flight went well."

"It did. What's up?"

"Why does something have to be up? Can't I just call to talk to my son?"

"You can, but not this early."

"Well, since you asked, there is something I'd like to discuss. Can you come by the house?"

"Uh oh. This must be serious."

"Just come to the house, boy."

"Okay. I'll be there in a few."

The Carters resided in a gated community on the outskirts of Chicago. Their abode was modest in comparison to the other opulent homes. They downsized once Nelson moved out, preferring a house than catered to their current needs instead of massive mansion they once owned. The days of lavish parties and family events were gone; now was a time for relaxation and reflection.

Mama waited for him in the front yard as the rideshare pulled up, greeting him with open arms.

"Hi, Mama."

"Hi son. Let's go out back to the garden."

Cynda

They strolled arm in arm around the house to the backyard. Mama was an excellent gardener. The yard was divided between food garden and flower garden, with a wide expanse between each edged by shade trees. They sat at the table.

"So what have you been up to?" Mama asked.

"I think you know," Nelson replied. "There are no secrets between you and Pops."

"I'm giving you a chance to tell me, since you didn't find the time to tell me before."

"Ouch," Nelson said. "Well, I'm about to invest all of my savings into the Atlanta project, and me and Veronica have split for real. I'm mean, we're still friends but I hate to inform you that there will be no grandkids from us."

Mama nodded. "I'm not going sit here and say I'm not disappointed. You two made a great couple, and we're practically in-laws to her parents."

"I'm sorry, Mama."

"No need to apologize. Things happen. At least you're still on good terms."

"I love Ronsie, but not in the way I should a partner, let alone a wife," Nelson said. "I didn't realize that until I met Cynda."

"Miss Cynda," Mama announced. "Seems she's become the center of your universe."

"She has," Nelson admitted. "I've never met anyone like her. She does so much for everyone but herself and stays positive despite that. She's smart, funny, beautiful, and down to earth. There's nothing fake about her."

Mama sighed. "Who knew my son would fall for an around the way girl?"

"A what?"

"Never mind," Mama said. "Just showing my age. So when do I meet her?"

"I don't know. Maybe never. She's not speaking to me right now."

"Because you told her there was a deal when there wasn't," Mama said.

"Yeah."

"Well, now you know how much she values honesty. First things first. I will not allow you to spend your savings on this project, no matter how much you believe in it."

"So you don't think it will be successful?" Nelson asked.

"No, just the opposite. I believe in you. Your father does, too. He just has a thing about people not doing what he tells them to do."

Mama reached into her pocket and gave him a check. Nelson looked at it and his eyes went wide.

"Wow!"

He tried to give it back to her but she held up her hand. "No. This is yours. Your daddy isn't the only one in this family with money. This business is a partnership, remember?"

"I didn't mean that," Nelson said. "Paper checks are old school. You can transfer the money."

"I know," Mama replied. "But it's not as dramatic. Now let's deal with Cynda. When will you see her again?"

"I'm assuming it will be at the partners meeting in Sao Paulo. Maybe."

"Well, if it is, make the best of it."

"I will."

Mama patted his hand. "Good. Now let me show you my flowers."

They strolled to a new planting.

"These are beautiful," Nelson said.

"They're delphiniums," Mama said.

Cynda

"So, how long do you think Pops will be mad at me?" Nelson asked.

"Not too much longer," Mama replied. "He was furious at first, but he calmed down a few days later after I explained to him he would have done the same thing for me. I'd still give him a few more days. Wait until the contract is signed. Once he knows there's no turning back, he'll come around."

"You think so?"

"You and your sister are all we have. We built this for ourselves and for you. We love you both, and we won't let a business deal come between us. You can be certain of that."

Nelson spent the rest of the morning in the garden with Mama, enjoying a light lunch of turkey sandwiches with tea. Although he was annoyed when Mama first called him, as he left home he was glad she did.

He skipped the workout and instead took a walk in downtown Chicago. He loved his hometown, frigid winters and all. He loved the energy, the diversity, and the opportunity despite the racism that simmered underneath. His mother and father made the best of it, creating a business that stood as a legacy for him and Darla, even if they decided to pursue different paths. And he wanted to share all this with Cynda. He wanted her to understand where he was from and how it made him who he was. And he wanted to share her life, too. She'd given him a glimpse of it, just enough to make him crave to know more. But that might not be. Unless he did something about it.

MILTON J DAVIS

29

As far as Nelson was concerned, this was the most important trip of his life. He'd taken an early morning flight to Sao Paulo so he'd have time to relax before the meeting. The ride from the airport through the chaotic traffic unnerved him a bit, but once he checked into his room he calmed down. He did a light workout then had a leisurely breakfast before returning to his room. He sat at his desk with his laptop and began typing. But this wasn't about the deal he'd come to sign. This was about Cynda. He typed over and over again, trying to come up with the right words to say. After about the fifteenth revision he shut down his computer. This wasn't working. He would have to just say what he felt, let it come from his heart. He had to be honest, no matter how bad it sounded.

Nelson took a quick shower then dressed for the meeting. The concierge hailed him a taxi, and he was on his way to Mauricio's office. The staff greeted him as he entered, and he was shown to the conference room. He was the last to arrive. Mauricio sat at the head of the table with Laura Benson sitting to his right. She smiled.

"Hello, Nelson," she said. "It's been a while. Thank you so much for this."

"It's amazing seeing you," Nelson replied. He did a quick scan of the room. Cynda wasn't there.

"Where's Cynda?" he asked.

Laura smirked. "She wasn't able to attend. She signed the papers in Atlanta."

"Oh."

Nelson took the empty seat to Mauricio's left and the meeting began. It was just a formality; everything had been agreed to beforehand. Mauricio passed the final contract to Laura, who signed and passed it to her left. It finally made it to Nelson. He signed then passed it to Mauricio. The deed was done. He was in all the way.

"Excelente!" Mauricio said. "I'm excited that we are all on this journey together. Now please follow me to the large conference room. A celebration is in order!"

As Mauricio led everyone to the large conference room, Nelson made his way to Laura.

"I'm so glad you agreed to this," Nelson said.

"You made a great save," Laura replied. "It took a while to convince Cynda."

"Is she okay?" Nelson asked.

"Oh, Cynda's just fine. I made her partner. She'll be leading our commercial properties division."

"That's fantastic. She deserves it."

"She deserves that and more. She just doesn't know it." Laura winked.

"So, why didn't she come?" Nelson asked.

"She's taking the rest she deserves, finally off to her dream destination."

"Paris," Nelson said.

Laura nodded. "I set up the trip for her. Organized her itinerary for two weeks. I know where she's going to be the entire trip. I did leave some room for exploring, but it's a great plan."

It took Nelson a moment to get what Laura was saying. When he did, he smiled.

"Would you be willing to share said itinerary with a desperately in love man?"

Laura smiled. "I'll text you."

Nelson waited until the phone pinged. He checked the text, then hugged Laura.

"Thank you so much!"

"You're welcome. Now go get that girl."

He hurried to Mauricio.

"Thanks for everything, Mauricio. I'd love to stay, but I have a last minute thing that just came up."

"Does it have something to do with a missing partner?"

"Yes."

"Then go. And good luck."

Nelson hugged Mauricio then hurried for the exit. He had a plane to catch.

* * *

"Everyone, welcome to Paris."

The flight attendant's words sent a chill through Cynda. She gazed down from her first class window seat as her flight circled Paris-Charles De Gaulle Airport, her heart beating like a hummingbird's wings. She'd dreamed of this moment, but deep inside, she never thought it would happen. Even with everything settling down around her, she envisioned the rest of her life making up for lost time. But now she was here, cruising over her dream destination, only moments away from touching the ground.

The flight attendant shared arrival details in French and English. Cynda understood both. Her years of studying French online were paying off. She still wasn't confident of her conversational French; she only had the computer to practice. But something was better than nothing, or so she heard. She was about to find out.

The plane landed and they disembarked. After passing through customs she walked through the airport to find a taxi to take her to her hotel. Standing near the door was a dark brown handsome man with sparkling white teeth holding a sign with her name. He noticed Cynda and shared the widest smile she'd ever seen in her life. The man walked up to her and extended his hand.

"Madame Cynda Jones, welcome to Paris!" the man said.

"Bon jour," Cynda replied. She didn't think it was possible, but the man's smile brightened.

"Your French is excellent! I'm Haruna Diallo. I'm your ride to your hotel."

They shook hands.

"Follow me," Haruna said. "We don't want to waste one second of your dream holiday."

Haruna's car was small yet comfortable. He stored Cinda's bags in the trunk, opened the door to the back seat for her and then they were on their way. Cynda moved closer to the window, drinking in every image.

"I'm in Paris. I'm in Paris!"

"Yes, you are," Haruna replied. "Where in America are you from?"

"Atlanta," Cynda said. "College Park to be exact."

"I'm familiar with it," Haruna replied. "I have a sister that lives in Atlanta. I visit her sometimes during holidays."

"Are you a Paris native?" Cynda asked.

"Yes. I was born here. My parents are from Senegal."

"That's great! Have you been to Senegal?"

"Many times," Haruna answered. "My family is very close."

"That must be amazing. This is my first time traveling outside of the U.S."

"Then let's make sure it's your best time. Madame Benson shared your itinerary with me. I hope that's okay."

"It is."

"Bon. I will be your contact. If you have any questions, feel free to text me. I understand you plan to see the city alone?"

"Yes," Cynda replied.

"Bon. Although a beautiful woman like you in the City of Love won't be alone for long unless you prefer."

"Haruna, are you flirting with me?"

Haruna laughed. "I'm just stating the obvious. Besides, Mrs. Diallo wouldn't approve. Again, if you have any difficulties, please feel free to call."

"Don't you have other clients?"

"Not for the next two weeks," Haruna replied. "Madame Benson has paid me handsomely for my time. I'm at your command."

"Wow."

Haruna took her to her destination, Hôtel Signature Saint Germain des Près. It was the perfect spot; the neighborhood was beautiful and centrally located. Haruna carried her bags into the lobby; a smiling young woman greeted them.

"Welcome to Hôtel Signature Saint Germain des Près!" the woman said in English.

"Merci beacoup," Cynda replied. The woman's eyes lit up.

"You speak French!"

"A little," Cynda replied.

"That's better than most. My name is Adeline. I'll show you to your room."

Cynda opened her bag to get a tip for Haruna, but he shook his head.

"Everything's been taken care of," he said. "Enjoy your stay, Cynda. Remember to call me if you need anything."

"I will."

Cynda followed Adeline to her room. She squealed when Adeline opened the door. It was small, cute, and had a lovely balcony overlooking the street. "This is perfect!" she said.

"I'm glad you think so," Adeline replied. "I'm sure you want to rest after your flight."

"No I don't," Cynda said. "I'm going for a stroll!" Cynda changed into her walking shoes then headed to the streets, mingling with the visitors and residents of Saint Germain. She ambled by the various galleries near her hotel, ate an amazing meal at Le Jardin, then continued her touring until just before dark. Although she had a full tour on her itinerary for the next day, there was no way she was going to put one thing off until then. She had to see the Eiffel Tower. She hurried back to the hotel. Adeline greeted her as she entered.

"Madame Cynda! How was your walk?"

"It was amazing! And call me Cynda, please. Adeline, how to I get to the Eiffel Tower?"

"Well, you could take the Metro, but a taxi is faster. I'll call one for you."

"Thank you!"

Cynda went to wait outside and moments later the taxi arrived. She climbed in and in minutes the tower came into view. She stepped out of the taxi and approached the iconic structure slowly, savoring every step. This was a dream come true. Cynda bought her ticket then waited for the elevator to the top. She decided to work on her French as she waited, small talking with some of the people waiting for the lift. When the doors opened, she took a deep breath then stepped inside.

Cynda enjoyed every minute of the view as they ascended. She wished Mama was here; she wished everyone was with her. The elevator reached the top and she stepped onto the platform. Cynda went directly to the edge, gazing on the scene below.

"Beautiful," she said.

"Yes, she is," someone replied.

Cynda turned. Nelson stood only a few feet away, holding a bouquet of flowers. He approached her slowly.

"I knew you would come here your first day," he said.

Cynda stepped away, a storm of emotions swirling inside her head. "What are you doing here? How did you know I was in Paris? And why did you come?"

"Laura told me you were here," Nelson said. "I left the contract signing and caught the first flight out. As to why I'm here, I think you know, and I'm hoping you feel the same way."

"How long have you been here?"

"All day."

Cynda fought the feelings that were rising in her, sensations threatening to overcome logic.

"You lied to me," she finally said.

"I know, and I was wrong. I didn't want to disappoint you. I thought I could work things out before you found out. I apologize. If I could do it differently I would."

Cynda took a step toward him. "Honesty is everything to me. There's no real relationship without it."

"So there's a chance?" Nelson asked.

This scene, this moment reminded her of her dream. "Maybe."

They both moved closer. Cynda gazed at the flowers.

"I love these," she said.

"And I love you," Nelson replied.

Cynda's eyes went wide. "Nelson. Let's think about this."

"I have, and I know this is how I feel. It's okay if you don't feel the same. I'm a patient person. And if it never happens for you, that's okay, too. I'd be a fool if I didn't take the chance of being with the most wonderful woman I've ever known." Nelson lowered the flowers. "If you want me to leave, I will."

Cynda couldn't deny her feelings any longer. She pushed the flowers aside then wrapped her arms around Nelson's shoulders. She felt his free arm wrap around her waist and they kissed. It was the kiss she wanted weeks ago, but it was happening in Paris, on the Eiffel Tower, just as she had imagined. When it was over, she knew.

"I love you, too," she whispered.

"So what do we do now?" Nelson asked.

"We enjoy this beautiful view and this wonderful night," Cynda said.

"And after that?"

Cynda smiled. "We have forever to figure it out."

The Beginning

ABOUT THE AUTHOR

Milton Davis is an award winning Black Speculative fiction author and owner of MVmedia, LLC, a publishing company specializing in Science Fiction and Fantasy based on African/African Diaspora history, culture, and traditions. Milton is the author of thirty novels and short story collections and editor of eleven anthologies. Cynda is his first romance novel. There may be more.